RETOLD CLASSICS

HUCKLEBERRY FINN

by

MARK TWAIN

Perfection Learning®

Writer: Wim Coleman, Educational Writer and Novelist
Editor-in-Chief: Kathleen Myers
Managing Editor: Beth Obermiller
Senior Editor: Marsha James
Editors: Randy Jedele, Christine LePorte
Cover Art: istockphoto.com
Inside Art: Paul Micich
Book Design: Emily Adickes
Consultants: Rhonda Fey, Gretchen Kauffman, Dr. Jona Mann, Lois Markham
Reviewers: Jim Fields, Pamela Friedman, Ken Holmes

Please visit our Web site at:
www.perfectionlearning.com

When ordering this book, please specify:
Softcover: ISBN 978-1-5631-2180-7 or **4314701**
Reinforced Library Binding: ISBN 978-0-7807-1213-3 or **4314702**
ebook: ISBN 978-0-7891-8836-6 or **43147D**

28 PP 19 18 17 16

Printed in the United States of America

TABLE OF CONTENTS

WELCOME TO RETOLD CLASSIC

HUCKLEBERRY FINN

Adventure, mischief, humor, and unforgettable characters are but a few of the elements that help make Mark Twain's *Huckleberry Finn* an American classic.

We call something a classic when it is so well-loved that it is saved and passed down to new generations. Classics have been around for a long time, but they're not dusty or out-of-date. That's because they are brought back to life by each new person who reads and enjoys them.

The Adventures of Huckleberry Finn is a novel written years ago that continues to entertain and influence readers today. The story offers exciting plots, important themes, fascinating characters, and powerful language. This is a story that many people have loved to read and share with one another.

RETOLD UPDATE

The *Retold Classic Huckleberry Finn* is a different from Twain's original story in two ways.

- Some chapters have been omitted. Brief summaries are provided for these parts so you can follow the complete story.

- The language has been updated. All the colorful, gripping, or comic details of the original story are here. Longer sentences and paragraphs have been shortened. And some old words have been replaced with modern language.

You will also find these special features. A word list has been added at the beginning of each chapter. The list should make reading easier. Each word defined on the list is printed in dark type within that chapter of the novel. If you forget the meaning of a word while you're reading, just check the list to review the definition.

You'll also see footnotes at the bottom of some pages. These notes identify people or places, explain ideas or words, or let you in on a joke.

Also, at the beginning of the book, you'll find a little information about Mark Twain. These revealing and sometimes amusing facts will give you insight into his life and work.

One last word. If you feel compelled to read the entire story, we encourage you to locate an original version to get more of Twain's rich characterization and humorous plots.

Now on to the novel. Remember, when you read this book, you bring the story back to life in today's world. We hope you'll discover why this novel has earned the right to be called an American classic.

Mark Twain

INSIGHTS INTO MARK TWAIN (1835–1910)

Mark Twain's real name was Samuel Langhorne Clemens. It was Clemens' love of the river that inspired his choice of a pen name. Mark twain is a river term meaning "two fathoms." A fathom is a measurement of water depth equaling six feet. When a riverboat crew heard the shout "Mark twain," they knew the water was deep enough for the boat to go ahead safely.

Early Influences

Twain was born in Florida, Missouri. Later his family moved to Hannibal, Missouri, where Twain spent most of his childhood.

Twain's life in Hannibal and his experiences on the river provided much of the material for *Huckleberry Finn.* Even some of the more far-fetched events in the story seem to have a basis in reality. For example, when Twain was eight years old, he discovered a murdered man in his father's office. A short time later, he witnessed a public shooting.

Views on Slavery

As a youth, Twain accepted slavery, as did most Southerners. Since it was a normal part of life where he lived, he probably never questioned it. But over the years, his attitude changed. He came to realize that slavery was inhuman and immoral.

As an adult, Twain did what he could to help African Americans, who were now freed by the U.S. Constitution. In fact, he paid for the education of two black students—one studying art in Paris and another studying law at Yale.

Perhaps Twain's most moving argument against slavery was his portrayal of Jim in *Huckleberry Finn.* Jim proves himself equal to whites in all respects. In fact, Jim is kinder and smarter than most of the other characters.

Controversy Surrounding the Book

Despite Twain's intentions, many readers have been offended by his book. Critics have tried to ban *Huckleberry Finn* from school libraries because Twain's characters use the word *nigger* to refer to blacks. Others have argued that Twain's negative picture of the South is unfair and misleading.

Those who defend the book say that Twain's language and descriptions are realistic. They see Twain's book as honest and believable.

What would Twain think about this debate? The inscription below his statue in the Hall of Fame for Great Americans makes his point. It reads, "Loyalty to a petrified opinion never yet broke a chain or freed a human soul."

Becoming a Writer

Twain dabbled in a variety of careers before becoming a writer. For a while he worked in a print shop. Then his spirit of adventure took over, and he became a riverboat pilot.

His adventures didn't end with the river. He traveled to Nevada to try to strike it rich in the silver mines. But after a time Twain gave up on this and became a reporter and editor. He also began writing stories.

After having some success with his written stories, Twain decided to branch out. So he began trying his luck at telling humorous tales in lecture halls out West.

His huge success there encouraged him to try speaking in the East. It soon became apparent that people all over the country loved to hear him talk.

Personal Life

When Twain was in his early thirties, he married Olivia Langdon. They had a son, who died in infancy, and three daughters.

Twain was determined that his family should not live in poverty as he once did. So he spent his money freely. The huge Twain house in Hartford, Connecticut, cost $120,000 to build. It was the only house in the area that had five bathrooms!

Mark Twain was very absentminded. He often forgot to put letters in envelopes before mailing them. Once he threw off his hat while on a walk and didn't miss it until he reached home. Another time he showed up for a formal dinner minus his collar and tie.

Twain was also careless with his friends' possessions. As a result, people became unwilling to loan him anything.

Once Twain asked a neighbor if he could borrow a certain book. The neighbor replied, "Why certainly, Mr. Clemens, you are welcome to read it. But I must ask you to read it here. I make it a rule never to let a book leave my library."

Some time later, the same neighbor asked Twain if he could borrow Twain's lawn mower. "Why, certainly," Twain replied. "You're welcome to use it. But I must ask you to use it here. I make it a rule never to let my lawn mower leave my lawn."

Mark Twain was a fun-loving man. He loved to play jokes on his friends. Once Twain was traveling with a friend. Twain told his friend that between them, they only had enough money for one train ticket. So he suggested that his friend hide under Twain's seat on the train. When the ticket collector came around, Twain gave him two tickets. He explained in a loud voice that his friend was a bit strange and liked to crouch under the seat while riding on trains.

Money Problems

Though Twain had a great flair for writing and telling stories, he had almost no business sense. It was only after many years that he realized that one of his publishers was cheating him out of large sums of money.

Twain, an inventor himself, was also an easy mark for other would-be inventors. His many bad investments—including a failed steam generator—plunged him into heavy debt. So he was forced to make a year-long world lecture tour to pay his bills.

Twain was able to solve his money problems, but he had other burdens to deal with in his personal life. His wife and two of his daughters died of illness. And his other daughter moved to Europe with her husband. As a result of these events, Twain spent his last years a lonely and bitter man.

Mark Twain was born when Halley's comet appeared in 1835. The comet approaches Earth about once every seventy-seven years. Twain predicted that he would die when the comet came back near the Earth. His prediction proved accurate.

It has been said that Twain received a dollar a word for his work. A fan once sent him a dollar and asked Twain to send him a word.

Twain quickly replied, sending the word "Thanks."

Other works by Twain:

The Adventures of Tom Sawyer, novel
"The Celebrated Jumping Frog of Calaveras County," short story
A Connecticut Yankee in King Arthur's Court, novel
"The Man That Corrupted Hadleyburg," short story
The Prince and the Pauper, novel
"What Is Man?" essay

THE ADVENTURES OF HUCKLEBERRY FINN

OR

TOM SAWYER'S COMRADE

by MARK TWAIN

NOTICE

Persons attempting to find a motive in this story
will be prosecuted;

persons attempting to find a moral in it
will be banished;

persons attempting to find a plot in it
will be shot.

BY ORDER OF THE AUTHOR
Per G.G., Chief of Ordnance.

Chapter 1

I Discover Moses and the Bulrushers

VOCABULARY PREVIEW

The following words appear in this chapter. Review the list and get to know the words before you read the chapter.

confidence—faith; belief
fidgety—restless; jumpy
mournful—sad; low-spirited
pecking—nagging
respectable—proper; decent

You don't know about me without you have read a book called *The Adventures of Tom Sawyer.* But that ain't no matter. That book was by Mr. Mark Twain, and he told the truth, mainly. There was things which he stretched, but mainly he told the truth.

That is nothing. I never seen anybody that never lied at one time or other. Not unless it was Aunt Polly, or the widow, or maybe Mary. Aunt Polly—she's Tom's Aunt Polly—and Mary, and the Widow Douglas is all told about in that book. And it's mostly a true book, with some stretchers, as I said before.

Now this is the way that book winds up. Tom and me found the money that the robbers hid in the cave. And it made us rich. We got six thousand dollars apiece—all gold. It was an awful sight of money when it was piled up. Well, Judge Thatcher, he took it and put it away to earn interest.[1] It fetched us a dollar a day apiece all year round. It was more than a body could tell what to do with.

The Widow Douglas, she took me for her son. She figured she would sivilize[2] me. But it was rough living in the house all the time, considering how horribly decent and regular the widow

1 *Interest* is money earned from savings. It is payment from the bank to a depositor.

2 *Sivilize* means "civilize." In the novel Twain misspells some words to show how the characters would pronounce or write them.

was in all her ways. So when I couldn't stand it no longer, I lit out. I got into my old rags again, and I moved back into my old sugar barrel. I was free and happy.

But Tom Sawyer, he hunted me up. He said he was going to start a band of robbers. I could join if I would go back to the widow and be **respectable**. So I went back.

The widow, she cried over me. She called me a poor lost lamb and a lot of other names, too. But she never meant no harm by it. Then she put me in them new clothes again. I couldn't do nothing but sweat and sweat, and feel all cramped up.

Well, then, the old things started again. The widow rung a bell for supper. You had to come on time. When you got to the table, you couldn't go right to eating. You had to wait for the widow to tuck down her head and grumble a little over the vittles.[3]

Really, though, there warn't nothing the matter with the food. That is, nothing except everything was cooked by itself. In a barrel of odds and ends it is different. Things get mixed up. The juice kind of swaps around, and things taste better.

After supper she got out her book. She learned me about Moses and the Bulrushers.[4] I was in a sweat to find out all about him. But by and by, she let it out that Moses had been dead for a fairly long time. Then I didn't care no more about him. I don't take no stock[5] in dead people.

Pretty soon I wanted to smoke and asked the widow to let me. But she wouldn't. She said it was a crude practice and wasn't clean. She told me I must try to not do it anymore.

That is just the way with some people. They get down on a thing when they don't know nothing about it. Here she was a-botherin' about Moses, which was no kin[6] to her. Besides, he was no use to anybody, being gone, you see. Yet she found a heap of fault in me doing anything that had some good in it. And

3 *Vittles* is a slang word for "food."

4 The widow's book is her Bible. Moses was a biblical prophet. As a baby, he was found floating on the Nile River in a basket made from bulrushes.

5 To *take stock* is slang for "believe" or "take seriously."

6 *Kin* is another word for "relative" or member of the same family.

she took snuff,[7] too. Of course, that was all right, because she done it herself.

Her sister, Miss Watson, was a fairly slim old maid with goggles. She had just come to live with the widow. Miss Watson started in at me with a spelling book. She worked me pretty hard for about an hour. Then the widow made her ease up. I couldn't have stood it much longer.

Then for an hour it was deadly dull, and I was **fidgety**. Miss Watson would say, "Don't put your feet up there, Huckleberry." And, "Don't scrunch up like that, Huckleberry. Set up straight." And pretty soon she would say, "Don't yawn and stretch like that, Huckleberry. Why don't you try to behave?"

Then she told me all about the bad place.[8] I said I wished I was there. She got mad then, but I didn't mean no harm. All I wanted was to go somewheres. All I wanted was a change. I warn't picky.

She said it was wicked to say what I said. She said she wouldn't say it for the whole world. She was going to live so as to go to the good place.[9] Well, I couldn't see no use in going where she was going. So I made up my mind I wouldn't try for it. But I never said so. That would only make trouble, and wouldn't do no good.

Now that she got started, she went on and told me about the good place. She said all a body would have to do there was play a harp and sing. She said you'd do this all day long, forever and ever. So I didn't think much of it. But I never said so.

I asked her if she reckoned Tom Sawyer would go there. She said not by a long way. I was glad about that. I wanted him and me to be together.

Miss Watson kept **pecking** at me, and it got tiresome and lonesome. By and by they fetched the niggers[10] in and had prayers. Then everybody was off to bed.

---

7 *Snuff* is powdered tobacco. Snuff is either sniffed, chewed, or placed against the gums.

8 The *bad place* is a polite phrase for "hell."

9 By *good place* Huck means "heaven."

10 At the time of the novel, *nigger* was often used to describe African Americans. Twain's telling of the story would not be truthful or realistic without using this term, although today it is an insulting word.

I went up to my room with a piece of candle and put it on the table. Then I set down in a chair by the window and tried to think of something cheerful. But it warn't no use. I felt so lonesome I most wished I was dead.

The stars were shining. The leaves rustled in the woods ever so **mournful**. I heard an owl way off. It was who-whooing about somebody that was dead. I heard a whippowill[11] and a dog, too. They were crying about somebody that was going to die. And the wind was trying to whisper something to me. I couldn't make out what it was. It made cold shivers run over me.

Then away out in the woods I heard another sound. It was the kind of sound a ghost makes when it wants to tell you something that's on its mind. Only it can't make itself understood. So it can't rest easy in its grave. It has to go around every night grieving.

I got so depressed and scared, I wished I had some company. Pretty soon a spider went crawling up my shoulder. I flipped it off and it lit in the candle. Before I could budge, it was all shriveled up. I didn't need anybody to tell me that that was an awful bad sign. It was bound to fetch me some bad luck.

I got so scared, I most shook the clothes off me. I got up and turned around in my tracks three times and crossed my breast every time. Then I tied up a little lock of my hair with a thread to keep witches away. But I hadn't no **confidence**. You do that when you've lost a horseshoe instead of nailing it over the door. But I hadn't heard anyone say it would keep off bad luck when you killed a spider.

I set down again, a-shakin' all over. I got out my pipe for a smoke. The house was as still as death, so the widow wouldn't know.

Well, after a long time I heard the clock way off in the town. It went boom—boom—boom—twelve licks. Then all was still again—stiller than ever.

Pretty soon I heard a twig snap down in the dark amongst the trees. Something was a-stirrin'. I set still and listened.

---

11 By *whippowill* Huck means "whippoorwill," a North American bird named for its whistling call, which sounds like "whip-poor-will."

Soon I could just barely hear a "*me-yow! me-yow!*" down there. That was good!

Says I, "*me-yow! me-yow!*" as soft as I could. Then I put out the light and scrambled out the window onto the shed. Then I slipped down to the ground and crawled in among the trees. And sure enough, there was Tom Sawyer waiting for me.

Chapter 2

Our Gang's Dark Oath

VOCABULARY PREVIEW

The following words appear in this chapter. Review the list and get to know the words before you read the chapter.

bothersome—causing trouble
misery—suffering; pain
muddled—mixed up; confused
oath—promise; pledge
ransomed—set free, usually after paying a price demanded by kidnappers, etc.
sued—brought to trial or court
trance—deep sleep; hypnotic state

We went creeping along a path amongst the trees back toward the end of the widow's garden. We had to stoop down so the branches wouldn't scrape our heads.

When we was passing by the kitchen, I fell over a root and made a noise. We crunched down and laid still. Miss Watson's big nigger, named Jim, was setting in the kitchen door. We could see him pretty clear, because there was a light behind him. He got up and stretched his neck out about a minute and listened. Then he says, "Who's there?"

He listened some more. Then he came creeping down and stood right between us. We could've touched him, nearly. Well, likely it was minutes and minutes that there warn't a sound. And we were all so close together.

There was a place on my ankle that got to itching. But I didn't dare scratch it. And then my ear began to itch. And next my back, right between my shoulders. Seemed like I'd die if I couldn't scratch.

Well, I've noticed that thing plenty of times since. Suppose you are with the well-to-do, or at a funeral, or trying to go to sleep when you ain't sleepy. Suppose you are anywheres where it won't do for you to scratch. Why, you will itch all over in more than a thousand places.

Pretty soon Jim says, "Say, who is you? Where is you? Dog my cats[1] if I didn't hear somethin'. Well, I know what I's goin' to do. I's goin' to set down here and listen till I hears it again."

So he set down on the ground between me and Tom. He leaned his back up against a tree and stretched his legs out. One of them almost touched one of mine.

My nose began to itch. It itched till the tears come into my eyes. But I dared not scratch. Then it begun to itch on the inside. Next I got to itching underneath. I didn't know how I was going to set still.

This **misery** went on as much as six or seven minutes. But it seemed a sight longer than that. I was itching in eleven different places now. I reckoned I couldn't stand it more than a minute longer. But I set my teeth hard and got ready to try.

Just then Jim begun to breathe heavy. Next he begun to snore. And then I was pretty soon comfortable again.

Tom made a sign to me. It was kind of a little noise with his mouth. And we went creeping away on our hands and knees.

When we was ten feet off, Tom whispered to me. He wanted to tie Jim to the tree for fun. But I said no. He might wake and make a disturbance. Then they'd find out I warn't in.

Then Tom said he hadn't got enough candles. He said he would slip in the kitchen and get some more. I didn't want him to try. I said Jim might wake up and come. But Tom wanted to risk it, so we slid in there and got three candles. Tom laid five cents on the table for pay.

Then we got out, and I was in a sweat to get away. But nothing would do for Tom. He had to crawl on his hands and knees to where Jim was. He wanted to play a trick on him. I waited, and it seemed a good while. Everything was so still and lonesome.

As soon as Tom was back, we headed out on the path. We went around the garden fence. By and by, we run off up to the steep top of the hill. It was on the other side of the house.

---

1 *Dog my cats* is an expression of surprise.

Tom said he had slipped Jim's hat off his head. He had hung it on a limb right over him. He said Jim stirred a little, but he didn't wake.

Afterward, Jim said the witches had bewitched him. He said they put him in a **trance** and rode him all over the state.[2] Then they set him under the trees again. And they hung his hat on a limb to show who done it.

Next time Jim told it, he said they rode him down to New Orleans. And after that, every time he told it, he spread it more and more. By and by, he said they rode him all over the world, and tired him most to death. He said his back was covered with saddle boils.[3]

Jim was awful proud about it. He got so he wouldn't hardly notice the other niggers who would come miles to hear him tell about it. He was more looked up to than any nigger in that country. Strange niggers would stand with their mouths open. They'd look him all over, same as if he was a wonder.

Niggers is always talking about witches in the dark by the kitchen fire. But whenever one was talking and letting on to know about such things, Jim would cut in. He'd say, "Hm! What do you know 'bout witches?" And that nigger was corked up, and had to take a back seat.

Jim always kept that five-cent piece around his neck with a string. He said it was a charm the devil give to him with his own hands. And the devil told Jim he could cure anybody with it. He said he could fetch witches whenever he wanted to just by saying something to it. But he never told what it was he said to it.

Niggers would come from all around. They would give Jim anything they had for a sight of that five-cent piece. But they wouldn't touch it, because the devil had had his hands on it.

Jim was most ruined for a servant. He got stuck up on account of having seen the devil and been rode by witches.

Well, Tom and me got to the edge of the hilltop. We looked

---

2 Huck is referring to the state of Missouri. The novel begins in St. Petersburg, a town Twain based on his hometown of Hannibal.

3 *Boils* are painful, red swellings on the skin. Saddle boils can develop under a horse's saddle when the horse is ridden too hard and long. Jim is exaggerating here.

away down into the village and could see three or four lights twinkling. There was sick folks there, maybe. The stars over us was sparkling ever so fine. And down by the village was the river. It was a whole mile broad, and awful still and grand.

We went down the hill and found Joe Harper and Ben Rogers, and two or three more of the boys. They was hid in the old tanyard.[4] We unhitched a small boat and rowed down the river two and a half miles.

We reached a big scar on the hillside and went ashore. We went to a clump of bushes, and Tom made everybody swear to keep the secret. Then he showed us a hole in the hill. It was right in the thickest part of the bushes.

Then we lit the candles, and crawled in on our hands and knees. After about two hundred yards, the cave opened up. Tom poked about amongst the passages. Pretty soon, he ducked under a wall. You wouldn't have noticed there was a hole there. We went along a narrow place and got into a kind of room. It was all damp and sweaty and cold. We stopped there.

Tom says, "Now, we'll start this band of robbers and call it Tom Sawyer's Gang. Everybody that wants to join has got to take an **oath**. He's got to write his name in blood."

Everybody was willing. So Tom got out a sheet of paper that he had wrote the oath on. He read it. It swore every boy to stick to the band, and never tell any of the secrets.

And if someone done anything to any boy in the band, another boy would be ordered to kill that person and his family. And he really must do it. He mustn't eat and he mustn't sleep till he'd killed them. Then he must hack a cross on the dead people's breasts, which was the sign of the band.

And nobody that didn't belong to the band could use that mark. And if he did, he must be **sued**. And if he done it again, he must be killed.

And if someone that belonged to the band told the secrets, he must have his throat cut. Then he'd have his body burnt up and the ashes scattered all around. His name would be blotted off the list with blood. It would never be mentioned again by the

4 A *tanyard* is a building where vats are kept for tanning (making) leather.

gang. It would have a curse put on it and be forgot forever.

We all agreed it was a real beautiful oath. We asked Tom if he got it out of his own head. He said some of it. But the rest was out of pirate books and robber books. He said every gang that was high quality had an oath.

Some thought it would be good to kill the families of boys that told the secrets. Tom said it was a good idea. So he took a pencil and wrote it in.

Then Ben Rogers says, "Here's Huck Finn. He ain't got no family. What are you going to do 'bout him?"

"Well, ain't he got a father?" says Tom Sawyer.

"Yes, he's got a father. But you can't never find him these days. He used to lay drunk with the hogs in the tanyard. But he ain't been seen in these parts for a year or more."

They talked it over, and they was going to rule me out. They said every boy must have a family or somebody to kill. Or else it wouldn't be fair and square for the others.

Well, nobody could think of anything to do. Everybody was stumped, and set still. I was most ready to cry. But all at once I thought of a way. I offered them Miss Watson—they could kill her.

Everybody said, "Oh, she'll do. That's all right. Huck can come in."

Then they all stuck a pin in their fingers to get blood. They signed their names with it, and I made my mark on the paper.[5]

"Now," says Ben Rogers, "what's the line of business for this Gang?"

"Nothing, only robbery and murder," Tom said.

"But who are we going to rob? Houses, cattle, or—"

"Stuff![6] Stealing cattle and such things ain't robbery," says Tom Sawyer. "It's burglary. We ain't burglars. That ain't no sort of style. We are highwaymen. We put masks on and stop stagecoaches and carriages on the road. We kill the people and take their watches and money."

"Must we always kill the people?"

---

5 Huck doesn't know how to read or write. Instead, he puts a mark on the paper for his signature.

6 *Stuff* is an exclamation of disgust.

"Oh, certainly. It's best. Some authorities think different. But mostly it's considered best to kill them. Except some that you bring to the cave here. We keep them till they're **ransomed**."

"Ransomed? What's that?"

"I don't know. But that's what they do. I've seen it in books. And so, of course, that's what we've got to do."

"But how can we do it if we don't know what it is?"

"Why, blame it all, we've got to do it. Didn't I tell you it's in the books? Do you want to go to doing different from what's in the books? Get things all **muddled** up?"

"Oh, that's very fine to say, Tom Sawyer. But how in the nation[7] are these fellows going to be ransomed? We don't even know how to do it to them! That's the thing I want to get at. Now, what do you reckon it is?"

"Well, I don't know. But maybe if we keep them till they're ransomed, it means that we keep them till they're dead."

"Now that's better. That's an answer. Why couldn't you have said that before? We'll keep them till they're ransomed to death. And a **bothersome** lot they'll be, too. They'll eat up all the food, and always try to get loose."

"How you talk, Ben Rogers. How can they get loose when there's a guard over them? He'll shoot them down if they move an inch."

"A guard! Well, that is good. So somebody's got to set up all night and never get any sleep. I think that's foolishness. Why can't a body take a club to them? We'll ransom them as soon as they get here!"

"Because it ain't in the books that way—that's why. Now, Ben Rogers, do you want to get things regular, or don't you? That's the idea.

"Don't you reckon that the people that made the books knows what's the correct thing to do? Do you reckon you can learn them anything? Not by a good deal. No, sir. We'll just go on and ransom them in the regular way."

"All right. I don't mind. But I say it's a foolish way, anyway. Say, do we kill the women, too?"

---

7 *Nation* is a polite version of "damnation."

"Well, Ben Rogers, if I was as stupid as you I wouldn't let on. Kill the women? No. Nobody ever saw anything in the books like that.

"You bring them to the cave, and you're always as polite as pie to them. And by and by they fall in love with you. And they'll never want to go home anymore."

"Well, if that's the way, I'm agreed. But I don't take no stock in it. Mighty soon we'll have the cave all cluttered up with women and fellows waiting to be ransomed. There won't be no place for the robbers. But go ahead. I ain't got nothing to say."

Little Tommy Barnes was asleep now. When they waked him up he was scared, and cried. He said he wanted to go home to his ma. He didn't want to be a robber anymore.

So they all made fun of him, and called him crybaby. And that made him mad. He said he would go straight and tell all the secrets. But Tom give him five cents to keep quiet. Tom said we would all go home and meet next week. Then we'd rob somebody and kill some people.

Ben Rogers said he couldn't get out much, only Sundays. So he wanted to begin next Sunday. But all the boys said it would be wicked to do it on Sunday. That settled the thing.

They agreed to get together and fix a day as soon as they could.

And then we elected Tom Sawyer first captain and Joe Harper second captain of the Gang. Then we started home.

I clumb up the shed and crept into my window just before day was breaking. My new clothes was all greased up and covered with clay, and I was dog-tired.

Chapter 3 (Summary)

We Ambuscade the A-rabs

The morning after the gang meeting, Miss Watson scolded Huck because of his dirty clothes. Then she took him aside and made him pray with her. She told Huck that he would get whatever he asked for. But he didn't believe her because he had never gotten the fishhooks he had prayed for earlier.

Later Huck did a lot of thinking about God and praying. He felt that if a person could really get something just by praying, then everyone would have all they wanted. And Miss Watson's lecture about praying for "spiritual gifts" and doing things for others made Huck feel that religion required too much work. Huck decided he preferred the widow's vision of God. That God didn't seem so hard to please. Huck finally concluded that he might be too stupid and stubborn for God to care about him anyway.

Huck also thought about his father, whom he hadn't seen for years. Huck dreaded the thought of a meeting, since Pap always mistreated him. But Huck had a feeling that Pap was bound to show up sooner or later.

All this thinking didn't keep Huck from playing. For a month he and the robber gang followed Tom Sawyer. Then all the boys quit since they never really robbed or killed anyone. The closest they came was when they tried to ambuscade, or attack, a group of Sunday School children. Tom tried to get Huck to believe that the children were really Spaniards and Arabs under a magic spell. But Huck doubted the truth of this. Finally he decided that the story was just another one of Tom's lies.

Chapter 4

The Hair-Ball Oracle

VOCABULARY PREVIEW

The following words appear in this chapter. Review the list and get to know the words before you read the chapter.

considerable—much; great
consideration—payment
counterfeit—imitation; fake
satisfactory—good; okay

Well, three or four months run along. It was well into the winter now. I had been to school most all the time. I could spell and read and write just a little. And I could say the multiplication table up to six times seven is thirty-five.

I don't reckon I could ever get any further than that. It didn't matter if I was to live forever. I don't take no stock in mathematics, anyway.

At first I hated school. But by and by, I got so I could stand it. Whenever I got uncommon tired, I played hooky. The whipping I got the next day done me good and cheered me up. So the longer I went to school the easier it got to be.

I was getting sort of used to the widow's ways, too. They warn't so rough on me. Living in a house and sleeping in a bed cramped me pretty tight mostly. But before the cold weather, I used to slide out and sleep in the woods sometimes. That was a rest to me.

I liked the old ways best. But I was getting so I liked the new ones, too, a little bit. The widow said I was coming along slow but sure. She said I was doing very **satisfactory**. She said she warn't ashamed of me.

One morning I happened to knock over the saltshaker at breakfast. I reached for some of it as quick as I could. I wanted to throw it over my left shoulder and keep off the bad luck. But

Miss Watson was in ahead of me and crossed me off.

She says, "Take your hands away, Huckleberry. What a mess you are always making!"

The widow put in a good word for me. But that warn't going to keep off the bad luck. I knowed that well enough.

I started out, after breakfast, feeling worried and shaky. I wondered where the bad luck was going to fall on me. And what it was going to be. There is ways to keep off some kinds of bad luck. But this warn't one of them kind. So I never tried to do anything. I just poked along low-spirited and on the watch-out.

I went down to the front garden. I clumb over the stile[1] where you go through the high board fence. There was an inch of new snow on the ground. And I seen somebody's tracks.

They had come up from the quarry and stood around the stile awhile. Then they went on around the garden fence. It was funny they hadn't come in, after standing around so. I couldn't make it out. It was very curious, somehow.

I was going to walk around, but I stooped down to look at the tracks first. I didn't notice anything at first, but next I did. There was a cross in the left bootheel made with big nails, to keep off the devil.

I was up in a second and running down the hill. I looked over my shoulder every now and then. But I didn't see nobody. I was at Judge Thatcher's as quick as I could get there.

He said, "Why, my boy, you are all out of breath. Did you come for your interest?"

"No, sir," I says. "Is there some for me?"

"Oh, yes, a half-yearly is in last night—over a hundred and fifty dollars. Quite a fortune for you. You had better let me invest it along with your six thousand. Because if you take it, you'll spend it."

"No, sir," I says. "I don't want to spend it. I don't want it at all—nor the six thousand, neither. I want you to take it. I want to give it to you—the six thousand and all."

He looked surprised. He couldn't seem to make it out. He says, "Why, what can you mean, my boy?"

I says, "Don't you ask me no questions about it, please.

---

1 A *stile* is a set of steps that goes over a fence. It's used in place of a gate.

You'll take it—won't you?"

He says, "Well, I'm puzzled. Is something the matter?"

"Please take it," says I, "and don't ask me nothing. Then I won't have to tell no lies."

He studied awhile, and then he says, "Oho-o! I think I see. You want to sell all your property to me—not give it. That's the correct idea."

Then he wrote something on a paper and read it over, and says, "There. You see it says 'for a **consideration**.' That means I have bought it from you and paid you for it. Here's a dollar for you. Now you sign it."

So I signed it, and left.

Miss Watson's nigger, Jim, had a hair ball as big as your fist. It had been taken out of the fourth stomach of an ox. He used to do magic with it. He said there was a spirit inside of it that knowed everything. So I went to him that night and told him Pap was here again. I found his tracks in the snow. What I wanted to know was, what he was going to do? And was he going to stay?

Jim got out his hair ball and said something over it. Then he held it up and dropped it on the floor. It fell pretty solid, and only rolled about an inch. Jim tried it again, and then another time. It acted just the same.

Jim got down on his knees. He put his ear against it and listened. But it warn't no use. He said it wouldn't talk. He said sometimes it wouldn't talk without money.

I told him I had an old slick **counterfeit** quarter. It warn't no good because the brass showed through the silver a little. It wouldn't pass, even if the brass didn't show. It was so slick it felt greasy. That would tell on it every time. I reckoned I wouldn't say nothing about the dollar I got from the judge. I said it was pretty bad money. But maybe the hair ball would take it. Maybe it wouldn't know the difference.

Jim smelt it and bit it and rubbed it. He said he would manage so the hair ball would think it was good. He said he would split open a raw Irish potato. He would stick the quarter in between and keep it there all night.

And the next morning you wouldn't see no brass. It wouldn't feel greasy no more. So anybody in town would take it in a minute, let alone a hair ball. Well, I knowed a potato would do that before, but I had forgot it.

Jim put the quarter under the hair ball. He got down and listened again. This time he said the hair ball was all right. He said it would tell my whole fortune if I wanted it to. I says, go on. So the hair ball talked to Jim, and Jim told it to me.

He says, "Your ole father don't know yit what he's a-goin' to do. Sometimes he spects he'll go away. En' den again he spects he'll stay. De best way is to rest easy en' let de ole man take his own way.

"There's two angels hoverin' 'round 'bout him. One of 'em is white en' shiny. De other one is black. De white one gits him to go right for a little while. Den de black one sail in en' bust it all up. A body can't tell yit which one goin' to get him at de end.

"But you is all right. You goin' to have **considerable** trouble in your life, en' considerable joy. Sometimes you goin' to git hurt, en' sometimes you goin' to get sick. But every time you's goin' to git well again.

"There's two girls flyin' 'bout you in your life. One of 'em's light and de other one is dark. One is rich en' de other is poor. You's goin' to marry de poor one first en' de rich one by en' by. You wants to keep 'way from de water as much as you can. Don't run no risk. 'Cause it's down in de bills[2] dat you's goin' to git hung."

When I lit my candle and went up to my room that night, there sat Pap—his own self!

---

2 *Down the bills* means "in store for you."

Chapter 5

Pap Starts In on a New Life

VOCABULARY PREVIEW

The following words appear in this chapter. Review the list and get to know the words before you read the chapter.

guardian—foster parent
jolt—sudden shock or surprise
meddle—interfere; butt in
navigate—pilot; steer

I had shut the door. Then I turned around, and there he was. I used to be scared of him all the time on account he tanned[1] me so much. I reckoned I was scared now, too. But in a minute I see I was mistaken.

That was the first **jolt**, as you may say. My breath sort of caught, since he was so unexpected. But right away after, I see I warn't scared of him worth bothering about.

He was most fifty, and he looked it. His hair was long and tangled and greasy, and hung down. You could see his eyes shining through like he was behind vines. It was all black, no gray. So was his long, mixed-up whiskers.

There warn't no color in his face, where his face showed. It was white. It was not like another man's white, but a white to make a body sick. It was a white to make a body's flesh crawl. It was a tree-toad white, a fish-belly white. As for his clothes—just rags, that was all.

He had one ankle resting on the other knee. The boot on that foot was busted and two of his toes stuck through. He wiggled them now and then. His hat was laying on the floor—an old black slouch[2] with the top caved in, like a lid.

---

1 *Tanned* is another word for "whipped."

2 A slouch hat is usually made from felt and has a wide, flexible brim.

I stood a-lookin' at him. He set there a-lookin' at me, with his chair tilted back a little. I set the candle down. I noticed the window was up. So he had clumb in by the shed. He kept a-lookin' me all over.

By and by he says, "Starchy clothes—very. You think you're a good deal of a big-bug,[3] don't you?"

"Maybe I am, maybe I ain't," I says.

"Don't you give me none of your lip," says he. "You've put on a lot of fancy ways since I been away. I'll take you down a peg before I get done with you.

"You're educated too, they say—can read and write. You think you're better than your father, now, don't you, because he can't? I'll take it out of you. Who told you you might **meddle** with such highfalutin'[4] foolishness, hey? Who told you you could?"

"The widow. She told me."

"The widow, hey? And who told the widow she could put in her shovel? This thing ain't none of her business!"

"Nobody never told her."

"Well, I'll learn her how to meddle. And looky here—you drop that school, you hear? I'll learn people to bring up a boy to put on airs over his own father and let on to be better than what he is. Don't let me catch you fooling around that school again. You hear?

"Your mother couldn't read. And she couldn't write, neither, before she died. None of the family couldn't before they died, I can't. And here you're a-swellin' yourself up like this. I ain't the man to stand it—you hear? Say, let me hear you read."

I took up a book and begun something. It was about General Washington and the wars. When I read about half a minute, he gave the book a whack with his hand. He knocked it across the house.

"It's so. You can do it. I had my doubts when you told me. Now looky here. You stop acting so fancy. I won't have it. I'll watch for you, my smarty. And if I catch you about that school

---

3 By *big-bug*, Pap means "hotshot."

4 *Highfalutin'* means "highbrow" or "fancy."

I'll tan you good. First thing you know, you'll get religion, too. I never see such a son."

He took up a little blue and yellow picture of some cows and a boy.

"What's this?"

"It's something they give me for learning my lessons good."

He tore it up and says, "I'll give you something better—I'll give you a cowhide."[5]

He set there a-mumblin' and a-growlin' a minute. And then he says, "Ain't you a sweet-scented dandy, though? A bed, and bedclothes, and a mirror. And a piece of carpet on the floor. And your own father has to sleep with the hogs in the tanyard. I never see such a son.

"I bet I'll take some of the fanciness out of you before I'm done with you. Why, there ain't no end to your airs. They say you're rich. Hey? How's that?"

"They lie—that's how."

"Looky here—mind how you talk to me. I'm a-standin' about all I can stand now. So don't give me no sass. I've been in town two days, and I ain't heard nothin' but about you bein' rich. I heard about it away down the river, too. That's why I come. You git me that money tomorrow. I want it."

"I ain't got no money."

"It's a lie. Judge Thatcher's got it. You git it. I want it."

"I ain't got no money, I tell you. You ask Judge Thatcher. He'll tell you the same."

"All right. I'll ask him. And I'll make him fork it over, too. Or I'll know the reason why. Say, how much you got in your pocket? I want it."

"I ain't got only a dollar, and I want that to—"

"It don't make no difference what you want it for. You just shell it out."

He took it and bit it to see if it was good. Then he said he was going downtown to get some whisky. He said he hadn't had a drink all day.

---

5 Pap means that he will use a leather strap, like a belt, and whip Huck.

When he got out on the shed, he put his head in again. He cussed me for putting on airs and trying to be better than him. Then I reckoned he was gone. But he come back and put his head in again. He told me to mind about that school. He was going to watch for me and lick me if I didn't drop that.

Next day he was drunk, and went to Judge Thatcher's. He threatened him, and tried to make him give up the money. But he couldn't. And then Pap swore he'd make the law force him.

The judge and the widow went to the law. They tried to get the court to take me away from him and let one of them be my **guardian**. But it was a new judge that had just come. He didn't know the old man.

So he said courts mustn't interfere and separate families if they could help it. He said he'd rather not take a child away from its father. So Judge Thatcher and the widow had to quit on the business.

That pleased the old man till he couldn't rest. He said he'd cowhide me till I was black and blue if I didn't raise some money for him. I borrowed three dollars from Judge Thatcher. Pap took it and got drunk.

He went a-blowin' around and cussin' and whoopin' and carryin' on. He kept it up all over town, with a tin pan, till most midnight. Then they jailed him. Next day they had him before court. They jailed him again for a week.

But he said he was satisfied. He said he was boss of his son. He'd make it warm for him.

When he got out of jail, the new judge said he was a-goin' to make a man of him. So he took him to his own house and dressed him up clean and nice. He had him to breakfast and dinner and supper with the family. He was just old pie[6] to him, so to speak.

And after supper the judge talked to Pap about temperance[7] and such things. Then Pap cried. He said he'd been a fool, and fooled away his life. But now he was a-goin' to turn over a new leaf. He'd be a man nobody wouldn't be ashamed of. He hoped the judge would help him and not look down on him.

---

6 *Old pie* means "old pal."

7 *Temperance* is refusing to drink alcohol.

The judge said he could hug him for them words. So he cried, and his wife, she cried again. Pap said he'd been a man that had always been misunderstood before. The judge said he believed it.

The old man said that what he wanted was sympathy. That's what a man needed when he was down. The judge said it was so. So they cried again.

And when it was bedtime Pap rose up and held out his hand. He says, "Look at it, gentlemen and ladies all. Take ahold of it. Shake it. There's a hand that was the hand of a hog. But it ain't so no more. It's the hand of a man that's started in on a new life. And he'll die before he'll go back.

"You mark them words. Don't forget I said them. It's a clean hand now. Shake it. Don't be afeard."

So they shook it, one after the other, all around. And they cried. The judge's wife, she kissed it. Then Pap, he signed a pledge[8]—made his mark.

The judge said it was the holiest time on record, or something like that. Then they tucked the old man into a beautiful room, which was the spare room.

In the night sometime he got powerful thirsty. So he clumb out onto the porch roof and slid down a post. He traded his new coat for a jug of forty-rod.[9] Then he clumb back in again and had a good old time.

Toward daylight he crawled out again, drunk as a fiddler. He rolled off the porch and broke his left arm in two places. He was most froze to death when somebody found him after sunup. Then they went to look at that spare room. But they had to take soundings before they could **navigate** it.[10]

The judge felt kind of sore. He said he reckoned a body could reform the old man with a shotgun, maybe. But he didn't know no other way.

---

8 The pledge Pap signs is his promise to give up drinking.

9 *Forty-rod* is a homemade whisky. It's very potent and supposedly knocks an individual 40 rods (60 yards).

10 A ship's navigator decides if the water is deep enough for safe passage. Huck means the room was in a such a mess that moving around was difficult.

Chapter 6

Pap Struggles with the Death Angel

VOCABULARY PREVIEW

The following words appear in this chapter. Review the list and get to know the words before you read the chapter.

infernal—devilish; wicked
objections—complaints; disapprovals
parcel—bunch; group
previous—before; earlier
prowling—sneaking
specimen—sample; example

Well, pretty soon the old man was up and around again. Then he went for Judge Thatcher in the courts to make him give up that money. And he went for me, too, for not stopping school.

He catched me a couple of times and beat me. But I went to school just the same. I dodged him or outrun him most of the time. I didn't want to go to school much before. But I reckoned I'd go now to spite Pap.

That law trial was a slow business. It appeared like they warn't ever going to get started on it. So every now and then, I'd borrow two or three dollars off of the judge for Pap. That would keep me from getting a cowhiding.

Every time he got money he got drunk. And every time he got drunk, he raised Cain around town. And every time he raised Cain he got jailed. He was just suited for it. This kind of thing was right in his line.

Well, he got to hanging around the widow's too much. So she told him at last to quit hanging around there. Otherwise, she would make trouble for him. Well, *wasn't* he mad? He said he would show who was Huck Finn's boss.

So he watched out for me one day in the spring. He catched me, and took me up the river about three mile in a skiff.[1] We crossed over to the Illinois shore where it was woody. There warn't no houses but an old log hut. It was in a place where the timber was thick. You couldn't find it if you didn't know where it was.

Pap kept me with him all the time. I never got a chance to run off. We lived in that old cabin. He always locked the door and put the key under his head at nights.

He had a gun which he had stole, I reckon. So we fished and hunted. And that was what we lived on.

Every little while he locked me in and went down to the store. It was three miles to the ferry.[2] He traded fish and game for whisky. Then he fetched it home and got drunk and had a good time, and licked me.

The widow, she found out where I was by and by. And she sent a man over to try to get hold of me. But Pap drove him off with the gun. It warn't long after that till I was used to being where I was, and liked it. All but the cowhide part.

It was kind of lazy and jolly. I lay off comfortable all day, smoking and fishing, and no books nor study. Two months or more run along. My clothes got to be all rags and dirt.

I didn't see how I'd ever got to like it so well at the widow's. You had to wash there, and eat on a plate, and comb up. You had to go to bed and get up regular. And you were forever bothering over a book. And you had Miss Watson pecking at you all the time.

I didn't want to go back no more. I had stopped cussing before, because the widow didn't like it. But now I took to it again because Pap hadn't no **objections**. It was pretty good times up in the woods there, take it all around.

But by and by, Pap got too handy with his hickory.[3] I couldn't stand it. I was all over welts. He got to going away so much, too, and locking me in.

---

1 A *skiff* is a small rowboat.

2 A *ferry* is a boat used for carrying people, animals, wagons, cars, etc., across a body of water. The store where Pap trades is located at the ferry landing.

3 Huck is referring to Pap's hickory stick, which he uses to whip Huck.

Once he locked me in and was gone three days. It was dreadful lonesome. I judged he had got drownded and I wasn't ever going to get out any more. I was scared. I made up my mind I would fix up some way to leave there.

I had tried to get out of that cabin many a time. But I couldn't find no way. There warn't a window to it big enough for a dog to get through. I couldn't get up the chimney—it was too narrow. And the door was thick, solid oak slabs.

Pap was pretty careful. He never left a knife or anything in the cabin when he was away. I reckon I had hunted the place over as much as a hundred times. Well, I was most all the time at it. It was about the only way to put in the time.

But this time I found something at last. I found an old rusty wood saw without any handle. It was laid in between a rafter and the clapboards of the roof. I greased it up and went to work.

We had an old horse blanket. It was nailed against the logs at the far end of the cabin behind the table. It kept the wind from blowing through the chinks and putting the candle out.

I got under the table and raised the blanket. I went to work to saw a section of the big bottom log out—big enough to let me through. Well, it was a good long job. But I was getting toward the end of it when I heard Pap's gun in the woods.

I got rid of the signs of my work. And I dropped the blanket and hid my saw. Pretty soon, Pap come in.

Pap warn't in good humor—so he was his natural self. He said he was downtown, and everything was going wrong. His lawyer said he reckoned Pap would win his lawsuit and get the money. That is, if they ever got started on the trial.

But then there was ways to put it off a long time. And Judge Thatcher knowed how to do it. Pap said people allowed there'd be another trial to get me away from him. They'd try to give me to the widow for my guardian. And they guessed it would win, this time.

This shook me up considerable. I didn't want to go back to the widow's anymore. I didn't want to be so cramped up and sivilized, as they called it.

Then the old man got to cussing. He cussed everything and everybody he could think of. And then he cussed them over again to make sure he hadn't skipped any. After that, he polished off with a kind of a general cuss all around.

He included a considerable **parcel** of people which he didn't know the names of. So he called them what's-his-name when he got to them. Then he went right along with his cussing.

He said he would like to see the widow get me. He said he would watch out for them. And just let them try to pull any such game on him. For he knowed of a place six or seven miles off to hide me in. They might hunt till they dropped and they wouldn't find me.

That made me pretty uneasy again, but only for a minute. I reckoned I wouldn't stay on hand till he got that chance.

The old man made me go to the skiff. I had to fetch the things he had got. There was a fifty-pound sack of cornmeal and a side of bacon. And there was gunpowder and a four-gallon jug of whisky. There was also an old book and two newspapers for wadding,[4] plus some other stuff.

I carried up a load. Then I went back and set down on the bow of the skiff to rest. I thought it all over. I reckoned I would walk off with the gun and some fishing lines. Then I would take to the woods and run away.

I guessed I wouldn't stay in one place. I'd just tramp right across the country, mostly at night. I'd hunt and fish to keep alive. I'd get as far away as I could. Neither the old man nor the widow couldn't ever find me anymore.

I judged I would saw out and leave that night if Pap got drunk enough. And I reckoned he would. I was so busy thinking that I didn't notice how long I was staying. Then the old man hollered. He asked me whether I was asleep or drownded, I got the things all up to the cabin. By then it was about dark. While I was cooking supper, the old man took a swig or two. He got sort of warmed up, and went to ripping again.

He had been drunk over in town, and laid in the gutter all night. He was a sight to look at. A body would have thought he was Adam.[5] He was just all mud.

---

4 *Wadding* was used to load gunpowder into a rifle.

5 Huck is making a reference to the biblical Adam (the first man), who was created from dirt.

Whenever his liquor begun to work, he most always went for the government. This time he says, "Call this a government! Why, just look at it and see what it's like. Here's the law a-standin' ready to take a man's son away from him. A man's own son! And he has taken all the worry and all the trouble and all the expense of raising him.

"Yes, and now that man has got that son raised at last. And that son's ready to go to work and begin to do something for him and give him a rest. Then the law up and goes for him. And they call that government!

"That ain't all, neither. The law backs that old Judge Thatcher up. It helps him to keep me out of my property.

"Here's what the law does. It takes a man worth six thousand dollars and upwards. It jams him into an old trap of a cabin like this. It lets him go round in clothes that ain't fittin' for a hog.

"They call that a government! A man can't get his rights in a government like this. Sometimes I've a mighty notion to just leave the country for good and all. Yes, and I told 'em so. I told old Thatcher so to his face. Lots of 'em heard me, and can tell what I said.

"Says I, 'For two cents I'd leave the blamed country. I'd never come a-near it again.' Them's the very words.

"I says, 'Look at my hat—if you call it a hat. The lid raises up and the rest of it goes down till it's below my chin. And then it ain't rightly a hat at all. It's more like my head was shoved up through a joint of stove pipe. Look at it,' says I. 'Such a hat for me to wear. One of the wealthiest men in this town, if I could get my rights.'

"Oh, yes, this is a wonderful government," says Pap, "wonderful. Why, looky here. There was a free nigger there from Ohio. He was a mulatto,[6] most as white as a white man. He had the whitest shirt on you ever see, too. And the shiniest hat.

"And there ain't a man in that town that's got as fine clothes as what he had. And he had a gold watch and chain. And a silver-headed cane. He was the awfulest old gray-headed bigwig in the state.

---

6 A *mulatto* is a person with one white parent and one black parent.

"And what do you think? They said he was a professor in a college. He could talk all kinds of languages, and knowed everything. And that ain't the worst. They said he could vote when he was at home.

"Well, that was too much for me. Thinks I, what is the country a-comin' to? It was election day. I was just about to go and vote myself, if I warn't too drunk to get there.

"But then they tell me there's a state in this country where they'd let that nigger vote. I gave it up. I says, 'I'll never vote again.' Them's the very words I said. They all heard me. And the country may rot for all I care. I'll never vote again as long as I live.

"And to see the cool way of that nigger! Why, he wouldn't have give me the road, if I hadn't shoved him out of the way. I says to the people, 'Why ain't this nigger put up at auction and sold? That's what I want to know.'

"And what do you reckon they said? Why, they said he couldn't be sold. He'd have to be in the state six months. And he hadn't been there that long yet.

"There now—that's a **specimen**. They call that a government that can't sell a free nigger. He's got to be in the state six months.

"Here's a government that calls itself a government. It lets on to be a government. It thinks it is a government. And yet it's got to be set still for six whole months. It can't even take ahold of a **prowling**, thieving, **infernal**, white-shirted free nigger,[7] and—"

Pap was a-goin' so, he never noticed where his old limber legs was taking him to. So he went head over heels over the tub of salt pork. He scraped both shins.

The rest of his speech was all the hottest kind of language.

Most of it was aimed at the nigger and the government. He did give the tub some, too, though, here and there.

He hopped around the cabin considerable. First on one leg and then on the other. He held first one shin and then the other one. At last, he let out with his left foot all of a sudden. And he gave the tub a rattling kick.

---

7 Laws governing the rights of blacks varied from state to state. At the time of this novel, a free black was in danger of being sold in Missouri.

But it warn't good judgment. That was the boot that had a couple of his toes leaking out the front end of it. So now he raised a howl that fairly made a body's hair raise.

And down he went in the dirt. He rolled there and held his toes. The cussing he done then topped anything he had ever done previous. He said so his own self afterwards. He had heard old Sowberry Hagan[8] in his best days. He said it topped him, too. But I reckon that was sort of piling it on, maybe.

After supper Pap took the jug. He said he had enough whisky there for two drunks and one delirium tremens.[9] That was always what he said. I judged he would be blind drunk in about an hour. Then I would steal the key, or saw myself out, one or the other.

He drank and drank and tumbled down on his blankets by and by. But luck didn't run my way. He didn't go sound asleep, but was uneasy.

He groaned and moaned. He thrashed around this way and that for a long time. At last I got sleepy. I couldn't keep my eyes open, no matter what I did. And so, before I knowed what I was about, I was sound asleep. The candle was still burning.

I don't know how long I was asleep. But all of a sudden there was an awful scream and I was up. There was Pap looking wild. He was skipping around every which way and was yelling about snakes. He said they was crawling up his legs. Then he would give a jump and scream. He said one had bit him on the cheek. But I couldn't see no snakes.

He started and run round and round the cabin. He kept hollering, "Take him off! Take him off! He's biting me on the neck!" I never saw a man look so wild in the eyes.

Pretty soon he was spent. He fell down panting. Then he rolled over and over, wonderful fast. He kicked things every which way. He struck and grabbed at the air with his hands. He screamed and said there was devils ahold of him.

---

8 Sowberry Hagan is probably a local character who is known for his cussing.

9 *Delirium tremens* is a nervous and mental disorder caused by alcoholism. Insomnia, restlessness, and hallucinations often accompany it.

He wore out by and by. He laid still awhile, moaning. Then he laid stiller, and didn't make a sound. I could hear the owls and the wolves way off in the woods. It seemed terrible still.

He was laying over by the corner. By and by, he raised up part way and listened. He tilted his head to one side.

He says, very low, "Tramp—tramp—tramp. That's the dead. Tramp—tramp—tramp. They're coming after me. But I won't go. Oh, they're here! Don't touch me—don't! Hands off—they're cold. Let go. Oh, let a poor devil alone!"

Then he went down on all fours and crawled off. He begged them to let him alone. And he rolled himself up in his blanket and huddled under the old pine table. He was still a-beggin'. And then he went to cryin'. I could hear him through the blanket.

By and by, he rolled out and jumped up on his feet. He looked wild. Then he saw me and went for me. He chased me round and round the place with a clasp knife.[10] He called me the Angel of Death and said he would kill me. Then I couldn't come for him no more.

I begged, and told him I was only Huck. But he laughed such a screechy laugh. He roared and cussed, and kept on chasing me.

Once I turned short and dodged under his arm. He made a grab and got me by the jacket between my shoulders. I thought I was gone. But I slid out of the jacket quick as lightning, and saved myself.

Pretty soon he was all tired out. He dropped down with his back against the door. He said he would rest a minute and then kill me. He put his knife under him and said he would sleep and get strong. Then he would see who was who.

So he dozed off pretty soon. By and by, I got an old chair. I clumb up as easy as I could, not to make any noise. And I got down the gun. I slipped the ramrod down it to make sure it was loaded.

Then I laid it across the turnip barrel, pointing it towards Pap. I set down behind it to wait for him to stir. And how slow and still the time did drag along.

---

10 A *clasp knife* is a one-bladed pocketknife.

Chapter 7

I Fool Pap and Get Away

VOCABULARY PREVIEW

The following words appear in this chapter. Review the list and get to know the words before you read the chapter.

abreast—beside
abused—mistreated; knocked around
browsing—looking over; checking
cranky—grouchy; crabby
hail—wave to; call out to
monstrous—huge; enormous

"Git up! What you about?"

I opened my eyes and looked around. I tried to make out where I was. It was after sunup, and I had been sound asleep. Pap was standing over me looking sour—and sick, too.

He says, "What you doin' with this gun?"

I judged he didn't know nothing about what he had been doing. So I says, "Somebody tried to get in so I was waiting for him."

"Why didn't you wake me up?"

"Well, I tried to, but I couldn't. I couldn't budge you."

"Well, all right. Don't stand there talking all day. Out with you and see if there's a fish on the lines for breakfast. I'll be along in a minute."

He unlocked the door and I cleared out up the riverbank. I noticed some pieces of limbs and such things floating down.

And there was a sprinkling of bark. So I knowed the river had begun to rise. I reckoned I would have great times now if I was over at the town.

The June rise used to be always luck for me. Because as soon as that rise begins, here comes cordwood[1] floating down.

1 *Cordwood* is wood that has been cut up.

And pieces of log rafts, too—sometimes a dozen logs together. So all you have to do is catch them. Then you sell them to the woodyards and the sawmill.

I went along up the bank with one eye out for Pap. I had the other one out for what the rise might bring along. Well, all at once here comes a canoe. It was just a beauty, too. It was about thirteen or fourteen foot long, riding high like a duck.

I shot headfirst off of the bank like a frog, clothes and all on. I struck out for the canoe. I just expected there'd be somebody laying down in it. People often did that to fool folks. They'd let a chap pull a skiff out and then they'd raise up and laugh at him.

But it warn't so this time. It was a drift canoe, sure enough. And I clumb in and paddled her ashore. Thinks I, the old man will be glad when he sees this. She's worth ten dollars.

But when I got to shore, Pap wasn't in sight yet. I ran the canoe into a little creek like a gully. It was all hung over with vines and willows. Then I struck another idea.

I judged I'd hide her good. Then I wouldn't have to take to the woods when I run off. I'd go down the river about fifty miles and camp in one place for good. I wouldn't have such a rough time tramping on foot.

It was pretty close to the hut. I thought I heard the old man coming all the time. But I got her hid.

Then I out and looked around a bunch of willows. There was the old man down the path a piece. He was just shooting down a bird with his gun. So he hadn't seen anything.

When he got along, I was hard at it taking up a trotline.[2] He **abused** me a little for being so slow. But I told him I fell in the river, and that was what made me so long. I knowed he would see I was wet. Then he would be asking questions. We got five catfish off the lines and went home.

We laid off after breakfast to sleep up. Both of us were about wore out. I got to thinking. Maybe I could fix up some way to keep Pap and the widow from trying to follow me.

It would be a more certain thing that way. Otherwise,

I would have to trust to luck to get far enough off before they missed me. You see, all kinds of things might happen.

2 A *trotline* is a fishing line that stretches out underwater. It is baited with a number of hooks.

Well, I didn't see no way for a while. But by and by, Pap raised up a minute. He drank another barrel of water, and he says, "Another time a man comes prowling 'round here, you wake me up, you hear? That man warn't here for no good. I'd a shot him. Next time you wake me up, you hear?"

Then he dropped down and went to sleep again. What he had been saying give me the very idea I wanted. I says to myself, I can fix it now. Nobody won't think of following me.

About twelve o'clock, we turned out and went up the bank. The river was coming up pretty fast. Lots of driftwood was going by on the rise. By and by, along comes part of a log raft. It was nine logs fast together. We went out with the skiff and towed it ashore.

Then we had dinner. Anybody but Pap would have waited and seen the day through. He could have caught more stuff. But that warn't Pap's style. Nine logs was enough for one time. He must shove right over to town and sell.

So he locked me in and took the skiff. At half past three, he started off towing the raft. I judged he wouldn't come back that night.

I waited till I reckoned he had got a good start. Then I out with my saw and went to work on that log again. Before he was to the other side of the river, I was out of the hole. Him and his raft was just a speck on the water away off yonder.

I took the sack of cornmeal and carried it to where the canoe was hid. I shoved the vines and branches apart and put it in. Then I done the same with the side of bacon. Then came the whisky jug.

I took all the coffee and sugar there was, and all the ammunition. I took the wadding. I took the bucket and the gourd. I gathered up a dipper and a tin cup, and my old saw and two blankets. And I took the skillet and the coffee pot.

I took fish lines and matches and other things. Everything that was worth a cent. I cleaned out the place. I wanted an ax, but there wasn't any. There was only the one out at the woodpile. And I knowed why I was going to leave that. I grabbed up the gun, and now I was done.

I had been crawling out of the hole and dragging out a lot of things. So I had wore out the ground a good deal. I fixed that as good as I could. I scattered dust on the place from the outside. This covered up the smoothness and the sawdust.

Then I fixed the piece of log back into its place. I put two rocks under it and another against it to hold it there. It was bent up at that place and didn't quite touch ground. If you stood four or five foot away and didn't know it was sawed, you wouldn't never notice it. Besides, this was the back of the cabin. It warn't likely anybody would go fooling around there.

It was all grass clear to the canoe. So I hadn't left a track. I hiked around to see. I stood on the bank and looked out over the river. All safe.

So I took the gun and went up a piece into the woods. I was hunting around for some birds when I saw a wild pig. Hogs often got away from the prairie farms. Then they ran wild in them bottoms. I shot this fellow and took him into camp.

I took the ax and smashed in the door. I beat it and hacked it considerable a-doin' it. I fetched the pig in and took him back nearly to the table. Then I hacked into his l throat with the ax. I laid him down on the ground to bleed. I say ground because it was ground. It was hard packed, and no boards.

Well, next I took an old sack and put a lot of big rocks in it—all I could drag. Starting from the pig, I dragged it to the door. I went through the woods down to the river and dumped it in. Down it sunk, out of sight. You could easy see that something had been dragged over the ground.

I did wish Tom Sawyer was there. I knowed he would take an interest in this kind of business. He'd throw in some fancy touches. Nobody could spread himself like Tom Sawyer in such a thing as that.

Well, last I pulled out some of my hair. I blooded the ax good, and stuck it on the back side. I slung the ax in the corner. Then I took up the pig and held him up to my breast with my jacket (so he couldn't drip). When I got a good piece below the house, I dumped him into the river.

Now I thought of something else. So I went and got the bag of meal and my old saw out of the canoe. These I brought to the house. I took the bag to where it used to stand. I ripped a hole in the bottom of it with the saw. There warn't no knives and forks on the place. Pap done everything with his clasp knife about the cooking.

Then I carried the sack about a hundred yards across the grass. I went through the willows east of the house. At last I came to a shallow lake that was five miles wide and full of rushes. It was full of ducks too, you might say, in the season. There was a slough or a creek leading out of it on the other side. It went miles away. I don't know where. But it didn't go to the river.

The meal sifted out and made a little track all the way to the lake. I dropped Pap's whetstone[3] there, too. It looked like it had been done by accident. Then I tied up the rip in the meal sack with a string so it wouldn't leak no more. Finally, I took it and my saw to the canoe again.

It was about dark now. So I dropped the canoe down the river, under some willows that hung over the bank. Then I waited for the moon to rise.

I made fast to a willow. Then I took a bite to eat. By and by, I laid down in the canoe to smoke a pipe and lay out a plan.

I says to myself, they'll follow the track of that sackful of rocks to the shore. Then they'll drag the river for me.

And they'll follow that meal track to the lake.

They'll go **browsing** down the creek that leads out of it. They'll try to find the robbers that killed me and took the things. They won't ever hunt the river for anything but my dead body. They'll soon get tired of that, and won't bother no more about me.

All right. I can stop anywhere I want to. Jackson's Island is good enough for me. I know that island pretty well. Nobody ever comes there. And then I can paddle over to town nights. I'll slink around and pick up things I want. Jackson's Island's the place.

I was pretty tired. The first thing I knowed I was asleep. Then I woke up. I didn't know where I was for a minute. I set up and looked around, a little scared. Then I remembered. The river looked miles and miles across. The moon was bright. I could

3 A *whetstone* is a rough stone used to sharpen blades.

have counted the drift logs that went a-slippin' along. They were black and still, hundreds of yards out from shore.

Everything was dead quiet. It looked late, and smelt late. You know what I mean. I don't know the words to put it in. I took a good yawn and a stretch. I was just going to unhitch and start, when I heard a sound way over the water.

I listened. Pretty soon I made it out. It was a dull kind of a regular sound. It came from oars working in rowlocks when it's a still night.

I peeped out through the willow branches. There it was—a skiff, way across the water. I couldn't tell how many was in it. It kept a-comin'. Then it was **abreast** of me. I see there warn't but one man in it. Thinks I, maybe it's Pap. But I warn't expecting him.

He dropped below me with the current. By and by, he came a-swingin' up shore in the easy water. He went by real close. I could have reached out the gun and touched him. Well, it was Pap, sure enough. And he was sober, too, by the way he laid his oars.

I didn't lose no time. The next minute I was a-spinnin' downstream, soft but quick. I stayed in the shade of the bank. I made two miles and a half. Then I struck out a quarter a mile or more toward the middle of the river. Pretty soon I would be passing the ferry landing. People might see me and **hail** me.

I got out amongst the driftwood. Then I laid down in the bottom of the canoe and let her float. I laid there, and had a good rest and a smoke out of my pipe. I looked away into the sky—not a cloud in it. The sky looks ever so deep when you lay down on your back in the moonshine. I never knowed it before. And how far a body can hear on the water such nights!

I heard people talking at the ferry landing. I heard what they said, too—every word of it. One man said it was getting towards the long days and the short nights now. The other one said this warn't one of the short ones, he reckoned.

And then they laughed. And he said it over again, and they laughed again. Then they waked up another fellow. They told him and laughed. But he didn't laugh. He let out something **cranky**, and said let him alone.

The first fellow said he reckoned he'd tell it to his old woman. She would think it was pretty good. But he said that warn't nothing to some things he had said in his time.

I heard one man say it was nearly three o'clock. He hoped daylight wouldn't wait more than about a week longer. After that, the talk got further and further away. I couldn't make out the words any more. But I could hear the mumble, and now and then a laugh, too. But it seemed a long ways off.

I was away below the ferry now. I rose up, and there was Jackson's Island. It was about two and a half miles downstream. It was heavily wooded and standing up out of the middle of the river.

The island looked big and dark and solid, like a steamboat without any lights. There warn't any signs of the bar[4] at the head. It was all under water now.

It didn't take me long to get there. The current was so swift, I shot past the head at a ripping rate. Then I got into the dead water.[5] I landed on the side towards the Illinois shore.

I run the canoe into a deep dent in the bank that I knowed about. I had to part the willow branches to get in. When I tied up the canoe, nobody could have seen it from the outside.

I went up and set down on a log at the head of the island. I looked out on the big river and the black driftwood. I looked away over to the town. It was three miles away. There was three or four lights twinkling.

A **monstrous** big lumber raft was about a mile upstream. It was coming along down, with a lantern in the middle of it. I watched it come creeping down. Then it was most abreast of where I stood.

I heard a man say, "Stern oars, there! Turn her head to starboard!"[6] I heard that just as plain as if the man was by my side.

There was a little gray in the sky now. I stepped into the woods. Then I laid down for a nap before breakfast.

---

4 *Bar* means "sandbar"—a high ridge of sand in the water. Since the river is high, this is now under water.

5 *Dead water* is water which has little or no current.

6 A *stern* is the rear portion of a boat (or raft). Starboard is to the right side as one faces the front of the boat.

Chapter 8

I Spare Miss Watson's Jim

VOCABULARY PREVIEW

The following words appear in this chapter. Review the list and get to know the words before you read the chapter.

brash—brave; bold
carcass—dead body; corpse
jabbered—chattered; babbled
lolled—rested; relaxed
tumbledown—rundown; ready to fall apart

The sun was high up when I waked. I judged it was after eight o'clock. I laid there in the grass and the cool shade, thinking about things. I felt rested and rather comfortable and satisfied. I could see the sun out at one or two holes. But mostly it was big trees all about. It was gloomy in there amongst them.

There was freckled places on the ground where the light sifted down through the leaves. The freckled places swapped about a little. That showed there was a little breeze up there. A couple of squirrels set on a limb. They **jabbered** at me very friendly.

I was powerful lazy and comfortable. I didn't want to get up and cook breakfast. Well, I was dozing off again, when I thinks I hears a deep sound of "boom!" It was coming from way up the river.

I rouses up, and rests on my elbow and listens. Pretty soon I hears it again. I hopped up, and went and looked out at a hole in the leaves.

I saw a bunch of smoke laying on the water a long ways up. It was about abreast of the ferry. And there was the ferryboat full of people floating along down.

I knowed what was the matter now. "Boom!" I saw the white smoke squirt out of the ferryboat's side. You see, they was firing a cannon over the water. They was trying to make my **carcass** come to the top.

I was pretty hungry. But it warn't going to do for me to start a fire. They might see the smoke. So I set there and watched the cannon smoke and listened to the boom.

The river was a mile wide there. It always looks pretty on a summer morning. So I was having a good enough time seeing them hunt for my remainders. If only I had a bite to eat.

Well, then I happened to think of something. They always put quicksilver[1] in loaves of bread and float them off. The loaves always go right to the drownded carcass and stop there. So, says I, I'll keep a lookout. If any of them's floating around after me, I'll give them a show.

I changed to the Illinois edge of the island. I thought I'd see what luck I could have there. And I warn't disappointed. A big double loaf come along. I most got it with a long stick. But my foot slipped and she floated out further.

Of course, I was where the current set in the closest to the shore. I knowed that well enough. But by and by, along comes another one. This time I won.

I took out the plug and shook out the little dab of quicksilver. I set my teeth in. It was "baker's bread"—what the well-to-do eat. It was none of your low-down corn pone.[2]

I got a good place amongst the leaves and set there on a log. I munched on the bread and watched the ferryboat. I was very well satisfied.

And then something struck me. I says, now I reckon the widow or the parson or somebody prayed that this bread would find me. And here it has gone and done it. So there ain't no doubt. There is something in that thing. At least, there is when a body like the widow or the parson prays. But it don't work for me. I reckon it don't work for only just the right kind.

I lit a pipe and had a good long smoke. I went on watching. The ferryboat was floating with the current. I reckoned I'd have a chance to see who was aboard when she come along. She could come in close, where the bread did.

She got pretty well along down towards me. Then I put out my pipe and went to where I fished out the bread. I laid down

---

1 *Quicksilver* is the liquid metal mercury.

2 *Core pone* is corn bread cooked without milk or eggs.

behind a log on the bank in a little open place. Where the log forked, I could peep through.

By and by, she come along. She drifted in real close. They could have run out a plank and walked ashore. Most everybody was on the boat. Pap, and Judge Thatcher, and Bessie Thatcher,[3] and Joe Harper. And also Tom Sawyer, and his old Aunt Polly, and Sid and Mary, and plenty more.

Everybody was talking about the murder. But the captain broke in and says, "Look sharp, now. The current sets in the closest here. Maybe he's washed ashore. He might have got tangled amongst the brush at the water's edge. I hope so, anyway."

I didn't hope so. They all crowded up and leaned over the rails, nearly in my face. They kept still, watching with all their might. I could see them first-rate, but they couldn't see me.

Then the captain sung out, "Stand away!"

And the cannon let off a blast right before me. It made me deaf with the noise and pretty near blind with the smoke. I judged I was gone. If they'd have had some bullets in, I reckon they'd have got the corpse they was after.

Well, I see I warn't hurt, thanks to goodness. The boat floated on. It went out of sight around the shoulder of the island. I could hear the booming now and then. It got further and further off. By and by, after an hour, I didn't hear it no more.

The island was three miles long. I judged they had got to the foot, and was giving it up. But they didn't yet awhile. They turned around the foot of the island. Then they started up the channel on the Missouri side, under steam.[4] They kept booming once in awhile as they went.

I crossed over to that side and watched them. When they got abreast the head of the island, they quit shooting. They dropped over to the Missouri shore and went home to the town.

I knowed I was all right now. Nobody else would come

---

3 In *The Adventures of Tom Sawyer*, Judge Thatcher's daughter was named Becky. Since several years passed between the writing of that book and *Huck Finn*, this fact may have slipped Twain's mind. (Or a typesetter may have made a mistake.)

4 A *channel* is a stretch of water joining two larger bodies of water. In this story, the word "channel" usually refers to the deepest part of the river. *Under steam* means "with engines going." Before the ferryboat turned to go up the Missouri side, it was floating downstream and did not need the power of the engine.

a-huntin' after me. I got my traps out of the canoe and made me a nice camp in the thick woods.

I made a kind of a tent out of my blankets. My things could be put under it so the rain couldn't get at them. I catched a catfish and cut him open with my saw. Towards sundown I started my campfire and had supper. Then I set out a line to catch some fish for breakfast.

When it was dark, I set by my campfire smoking. I felt pretty well satisfied. But by and by it got sort of lonesome. So I went and set on the bank. I listened to the current swashing along. And I counted the stars and drift logs and rafts that come down. Then I went to bed. There ain't no better way to put in time when you are lonesome. You can't stay that way, you soon get over it.

And so for three days and nights. No difference—just the same thing. But the next day I went exploring around down through the island.

I was boss of it. It all belonged to me, so to say. And I wanted to know all about it. But mainly I wanted to put in the time.

I found plenty of strawberries, ripe and prime. And green summer grapes and green raspberries. And the green blackberries was just beginning to show. They would all come handy by and by, I judged.

Well, I went fooling along in the deep woods. I judged I warn't far from the foot of the island. I had my gun along, but I hadn't shot nothing. It was for protection. I thought I would kill some game near home.

About this time, I mighty near stepped on a good-sized snake. It went sliding off through the grass and flowers. I went after it, trying to get a shot at it.

I clipped along. Then all of a sudden, I bounded right on to the ashes of a campfire. It was still smoking.

My heart jumped up amongst my lungs. I never waited to look further. I uncocked my gun and went sneaking back on my tiptoes as fast as ever I could.

Every now and then I stopped a second amongst the thick leaves and listened. But my breath come so hard I couldn't hear nothing else. I slunk along another piece further. Then I listened again, and so on, and so on.

If I saw a stump, I took it for a man. If I trod on a stick and broke it, it made me feel like a person had cut one of my breaths in two. It felt like I only got half a breath, and the short half, too.

When I got to camp, I warn't feeling very **brash**. I warn't very lively. But I says, this ain't no time to be fooling around.

So I got all my traps into my canoe again, so as to have them out of sight. And I put out the fire and scattered the ashes around. I made it look like an old last year's camp. And then I clumb a tree.

I reckon I was up in the tree two hours. But I didn't see nothing. I didn't hear nothing. I only thought I heard and seen as much as a thousand things.

Well, I couldn't stay up there forever. So at last I got down. But I kept in the thick woods and on the lookout all the time. All I could get to eat was berries and what was left over from breakfast.

By the time it was night, I was pretty hungry. Then it got good and dark. I got in the canoe and slid out from shore before moonrise. I paddled over to the Illinois bank—about a quarter of a mile.

I went out in the woods and cooked supper. I had about made up my mind I would stay there all night. But then I hear a *plunkety-plunk, plunkety-plunk*. And I says to myself, horses coming.

Next I hear people's voices. I got everything into the canoe as quick as I could. Then I went creeping through the woods to see what I could find out. I hadn't got far when I hear a man say, "We better camp here if we can find a good place. The horses is about beat out. Let's look around."

I didn't wait. I shoved out and paddled away easy. I tied up in the old place and reckoned I would sleep in the canoe.

I didn't sleep much. I couldn't, somehow, for thinking. And every time I waked up, I thought somebody had me by the neck. So the sleep didn't do me no good.

By and by, I says to myself, I can't live this way. I'm a-goin' to find out who it is that's here on the island with me. I'll find it out or bust. Well, I felt better right off.

So I took my paddle and slid out from shore just a step or

two. Then I let the canoe drop along amongst the shadows. The moon was shining. Outside of the shadows, it made it most as light as day. I poked along well onto an hour. Everything was still as rocks and sound asleep.

Well, by this time, I was most down to the foot of the island. A little ripply, cool breeze begun to blow. That was as good as saying the night was about done. I give the canoe a turn with the paddle and brung her nose to shore. Then I got my gun and slipped out. I went into the edge of the woods.

Then I sat down there on a log and looked out through the leaves. I saw the moon go down, and the darkness begin to blanket the river. But in a little while I saw a pale streak over the treetops. I knowed day was coming.

So I took up my gun. I slipped off towards where I had run across that campfire. Every minute or two I stopped to listen. But I hadn't no luck somehow. I couldn't seem to find the place.

But by and by, sure enough, I catched a glimpse of fire through the trees. I went for it, cautious and slow. By and by, I was close enough to have a look.

There laid a man on the ground. It most give me the shivers. He had a blanket around his head, and his head was nearly in the fire. I set there behind a clump of bushes about six foot away from him. I kept my eyes on him steady.

It was getting gray daylight now. Pretty soon he yawned and stretched himself. He threw off the blanket. And it was Miss Watson's Jim! I bet I was glad to see him.

I says, "Hello, Jim!" and skipped out.

He bounced up and stared at me wild. Then he drops down on his knees. He puts his hands together and says, "Don't hurt me—don't! I ain't ever done no harm to a ghost. I always liked dead people. I done all I could for 'em. You go en' git in de river again, where you belongs. Don't do nothin' to Ole Jim. I was always your friend."

Well, I warn't long making him understand I warn't dead. I was ever so glad to see Jim. I warn't lonesome now. I told him I warn't afraid of him telling the people where I was. I talked along. But he only set there and looked at me. He never said nothing.

Then I says, “It’s good daylight. Let’s get breakfast. Make up your campfire good.”

“What’s de use of makin’ up de campfire to cook strawberries and such truck?[5] But you got a gun, ain’t you? Den we can git somethin’ better den strawberries.”

“Strawberries and such truck,” I says. “Is that what you live on?”

“I couldn’t git nothin’ else,” he says.

“Why, how long you been on the island, Jim?”

“I come here de night after you’s killed.”

“What, all that time?”

“Yes-indeedy.”

“And ain’t you had nothing but that kind of stuff to eat?”

“No, sir—nothin’ else.”

“Well, you must be most starved, ain’t you?”

“I reckon I could eat a horse. I think I could. How long you been on de island?”

“Since the night I got killed.”

“No! Why, what has you lived on? But you got a gun. Oh, yes, you got a gun. Dat’s good. Now you kill somethin’ and I’ll make up de fire.”

So we went over to where the canoe was. He built a fire in a grassy open place amongst the trees. I fetched meal and bacon and coffee. And I got the coffee pot and frying pan, and sugar and tin cups.

The nigger was pretty impressed. He reckoned it was all done with witchcraft. I catched a good big catfish, too. And Jim cleaned him with his knife, and fried him.

When breakfast was ready, we **lolled** on the grass and eat it smoking hot. Jim ate it down with all his might. He was most about starved. Then when we had got pretty well stuffed, we laid off and lazied.

By and by, Jim says, “But looky here, Huck. Who was it dat was killed in dat hut if it warn’t you?”

Then I told him the whole thing. He said it was smart. He said Tom Sawyer couldn’t get up no better plan than what I had.

Then I says, “How do you come to be here, Jim? And how’d you get here?”

---

5 *Truck* is junk or garbage. Jim is referring to whatever he could find to eat on the island.

He looked pretty uneasy. He didn't say nothing for a minute. Then he says, "Maybe I better not tell."

"Why, Jim?"

"Well, there's reasons. But you wouldn't tell on me if I was to tell you. Would you, Huck?"

"Blamed if I would, Jim."

"Well, I believe you, Huck. I—I run off."

"Jim!"

"But mind, you said you wouldn't tell. You know you said you wouldn't tell, Huck."

"Well, I did. I said I wouldn't, and I'll stick to it. Honest injun, I will. People might call me a low-down Abolitionist.[6]

They might despise me for keeping mum. But that don't make no difference. I ain't a-goin' to tell, and I ain't a-goin' back there, anyways. So now, let's know all about it."

"Well, you see, it was dis way. Ole missus—dat's Miss Watson—she pecks on me all de time. En' she treats me pretty rough. But she always said she wouldn't sell me down to Orleans. But I noticed there was a nigger trader round de place considerable lately. En' I begin to get uneasy.

"Well, one night, I creeps to de door pretty late. En' de door warn't quite shut. En' I hear old missus tell de widow she goin' to sell me down to Orleans.

"She didn't want to," Jim says. "But she could git eight hundred dollars for me. It was such a big stack of money she couldn't resist. De widow, she try to git her to say she wouldn't do it. But I never waited to hear de rest. I lit out mighty quick, I tell you.

"I took out runnin' down de hill. I 'spect to steal a skiff along de shore somewhere above de town. But there was people a-stirrin' yit. So I hid in de ole **tumbledown** cooper[7] shop on de bank. I waited there for everybody to go 'way.

"Well, I was there all night. There was somebody 'round all de time. 'Long 'bout six in de mornin', skiffs begin to go by. En' it got to be 'bout eight or nine. En' every skiff dat went 'long was talkin' 'bout how your pap come over to de town. En' he say you's killed.

---

6 In the nineteenth century, an abolitionist was one opposed to slavery.

7 A cooper makes or repairs barrels.

"Dese last skiffs was full of ladies en' gentlemen. Dey was a-goin' over for to see de place. Sometimes dey'd pull up at de shore and take a rest before they started across. So by de talk, I got to know all 'bout de killin'.

"I was powerful sorry you's killed, Huck. But I ain't no more now.

"I laid there under de shavings all day," Jim says. "I was hungry, but I warn't afraid. 'Cause I knowed old missus en' de widow was goin' to start to de camp meetin'[8] right after breakfast. They'd be gone all day.

"En' dey knows I goes off with de cattle 'bout daylight. So dey wouldn't expect to see me 'round de place. En' so dey wouldn't miss me till after dark in de evenin'.

"De other servants wouldn't miss me. Dey'd take off for a holiday, soon as de ole folks was out of de way.

"Well, when it comes dark, I took out up de river road. I went 'bout two miles or more to where there warn't no houses. I'd made up my mind 'bout what I's a-goin' to do.

"You see, I couldn't keep tryin' to git away afoot. De dogs would track me. I could steal a skiff to cross over. But dey'd miss dat skiff, you see. En' dey'd know 'bout where I'd land on de other side, en' where to pick up my track. So I says, a raft is what I's after. It don't make no track.

"I see a light a-comin' 'round de point by and by. So I wade in en' shove a log ahead of me. I swum more than halfway across de river, en' got in amongst de driftwood. I kept my head down low. I kind of swum against the current till de raft come along. Den I swum to de stern of it and took ahold.

"It clouded up en' was pretty dark for a little while. So I clumb up en' laid down on de planks. De men was all 'way yonder in de middle. Dat was where de lantern was.

"De river was a-risin', en' there was a good current. So I reckoned that by four in de mornin', I'd be twenty-five miles down de river. En' den I'd slip in just before daylight en' swim ashore. Den I'd take to de woods on de Illinois side.

"But I didn't have no luck," says Jim. "We was 'most down to de head of de island. Den a man begin to come aft[9] with de lantern.

---

8 A *camp meeting* is a religious meeting, usually held outdoors or in a tent.

9 *Aft* means "near the back" of a boat or ship.

I see it warn't no use for to wait. So I slid overboard en' struck out for de island.

"Well, I had a notion I could land 'most anywheres. But I couldn't. De bank was too steep. I was 'most to de foot of de island before I found a good place. I went ashore and into de woods. I judged I wouldn't fool with rafts no more. Not as long as dey move the lantern 'round so.

"I had my pipe en' a plug of tobacco en' some matches in my cap. Dey warn't wet, so I was all right."

I says, "And so you ain't had no meat nor bread to eat all this time? Why didn't you get mud-turtles?"

"How you goin' to git 'em? You can't slip up on 'em en' grab 'em. En' how's a body goin' to hit 'em with a rock? How could a body do it in de night? En' I warn't goin' to show myself on de bank in de daytime."

"Well, that's so. You've had to keep in the woods all the time, of course. Did you hear 'em shooting the cannon?"

"Oh, yes. I knowed dey was after you. I see 'em go by here—watched 'em through de bushes."

Some young birds come along. They were flying a yard or two at a time and lighting. Jim said it was a sign it was going to rain. He said it was a sign when young chickens flew that way. So he reckoned it was the same way when young birds done it.

I was going to catch some of them. But Jim wouldn't let me. He said it was death. He said his father laid mighty sick once. Some of them catched a bird. And his old granny said his father would die. And he did.

And Jim said you mustn't count the things you are going to cook for dinner. That would bring bad luck. The same if you shook the tablecloth after sundown.

And he said, what if a man owned a beehive and that man died? The bees must be told about it before sunup next morning. Or else the bees would all weaken down. They'd quit work and die.

Jim said bees wouldn't sting idiots. But I didn't believe him. I had tried them lots of times myself. They wouldn't sting me.

I had heard about some of these things before. But not all of them. Jim knowed all kinds of signs. He said he knowed most everything. I said it looked to me like all the signs was about bad luck. So I asked him if there warn't any good-luck signs.

He says, "Mighty few. And dey ain't no use to a body. What you want to know when good luck's a-comin' for? Want to keep it off?"

And he said, "Suppose you's got hairy arms en' a hairy chest. It's a sign dat you's a-goin' to be rich. Well, there's some use in a sign like that. 'Cause it's so far ahead.

"You see, maybe you's got to be poor a long time first. En' so you might git discouraged en' kill yourself. And all because you didn't know by de sign dat you goin' to be rich by and by."

"Have you got hairy arms and a hairy chest, Jim?"

"What's de use to ask dat question? Don't you see I has?"

"Well, are you rich?"

"No, but I been rich once. And I's goin' to be rich again. Once I had fourteen dollars. But I took to speculatin',[10] en' got busted out."

"What did you speculate in, Jim?"

"Well, first I tackled stock."

"What kind of stock?"

"Why, livestock—cattle, you know. I put ten dollars in a cow. But I ain't goin' to risk no more money in stock. De cow up and died on my hands."

"So you lost the ten dollars."

"No, I didn't lose it all. I only lost 'bout nine of it. I sold de hide and tallow[11] for a dollar en' ten cents."

"You had five dollars and ten cents left. Did you speculate any more?"

"Yes. You know that one-legged nigger dat belongs to old Mr. Bradish? Well, he set up a bank. He say anybody dat put in a dollar would git four dollars more at de end of de year.

"Well," Jim says, "all de niggers went in. But dey didn't have much. I was de only one dat had much. So I stuck out for more than four dollars. I said if I didn't git it, I'd start a bank myself.

"Well, of course dat nigger want to keep me out of business.

---

10 *Speculatin'* means to gamble and take risks with money, hoping to make more money.

11 *Tallow* is the fat of cattle or sheep. It is used to making soap or candles.

He says there warn't business enough for two banks. So he say I could put in my five dollars. En' he say he pay me thirty-five at de end of de year.

"So I done it. Den I reckoned I'd invest de thirty-five dollars right off en' keep things a-movin'. There was a nigger named Bob. He had catched a flatboat,[12] en' his master didn't know it. En' I bought it off n him. En' I told him to take de thirty-five dollars when de end of de year come.

"But somebody stole de flatboat dat night. En' next day de one-legged nigger say de bank's busted. So we didn't none of us git no money."

"What did you do with the ten cents, Jim?"

"Well, I was goin' to spend it. But I had a dream. En' de dream told me to give it to a nigger name Balum. Balum's Ass, dey call him for short. He's one of dem chuckleheads, you know.

"But he's lucky, dey say. En' I see I warn't lucky. De dream say, let Balum invest de ten cents. He'd make me some money.

"Well, Balum, he took de money. En' when he was in church, he hear de preacher talk. En' dis preacher say dat whoever give to de poor lent to de Lord. En' he was bound to get his money back a hundred times. So Balum, he took and give de ten cents to de poor. And he laid low to see what was goin' to come of it."

"Well, what did come of it, Jim?"

"Nothin' never come of it. I couldn't manage to collect dat money no way. En' Balum, he couldn't either. I ain't goin' to lend no more money without I see de security.[13]

"Bound to git your money back a hundred times, de preacher says! If I could git de ten cents back, I'd call it square. En' I'd be glad of de chance."

"Well, it's all right anyway, Jim. You're going to be rich again some time or other."

"Yes. En' I's rich now, come to look at it. I owns myself. En' I's worth eight hundred dollars. I wish I had de money. I wouldn't want no more."

---

12 A *flatboat* is a boat with a flat bottom and square ends. Heavy or bulky freight is transported on a flatboat, especially in shallow water.

13 *Security* is something given as a promise of repayment.

Chapter 9

The House of Death Floats By

VOCABULARY PREVIEW

The following words appear in this chapter. Review the list and get to know the words before you read the chapter.

ghastly—frightful; scary
haul—loot; takings
tolerable—average; reasonable

I wanted to go and look at a place right about the middle of the island. I'd found it when I was exploring. So we started and soon got to it. The island was only three miles long and a quarter of a mile wide.

This place was **tolerable** long. It had a steep hill or ridge about forty foot high. We had a rough time getting to the top. The sides was steep and the bushes thick. We tramped and clumb around all over it.

By and by, we found a good big cavern in the rock. It was near the top on the side towards Illinois. The cavern was as big as two or three rooms bunched together. Jim could stand up straight in it. It was cool in there. Jim was for putting our traps in there right away. But I said we didn't want to be climbing up and down there all the time.

Jim said we should hide the canoe in a good place. Then we could put all the traps in the cavern. We could rush there if anybody was to come to the island. They would never find us without dogs.

And besides, he said, them little birds had said it was going to rain. Did I want the things to get wet? So we went back and got the canoe. We paddled up abreast of the cavern. We lugged all the traps up there.

Then we looked for a place close by to hide the canoe in. We found a spot amongst the thick willows and hid it. We took some fish off of the lines and set them again. Then we begun to get ready for dinner.

The door of the cavern was big enough to roll a barrel in. On one side of the door, the floor stuck out a little bit. It was flat and a good place to build a fire on. So we built it there and cooked dinner. We spread the blankets inside for a carpet and ate our dinner in there. We put all the other things handy at the back of the cavern.

Pretty soon it darkened up and begun to thunder and lightning. So the birds was right about it. Directly it begun to rain. And it rained like all fury, too. I never saw the wind blow so. It was one of those regular summer storms.

It got so dark that it looked all blue-black outside, and lovely. And the rain thrashed along real thick. The trees off a little ways looked dim and spider-webby.

And then here would come a blast of wind. It would bend the trees down and turn up the pale underside of the leaves. Then a perfect ripper of a gust would follow along. It would set the branches to tossing their arms as if they was just wild.

And next, when it was just about the bluest and blackest —fst! It was as bright as glory. You'd have a little glimpse of treetops a-plungin' about way off yonder in the storm. You could see hundreds of yards further than you could see before.

It was dark as sin again in a second. And now you'd hear the thunder let go with an awful crash. Then it went rumbling, grumbling, tumbling down the sky towards the underside of the world. It was like rolling empty barrels downstairs. And I mean long stairs, where they bounce a good deal, you know.

"Jim, this is nice," I says. "I wouldn't want to be nowhere else but here. Pass me along another hunk of fish and some hot corn bread."

"Well, you wouldn't have been here if it hadn't been for Jim. You'd have been down there in de woods without any dinner. En' gittin' mos' drownded, too. Dat you would, honey. Chickens knows when it's goin' to rain. En' so do de birds, chile."

The river went on raising and raising for ten or twelve days. At last it was over the banks. The water was three or four feet deep on the island in the low places and on the Illinois bottom.

On that side, it was a good many miles wide. But on the Missouri side it was the same old distance across—a half a mile.

The Missouri shore was just a wall of high bluffs.

Daytimes, we paddled all over the island in the canoe. It was mighty cool and shady in the deep woods. It didn't matter if the sun was blazing outside. We went winding in and out amongst the trees. Sometimes the vines hung real thick. Then we had to back away and go some other way.

Well, on every old broken-down tree you could see rabbits and snakes and such things. And when the island had been overflowed a day or two, they got tame on account of being hungry. You could paddle right up and put your hand on them if you wanted to. But not the snakes and turtles. They would slide off in the water. The ridge our cavern was in was full of them. We could have had pets enough if we'd wanted them.

One night, we catched a little section of a lumber raft with nice pine planks. It was twelve foot wide and about fifteen or sixteen foot long. The top stood above water six or seven inches. It was a solid, level floor.

We could see sawlogs[1] go by in the daylight sometimes. But we let them go. We didn't show ourselves in daylight.

Another night, we was up at the head of the island. It was just before daylight. And here comes a frame house down the river, on the west side. She was a two-story and tilted over considerable.

We paddled out and got aboard. We clumb in at an upstairs window. But it was too dark to see yet. So we made the canoe fast and set in her to wait for daylight.

The light begun to come before we got to the foot of the island. Then we looked in at the window. We could make out a bed, and a table, and two old chairs. There were lots of things around on the floor. There was clothes hanging against the wall. There was something laying on the floor in the far corner. It looked like a man.

So Jim says, "Hello, you!"

But it didn't budge. So I hollered again, and then Jim says, "De man ain't asleep—he's dead. You hold still—I'll go en' see."

He went, and bent down and looked, and says, "It's a dead man. Yes, indeedy. Naked, too. He's been shot in de back. I

---

1 A *sawlog* is a log the right size to be cut into lumber.

reckon he's been dead two or three days. Come in, Huck. But don't look at his face. It's too **ghastly**."

I didn't look at him at all. Jim throwed some old rags over him. But he needn't have done it. I didn't want to see him. There was heaps of old greasy cards scattered around over the floor. There was old whisky bottles, too, and a couple of masks made out of black cloth.

All over the walls was the most ignorant kind of words and pictures made with charcoal. There was two old dirty calico[2] dresses, and a sunbonnet. And there was some women's underclothes hanging against the wall, and some men's clothing, too.

We put the lot into the canoe—it might come good. There was a boy's old speckled straw hat on the floor. I took that, too. And there was a bottle that had milk in it. It had a rag stopper for a baby to suck. We would have took the bottle, but it was broke.

There was a seedy old chest, and an old hair trunk[3] with the hinges broke. They stood open, but there warn't nothing left in them that was any account. Things was scattered all about. So we reckoned the people left in a hurry. They warn't fixed so as to carry off most of their stuff.

We got an old tin lantern and a butcher knife without any handle. We got a brand-new Barlow knife[4] worth two bits in any store. And we got a lot of tallow candles, a tin candlestick, and a gourd, and a tin cup. We also took a ratty old bedquilt off the bed.

We also got a purse. It had needles and pins and beeswax and buttons and thread and all such truck in it. We got a hatchet with some nails. Also a fish line as thick as my little finger with some monstrous hooks on it. And we got a roll of buckskin,[5] and a leather dog collar, and a horseshoe.

We also got some vials of medicine that didn't have no label on them. And just as we was leaving, I found a tolerable good currycomb.[6]

---

2 *Calico* is a printed cotton fabric.

3 A hair trunk is covered with animal hide that still has hair on it.

4 A *Barlow knife* is a pocketknife, named for its inventor.

5 *Buckskin* is leather made from a deer's hide.

6 A currycomb is used to groom horses.

And Jim, he found a ratty old fiddle bow, and a wooden leg. The straps was broke off of it. But barring that, it was a good enough leg. It was too long for me, though, and not long enough for Jim. And we couldn't find the other one, though we hunted all around.

And so, take it all around, we made a good **haul**. We was ready to shove off. By that time, we was a quarter of a mile below the island. And it was pretty broad day. So I made Jim lay down in the canoe and cover up with the quilt. If he set up, people could tell he was a nigger a good ways off.

I paddled over to the Illinois shore, and drifted down most a half a mile doing it. I crept up the dead water under the bank. We hadn't no accidents and didn't see nobody. We got home all safe.

Chapter 10

What Comes of Handlin' Snakeskin

VOCABULARY PREVIEW

The following words appear in this chapter. Review the list and get to know the words before you read the chapter.

pert—smart-mouthed
rubbish—trash; stuff
rummaged—searched
varmint—pest; pesky anmial

After breakfast, I wanted to talk about the dead man. I wanted to guess about how he come to be killed. But Jim didn't want to. He said it would fetch bad luck.

And besides, he said, he might come and haunt us. He said a man that warn't buried was likely to go a-hauntin' around. More likely than one that was planted and comfortable.

That sounded pretty reasonable, so I didn't say no more. But I couldn't keep from studying over it. I wished I knowed who shot the man, and what they done it for.

We **rummaged** through the clothes we'd got. We found eight dollars in silver. It was sewed up in the lining of an old blanket overcoat.

Jim said he reckoned the people in that house stole the coat. If they'd knowed the money was there, they wouldn't have left it. I said I reckoned they killed the man, too. But Jim didn't want to talk about that.

I says, "Now you think it's bad luck. But what did you say when I fetched in the snakeskin? The one that I found on the top of the ridge day before yesterday? You said it was the worst bad luck in the world to touch a snakeskin with my hands.

"Well, here's your bad luck!" I says. "We've raked in all this truck and eight dollars besides. I wish we could have some bad luck like this every day, Jim."

"Never you mind, honey. Never you mind. Don't you git too **pert**. It's a-comin'. Mind I tell you, it's a-comin'."

It did come, too. It was a Tuesday that we had that talk. Well, after dinner Friday, we was laying around in the grass at the upper end of the ridge.

We got out of tobacco. I went to the cavern to get some and found a rattlesnake in there. So I killed him. Then I curled him up on the foot of Jim's blanket. It looked ever so natural. I thought there'd be some fun when Jim found him there.

Well, by night I forgot all about the snake. Then Jim flung himself down on the blanket while I struck a light. The snake's mate was there, and bit him.

Jim jumped up yelling. The first thing the light showed was the **varmint**. He was curled up and ready for another spring. I laid him out in a second with a stick. Jim grabbed Pap's whisky jug and begun to pour it down. He was barefooted, and the snake bit him right on the heel. That all comes of my being such a fool for not remembering. Wherever you leave a dead snake, its mate always comes there and curls around it.

Jim told me to chop off the snake's head and throw it away. Then I was to skin the body and roast a piece of it. I done it, and he eat it. He said it would help cure him.

He made me take off the rattles and tie them around his wrist, too. He said that would help. Then I slid out quiet. I throwed the snakes clear away amongst the bushes. I warn't going to let Jim find out it was my fault. Not if I could help it.

Jim sucked and sucked at the jug. Now and then he got out of his head. He pitched around and yelled. But every time he come to himself, he went to sucking at the jug again. His foot swelled up pretty big. So did his leg. But by and by, the drunkenness begun to come. So I judged he was all right. But I'd rather have been bit with a snake than Pap's whisky. Jim was laid up for four days and nights. Then the swelling was all gone and he was around again.

I made up my mind. I wouldn't ever take ahold of a snakeskin again with my hands. Now I could see what had come of it.

Jim said he reckoned I would believe him next time. And he said that handling a snakeskin was awful bad luck. Maybe we hadn't seen the end of it yet. He said he'd rather see a new moon over his left shoulder as much as a thousand times. That would be better than taking up a snakeskin in his hand.

Well, I was getting to feel that way myself. But I've always been careful not to look at the new moon over my left shoulder. I reckon that's one of the most careless and foolish things a body can do. Old Hank Bunker done it once. He even bragged about it. In less than two years, he got drunk and fell off a shot tower. He spread himself out so that he was just a kind of a layer, as you may say. And they slid him edgeways between two barn doors for a coffin. Then they buried him.

So they say, but I didn't see it. Pap told me. But anyway, it all come of looking at the moon that way, like a fool.

Well, the days went along. The river went down between its banks again. About the first thing we done was to bait one of the big hooks. We used a skinned rabbit. We set it and caught a catfish that was as big as a man. It was six foot two inches long. And it weighed over two hundred pounds.

We couldn't handle him, of course. He would have flung us into Illinois. We just set there and watched him rip and tear around. At last he drownded.

We found a brass button in his stomach. There was a round ball, too, and lots of **rubbish**. We split the ball open with a hatchet. There was a spool in it. Jim said he'd had it there a long time, to coat it over so and make a ball of it.

It was as big a fish as was ever catched in the Mississippi, I reckon. Jim said he hadn't ever seen a bigger one. He would have been worth a good deal over at the village.

They sell such a fish as that by the pound in the markethouse there. Everybody buys some of him. His meat's as white as snow and makes a good fry.

Next morning, I said it was getting slow and dull. I wanted to get a-stirrin' up some way. I said I reckoned I would slip over the river. Then I could find out what was going on.

Jim liked that notion. But he said I must go in the dark and look sharp. Then he studied it over. He said, couldn't I put on some of them old things? I could dress up like a girl.

That was a good notion, too. So we shortened up one of the calico gowns. I turned up my trouser legs to my knees and got into it. Jim hitched it behind with the hooks. It was a fair fit.

I put on the sunbonnet and tied it under my chin. Then a body couldn't look in and see my face. It was like looking down a joint of stovepipe. Jim said nobody would know me, even in the daytime, hardly.

I practiced around all day to get the hang of things. By and by, I could do pretty well in them. Only Jim said I didn't walk like a girl. He said I must quit pulling up my gown to get at my britches pocket. I took notice, and done better.

I started up the Illinois shore in the canoe just after dark. I went across to the Missouri side from a little below the ferry landing. The drift of the current fetched me in at the bottom of the town. I tied up and started along the bank.

There was a light burning in a little shanty. It hadn't been lived in for a long time. I wondered who lived there. I slipped up and peeped in at the window.

There was a woman about forty years old in there. She was knitting by a candle that was on a pine table. I didn't know her face. She was a stranger. You couldn't find a face in that town that I didn't know.

Now this was lucky, because I was weakening. I was getting afraid I had come. People might know my voice and find me out.

This was such a little town, though. What if this woman had been here just two days? She could still tell me all I wanted to know. So I knocked at the door. And I made up my mind so I wouldn't forget I was a girl.

Chapter 11

They're After Us!

VOCABULARY PREVIEW

The following words appear in this chapter. Review the list and get to know the words before you read the chapter.

contrived—invented; made up
innocent—childlike; simple
pivot—point on which something turns
prompt—immediate; right away
slouched—shuffled
wrenched—twisted; sprained

Come in," says the woman, and I did. She says, "Take a chair."

I done it. She looked me all over with her little shiny eyes, and says, "What might your name be?"

"Sarah Williams."

"Where about do you live? In this neighborhood?"

"No'm. In Hookerville, seven miles below. I've walked all the way and I'm all tired out."

"Hungry, too, I reckon. I'll find you something."

"No'm. I ain't hungry. I was hungry. But I stopped two miles below here at a farm. So I ain't hungry no more. That's what makes me so late.

"My mother's down sick, and out of money and everything. I come to tell my uncle Abner Moore. He lives at the upper end of the town, she says. I ain't ever been here before. Do you know him?"

"No. But I don't know everybody yet. I haven't lived here quite two weeks. It's a considerable ways to the upper end of the town. You better stay here all night. Take off your bonnet."

"No," I says. "I'll rest awhile, I reckon, and go on. I ain't afeard of the dark."

She said she wouldn't let me go by myself. Her husband would be in by and by, maybe in a hour and a half. She'd send him along with me.

Then she got to talking about her husband, and about her relations up the river, and her relations down the river. She talked about how much better off they used to be. She said they didn't know but they'd made a mistake coming to our town. Maybe they should have let well alone.

She went on and on. I was afraid I had made a mistake coming to her to find out what was going on in the town. But by and by, she moved on to Pap and the murder. Then I was pretty willing to let her chatter right along.

She told about me and Tom Sawyer finding the twelve thousand dollars (only she got it twenty). And she told all about Pap and what a hard lot he was, and what a hard lot I was. At last she got down to where I was murdered.

I says, "Who done it? We've heard considerable about these goings on down in Hookerville. But we don't know who 'twas that killed Huck Finn."

"Well, people here would like to know who killed him. I reckon there's a right smart chance of that. Some think old Finn done it himself."

"No—is that so?"

"Most everybody thought it at first. He'll never know how close he come to getting lynched.[1] But before night they changed around. They judged it was done by a runaway nigger named Jim."

"Why he—"

I stopped. I reckoned I better keep still. She kept right on talking. She never noticed I had put in at all.

"The nigger run off the very night Huck Finn was killed. So there's a reward out for him—three hundred dollars. And there's a reward out for old Finn, too—two hundred dollars.

"You see, he come to town in the morning after the murder, and told about it. He was out with 'em on the ferryboat hunt. Right away after, he up and left. Before night, they wanted to lynch him, but he was gone, you see.

---

1 To be *lynched* is to be hung by a mob without a trial.

"Well, next day they found out the nigger was gone. They found out he hadn't been seen since ten o'clock, the night the murder was done. So then they put it on him, you see.

"And while they was full of it, next day, back comes Old Finn. He went boo-hooing to Judge Thatcher. He asked for money to hunt for the nigger all over Illinois with.

"The judge gave him some, and that evening old Finn got drunk. He was around till after midnight. He had a couple of mighty hard-looking strangers with him. Then he went off with them.

"Well," she goes on, "he ain't come back since. And they ain't looking for him to come back till this thing blows over a little. For people thinks now that he killed his boy. They think he fixed things so folks would think robbers done it. Then he'd get Huck's money without bothering a long time with a lawsuit. People do say he warn't any too good to do it.

"Oh, he's sly, I reckon. If he don't come back for a year, he'll be all right. You can't prove anything on him, you know. Everything will be quieted down then. And he'll walk into Huck's money as easy as nothing."

"Yes," I says, "I reckon so, ma'am. I don't see nothing in the way of it. Has everybody quit thinking the nigger done it?"

"Oh, no, not everybody. A good many thinks he done it. But they'll get the nigger pretty soon now. Maybe they can scare it out of him."

"Why, are they after him yet?"

"Well, you're **innocent**, ain't you! Does three hundred dollars lay around every day for people to pick up? Some folks think the nigger ain't far from here. I'm one of them. But I ain't talked it around.

"A few days ago, I was talking with an old couple. They lives next door in the log shanty. They happened to say hardly anybody ever goes to that island over yonder—the one they call Jackson's Island. 'Don't anybody live there?' says I. 'No, nobody, says they.'

"I didn't say anymore, but I done some thinking. I was pretty near certain I'd seen smoke over there a day or two before that. It was near the head of the island. So I says to myself, like as not, that nigger's hiding over there. Anyway, says I, it's worth the trouble to give the place a hunt.

"I ain't seen any smoke since, so I reckon maybe he's gone, if it was him. But my husband's going over to see—him and another man. He was gone up the river, but he got back today. I told him as soon as he got here two hours ago."

I had got so uneasy I couldn't set still. I had to do something with my hands. So I took up a needle off of the table and went to threading it. My hands shook, and I was making a bad job of it.

When the woman stopped talking, I looked up. She was looking at me pretty curious, and smiling a little. I put down the needle and thread. I let on to be interested—and I was, too.

I says, "Three hundred dollars is a power of money. I wish my mother could get it. Is your husband going over there tonight?"

"Oh, yes. He went uptown with the man I was telling you of. They're going to get a boat and see if they can borrow another gun. They'll go over after midnight."

"Couldn't they see better if they was to wait till daytime?"

"Yes. And couldn't the nigger see better, too? After midnight, he'll likely be asleep. They can slip around through the woods and hunt up his campfire, if he's got one. They'll do all the better for the dark."

"I didn't think of that."

The woman kept looking at me pretty curious. I didn't feel a bit comfortable. Pretty soon she says, "What did you say your name was, honey?"

"M—Mary Williams."

Somehow, it didn't seem to me that I said it was Mary before. So I didn't look up. Seemed to me I said it was Sarah. So I felt sort of cornered. I was afeard maybe I was looking it, too.

I wished the woman would say something more. The longer she set still, the uneasier I was. But now she says, "Honey, I thought you said it was Sarah when you first come in?"

"Oh, yes'm, I did. Sarah Mary Williams. Sarah's my first name. Some calls me Sarah, some calls me Mary."

"Oh, that's the way of it?"

"Yes'm."

I was feeling better then. But I wished I was out of there, anyway. I couldn't look up yet.

Well, the woman fell to talking again. She told about how hard times was, and how poor they had to live. She talked about how the rats was as free as if they owned the place, and so forth and so on. Then I got easy again.

She was right about the rats. You'd see one stick his nose out of a hole in the corner every little while. She said she had to have things handy to throw at them when she was alone. Otherwise, they wouldn't give her no peace.

She showed me a bar of lead twisted up into a knot. She said she was a good shot with it generally. But she'd **wrenched** her arm a day or two ago. She didn't know whether she could throw true now. But she watched for a chance. Directly, she banged away at a rat, but she missed him wide. She said, "Ouch!" because it hurt her arm so.

Then she told me to try for the next one. I wanted to be getting away before the old man got back. But of course I didn't let on. I got the bar of lead. The first rat that showed his nose, I let have it. And if he'd have stayed where he was, he'd have been a tolerable sick rat.

She said that was first-rate. She reckoned I would go for the next one. She went and got the lump of lead and fetched it back. And she brought along a handful of yarn which she wanted me to help her with.

I held up my two hands and she put the yarn over them.

She went on talking about her and her husband's matters. But she broke off to say, "Keep your eye on the rats. You'd better have the lead in your lap, handy."

So she dropped the lump into my lap just at that moment. I clapped my legs together on it and she went on talking. But only about a minute. Then she took off the yarn and looked me straight in the face, but very pleasant, and says, "Come, now, what's your real name?"

"Wh—hat, ma'am?"

"What's your real name? Is it Bill, or Tom, or Bob? Or what is it?"

I reckon I shook like a leaf. I didn't know hardly what to do.

But I says, "Please don't poke fun at a poor girl like me, ma'am. If I'm in the way here, I'll—"

"No, you won't. Set down and stay where you are. I ain't going to hurt you. And I ain't going to tell on you, neither. You just tell me your secret, and trust me. I'll keep it. And what's more, I'll help you. So'll my old man, if you want him to.

"You see, you're a runaway apprentice,[1] that's all. It ain't anything. There ain't no harm in it. You've been treated bad, and you made up your mind to run. Bless you, child, I wouldn't tell on you. Tell me all about it now, that's a good boy."

So I said it wouldn't be no use to try to play it any longer. I would just make a clean break and tell her everything. But she mustn't go back on her promise.

Then I told her my father and mother was dead. The law had bound me out to a mean old farmer. He lived in the country thirty miles back from the river. He treated me so bad, I couldn't stand it no longer.

He went away to be gone a couple of days. And so I took my chance. I stole some of his daughter's old clothes and cleared out. I had been three nights coming the thirty miles. I traveled nights, and hid daytimes and slept. The bag of bread and meat I carried from home lasted me all the way. I still had a-plenty.

I said I believed my uncle Abner Moore would take care of me. So that was why I struck out for this town of Goshen.

"Goshen, child? This ain't Goshen. This is St. Petersburg.

Goshen's ten miles further up the river. Who told you this was Goshen?"

"Why, a man I met at daybreak this morning. He told me just as I was going to turn into the woods for my regular sleep. He told me when the roads forked I must take the right hand. And five miles would fetch me to Goshen."

"He was drunk, I reckon. He told you just exactly wrong."

"Well, he did act like he was drunk. But it ain't no matter now. I got to be moving along. I'll get to Goshen before daylight."

"Hold on a minute. I'll put you up a snack to eat. You might want it."

---

1 An apprentice worked for a craftsman for a set number of years.

So she put me up a snack, and says, "Say, when a cow's lying down, which end of her gets up first? Answer up **prompt** now—don't stop to study it. Which end gets up first?"

"The hind end, ma'am."

"Well, then, a horse?"

"The forward end, ma'am."

"Which side of a tree does the moss grow on?"

"North side."

"Say fifteen cows is grazing on a hillside. How many of them eats with their heads pointed in the same direction?"

"The whole fifteen, ma'am."

"Well, I reckon you have lived in the country. I thought maybe you was trying to fool me again. What's your real name, now?"

"George Peters, ma'am."

"Well, try to remember it, George. Don't forget and tell me it's Alexander before you go. And if I catch you, don't try to get out by saying it's George Alexander. And don't go about women in that old calico. You do a girl tolerable poor, but you might fool men, maybe.

"Bless you, child, learn how to thread a needle. Don't hold the thread still and fetch the needle up to it. Hold the needle still and poke the thread at it. That's the way a woman most always does. But a man always does it the other way.

"And watch how you throw at a rat or anything. Pick yourself up on tiptoe. Throw your hand up over your head as clumsy as you can. Miss your rat by about six or seven feet.

"Throw stiff-armed from the shoulder. Act like there was a **pivot** there for it to turn on. That's how a girl would do. Don't throw from the wrist and elbow, with your arm out to one side, like a boy.

"And mind how a girl tries to catch anything in her lap. She throws her knees apart. She don't clap them together. That's the way you did when you catched the lump of lead. Why, I spotted you for a boy when you was threading the needle. I **contrived** the other things just to make certain.

"Now trot along to your uncle, Sarah Mary Williams George Alexander Peters. If you get into trouble, you send word to Mrs.

Judith Loftus. That's me. I'll do what I can to get you out of it.

"Keep the river road all the way. The next time you tramp, take shoes and socks with you 'cause the river road's a rocky one. Your feet will be in bad shape when you get to Goshen, I reckon."

I went up the bank about fifty yards. Then I doubled on my tracks and slipped back to where my canoe was. It was a good piece below the house. I jumped in, and was off in a hurry.

I went upstream far enough to make the head of the island. Then I started across. I took off the sunbonnet, for I didn't want no blinders on then.

When I was about the middle, I heard the clock begin to strike. So I stops and listens. The sound come faint over the water but clear—eleven.

I struck the head of the island. I never waited to catch my breath, though I was most winded. I shoved right into the timber where my old camp used to be. I started a good fire there on a high and dry spot.

Then I jumped in the canoe and dug out for our place as hard as I could go. It was a mile and a half below. I landed, and **slouched** through the timber and up the ridge and into the cavern. There Jim laid, sound asleep on the ground. I woke him up and says, "Get up and moving, Jim! There ain't a minute to lose. They're after us!"

Jim never asked no questions. He never said a word. But the way he worked for the next half an hour showed about how he was scared. By that time everything we had in the world was on our raft. She was ready to be shoved out from the willow cove where she was hid. We put out the campfire at the cavern the first thing. We didn't show a candle outside after that.

I took the canoe out from the shore a little piece and took a look. If there was a boat around, I couldn't see it. Stars and shadows ain't good to see by. Then we got out the raft and slipped along down in the shade. We went past the foot of the island dead still—never saying a word.

Chapter 12 (Summary)

"Better Let Blamed Well Alone"

Around one o'clock in the morning, the raft slipped past the island, so Jim and Huck felt safe once again.

As time went on, Huck and Jim grew more used to life on the river. Jim built a wigwam on the raft for shelter in bad weather. The two also set up a routine. During the days they hid the raft and slept on shore. At night they floated down the river. Every evening Huck went ashore for supplies. He bought meal and bacon in the nearest village and "borrowed" food from the fields.

The two continued on this way, passing St. Louis. Then one night a big storm came up. As the raft glided down the river, a big bolt of lightning brightened up the water. In the sudden light, Huck spied a wrecked steamboat on a nearby rock.

Although Jim argued against the idea, he and Huck went aboard the boat to have an adventure. When they got inside and heard voices, Jim started to hightail it back to the raft. But Huck's curiosity got the better of him. He crept toward the men's voices and came to a room with three thieves, one of them tied up. The other two were arguing about murdering the third one because he had tried to cheat them.

Huck lit out to find Jim. He was surprised to see that Jim was still on the steamboat. He told Jim about the thieves and urged that they set the outlaws' boat adrift so the men would be stuck on the steamboat.

But he hadn't counted on hearing Jim's news: the raft had broken loose. Now Jim and Huck were stranded on the wrecked boat.

Chapter 13 (Summary)

Honest Loot from the *Walter Scott*

Huck almost fainted at the thought of being stuck on the wreck with three criminals. Then he realized the only way he and Jim could escape was to steal the outlaws' boat.

Huck and Jim acted on the idea at once. They located the boat, jumped in, and cut it loose. Soon the boat was swallowed up in darkness, and Huck and Jim were out of harm's way. After rowing down the river for a while, Huck and Jim were overjoyed to see their raft a little ways ahead of them. They headed for the raft and soon overtook it.

But Huck began to feel guilty about leaving the thieves stranded. He knew the men would probably die when the wreck broke up.

So Huck went ashore to find help for the outlaws. He stumbled upon the owner of a ferryboat and made up a wild story about Huck's family being on the wreck. To Huck's relief, the ferryboat captain started out for the rescue.

Then Huck spied the wrecked steamboat moving down the river. It was almost sunk, and Huck knew that there was no one alive on her. He felt sad but took comfort in knowing he had done what he could.

Huck returned to the raft and Jim. It was almost dawn, so they hid the raft near an island and settled down to sleep.

Chapter 14

Was Solomon Wise?

VOCABULARY PREVIEW

The following words appear in this chapter. Review the list and get to know the words before you read the chapter.

consequence—importance; value
dispute—argument; conflict
flutter—swishing; rippling
gaudy—cheap; flashy
ridiculous—senseless; pointless

By and by, we got up. We looked over the truck the gang had stole off the wreck. We found boots and blankets and clothes and all sorts of other things. There were a lot of books, and a spyglass, and three boxes of seegars.[1]

We hadn't ever been this rich before in neither of our lives. The seegars was prime. We laid off all afternoon in the woods talking. I was reading the books. We were having a general good time.

I told Jim all about what happened inside the wreck and at the ferryboat. I said these kinds of things was adventures. But he said he didn't want no more adventures.

He said he remembered when I went in the texas[2] and he crawled back to get on the raft. When he found her gone he nearly died. He judged it was all up with him, no matter how he figured it.

If he didn't get saved, he'd get drownded. And if he did get saved, whoever saved him would send him back home so as to get the reward. And then Miss Watson would sell him South, sure. Well, he was right. He was most always right. He had an uncommon level head for a nigger.

---

1 *Seegars* is Huck's way of saying "cigars."

2 *The texas* is the name of the officers' sleeping quarters on a steamboat. The texas is located just below the pilothouse.

I read considerable to Jim about kings and dukes and earls and such. I read about how **gaudy** they dressed, and how much style they put on. And how they called each other your majesty and your grace, and your lordship, and so on, instead of mister.

And Jim's eyes bugged out. He was interested. He says, "I didn't know dey was so many of dem. I ain't heard 'bout none of 'em, scarcely, but old King Solomon.[3] Unless you counts dem kings dat's in a pack of cards. How much do a king git?"

"Get?" I says. "Why, they get a thousand dollars a month if they want it. They can have just as much as they want. Everything belongs to them."

"Ain't dat gay? En' what dey got to do, Huck?"

"They don't do nothing! Why, how you talk! They just set around."

"No. Is dat so?"

"Of course it is. They just set around. Except, maybe, when there's a war. Then they go to war. But other times they just lazy around. Or they go hawking.[4] Just hawking and sp—Sh!—Do you hear a noise?"

We skipped out and looked. But it warn't nothing but the **flutter** of a steamboat wheel. It was away down, coming around the point. So we come back.

"Yes," says I. "And other times when things is dull, they fuss with parlyment.[5] If everybody don't go just so, he whacks their heads off. But mostly, they hang 'round the harem."

"'Round de which?"

"Harem."

"What's de harem?"

"The place where he keeps his wives. Don't you know about the harem? Solomon had one. He had about a million wives."

---

3 King Solomon, the son of David and Bathsheba, was a king of ancient Israel. Solomon is known for his wisdom.

4 *Hawking* is training and using hawks for sports.

5 *Parlyment* is Huck's way of saying "parliament," the governing body in some countries, including England. It is similar to the U.S. Congress.

"Why, yes, dat's so. I—I'd done forgot it. A harem's a boardin' house,[6] reckon. Most likely dey had noisy times in de nursery. En' I reckon de wives quarrels considerable. En' dat increase de racket.

"Yit dey say Solomon de wisest man dat ever lived. I don't take no stock in dat. Here's why: Would a wise man want to live in de midst of such a blim-blammin' all de time? No—'deed he wouldn't. A wise man would take en' build a boiler-factory. En' den he could shut down de boiler-factory when he want to rest."

"Well, but he was the wisest man, anyway. Because the widow, she told me so, her own self."

"I don't care what de widder say. He warn't no wise man, neither. He had some of de dad-fetchedest[7] ways I ever see. Does you know 'bout dat chile he was goin' to chop in two?"

"Yes, the widow told me all about it."

"Well, den! Warn't dat de beatenest notion in de world? You just take a look at it a minute. Dah's de stump, dah—dat's one of de women. Here's you—dat's de other one. I's Solomon. En' dis here dollar bill's de chile.

"Both of you claims it. What does I do? Does I check around amongst de neighbors? Does I try to find out which of you de bill do belong to? En' do I hand it over to de right one, all safe and sound? Do I do it like anybody dat had any good sense would?

"No. I take en' whack de bill in two. En' I give half of it to you, en' de other half to de other woman. Dat's de way Solomon was goin' to do with de chile.

"Now I want to ask you: what's de use in dat half a bill? You can't buy nothin' with it. En' what use is half a chile?

I wouldn't give a dern for a million of 'em."

"But hang it, Jim, you've clean missed the point. Blame it, you've missed it by a thousand miles."

"Who? Me? Go 'long. Don't talk to me 'bout your points. I reckon I knows sense when I sees it. En' dey ain't no sense in such doings as dat. De **dispute** warn't 'bout half a chile. De dispute was 'bout a whole chile.

---

6 A *boardinghouse* is a house where people pay for rooms and meals. It is, needless to say, not at all like a harem.

7 *Dad-fetchedest* is Jim's way of saying "damnedest."

"You can't settle a dispute 'bout a whole chile with half a chile. If a man thinks he can, he don't know enough to come in out of the rain. Don't talk to me about Solomon, Huck. I knows him backwards and forwards."

"But I tell you, you don't get the point."

"Blame de point! I reckon I knows what I knows. En' mind you, de real point is down further. It's down deeper. It lays in de way Solomon was raised.

"You take a man dat's got only one or two children. Is dat man goin' to be wasteful of children? No, he ain't. He can't afford it. He knows how to value 'em.

"But you take a man dat's got 'bout five million children runnin' 'round de house. It's different. He as soon chop a chile in two as a cat. There's plenty more. A chile or two, more or less, warn't no **consequence** to Solomon!"

I never saw such a nigger. If he got a notion in his head once, there warn't no getting it out again. He was the most down on Solomon of any nigger I ever saw. So I went to talking about other things. I let Solomon slide.

I told about Louis Sixteenth that got his head cut off in France long time ago. And I told about his little boy the dolphin. He would have been king. But they took and shut him up in jail. Some said he died there.[8]

"Poor little chap."

"But some says he got out and got away. They says he come to America."

"Dat's good. But he'll be pretty lonesome. There ain't no kings here, is there, Huck?"

"No."

"Den he can't get no situation. What's he goin' to do?"

"Well, I don't know. Some of them gets on the police. And some of them learns people how to talk French."

"Why, Huck, don't de French people talk de same way we does?"

---

8 Louis XVI and his wife, Marie Antoinette, were beheaded during the French Revolution in 1793. *Dolphin* is Huck's way of saying "dauphin," the eldest son of the king of France. The dauphin in this case was Charles Louis. Although it is not known for sure, the boy probably died in prison around 1795.

"No, Jim. You couldn't understand a word they said. Not a single word."

"Well, now, I be ding-busted![9] How do dat come?"

"I don't know. But it's so. I got some of their jabber out of a book. Suppose a man was to come up to you and say 'Polly-voo-franzy?'[10] What would you think?"

"I wouldn't think nothin'. I'd take him en' bust him over de head. Dat is, if he warn't white. I wouldn't allow no nigger to call me dat."

"Shucks, it ain't calling you anything. It's only saying, do you know how to talk French?"

"Well, den, why couldn't he say it?"

"Why, he is a-sayin' it. That's a Frenchman's way of sayin' it."

"Well, it's a blamed **ridiculous** way. I don't want to hear no more about it. There ain't no sense in it."

"Looky here, Jim. Does a cat talk like we do?"

"No, a cat don't."

"Well, does a cow?"

"No, a cow don't neither."

"Does a cat talk like a cow, or a cow talk like a cat?"

"No, dey don't."

"It's natural and right for them to talk different from each other. Ain't it?"

"Course."

"And ain't it natural and right for a cat and a cow to talk different from us?"

"Why, most surely it is."

"Well, then," says I, "why ain't it natural and right for a Frenchman to talk different from us? You answer me that."

"Is a cat a man, Huck?"

"No."

"Well, den, there ain't no sense in a cat talkin' like a man. Is a cow a man?—er is a cow a cat?"

---

9 *Ding-busted* is another slang term of Jim's for "damned."

10 *Polly-voo-franzy?* is Huck's way of asking "Parlez-vous Francais?" which is French for "Do you speak French?"

"No, she ain't either of them."

"Well, den, she ain't got no business to talk like either one or the other of 'em. Is a Frenchman a man?"

"Yes."

"Well, den! Dad blame it, why don't he talk like a man? You answer me dat!"

I see it warn't no use wasting words. You can't learn a nigger to argue. So I quit.

Chapter 15

Fooling Poor Old Jim

VOCABULARY PREVIEW

The following words appear in this chapter. Review the list and get to know the words before you read the chapter.

aggravate—anger; irritate
dismal—gloomy; cheerless
interpret—explain; figure out
littered—messed up; cluttered
quarrelsome—unfriendly; likely to quarrel or argue

We judged that three nights more would fetch us to Cairo, which was at the bottom of Illinois where the Ohio River comes in. That was what we was after. We would sell the raft and get on a steamboat. Then we would go way up the Ohio amongst the free states. We would be out of trouble then.

Well, the second night a fog begun to come on. We made for a towhead[1] to tie to. It wouldn't do to try to run in a fog. I paddled ahead in the canoe with the line to make fast. But there warn't anything but little saplings to tie to.

I passed the line around one of them right on the edge of the cut bank. But there was a stiff current. The raft come rushing down real lively. She tore the sapling out by the roots and away she went.

I saw the fog closing down. It made me sick and scared.

I couldn't budge for most a half a minute, it seemed to me. And then there warn't no raft in sight. You couldn't see twenty yards. I jumped into the canoe and run back to the stern. I grabbed the paddle and set her back a stroke. But she didn't come. I was in such a hurry, I hadn't untied her.

---

1 A *towhead* is a sandbar in a river.

I got up and tried to untie her. But I was so excited my hands shook. I couldn't hardly do anything with them. As soon as I got started, I took out after the raft. I went hot and heavy, right down the towhead.[1]

That was all right as far as it went. But the towhead warn't sixty yards long. The minute I flew by the foot of it, I shot out into the solid white fog. I hadn't no more idea which way I was going than a dead man.

Thinks I, it won't do to paddle. First I know, I'll run into the bank or a towhead or something. I got to set still and float. Yet it's mighty fidgety business to have to hold your hands still at such a time. I whooped and listened. Away down there somewheres I hears a small whoop. Up comes my spirits.

I went tearing after it, listening sharp to hear it again. The next time it come, I see I warn't heading for it. Instead, I was heading away to the right of it. And the next time I was heading away to the left of it.

And I warn't gaining on it much, either. For I was flying around, this way and that and the other. But it was going straight ahead all the time.

I did wish the fool would think to beat a tin pan, and beat it all the time. But he never did. It was the still places between the whoops that was making the trouble for me.

Well, I fought along. And directly I hears the whoop behind me. I was tangled good now. That was somebody else's whoop, or else I was turned around. I throwed the paddle down and heard the whoop again. It was behind me yet, but in a different place. It kept coming, and kept changing its place. I kept answering.

By and by, it was in front of me again. I knowed the current had swung the canoe's head downstream. I was all right if that was Jim and not some other raftsman hollering. I couldn't tell nothing about voices in a fog. Nothing don't look nor sound natural in a fog.

The whooping went on. In about a minute, I came a-rushin' down on a cut bank. It had smoky ghosts of big trees on it. The current throwed me off to the left and shot by. I was amongst a lot of snags. They fairly roared, the current was tearing by them so swift.

In another second or two, it was solid white and still again. I set perfectly still, listening to my heart thump. I reckon I didn't draw a breath while it thumped a hundred.

I just give up then. I knowed what the matter was. That cut bank was an island, and Jim had gone down the other side of it. It warn't no towhead that you could float by in ten minutes. It had the big timber of a regular island. It might be five or six miles long and more than a half a mile wide.

I kept quiet, with my ears cocked, for about fifteen minutes, I reckon. I was floating along, of course, four or five miles an hour.

But you don't ever think of that. No, you feel like you are laying dead still on the water. A little glimpse of a snag might slip by. But you don't think to yourself how fast you're going. You catch your breath and think, my! how that snag's tearing along.

Maybe you think it ain't **dismal** and lonesome out in a fog that way by yourself in the night. You try it once. You'll see.

Next, for about a half an hour, I whoops now and then. At last I hears the answer a long ways off. I tries to follow it, but I couldn't do it. Directly, I judged I'd got into a nest of towheads. I had dim glimpses of them on both sides of me. Sometimes there was just a narrow channel between.

Some of them I couldn't see. But I knowed they was there. I'd hear the wash of the current against the old dead brush and trash that hung over the banks.

Well, I warn't long losing the whoops down amongst the towheads. I only tried to chase them a little while, anyway.

It was worse than chasing a Jack-o'-lantern.[2] You never knowed a sound to dodge around so, and swap places so quick and so much.

I had to claw away from the bank pretty lively four or five times. I came close to knocking the islands out of the river. So I judged the raft must be butting into the bank every now and then. Or else it would get further ahead and clear out of hearing. It was floating a little faster than what I was.

Well, I seemed to be in the open river again, by and by. But I couldn't hear no sign of a whoop nowheres. I reckoned Jim had fetched up on a snag, maybe, and it was all up with him.

I was good and tired, so I laid down in the canoe. I said I wouldn't bother no more. I didn't want to go to sleep, of course. But I was so sleepy, I couldn't help it. So I thought I would take just one little cat nap.

But I reckon it was more than a cat nap. For when I waked up, the stars was shining bright. The fog was all gone. And I was spinning down a big bend, stern first.

First, I didn't know where I was. I thought I was dreaming. Then things began to come back to me. But they seemed to come up dim out of last week.

It was a monstrous big river here. It had the tallest and the thickest kind of timber on both banks. It was just a solid wall, as well as I could see by the stars.

I looked away downstream and saw a black speck on the water. So I took after it and got to it. But it warn't nothing but a couple of sawlogs made fast together. Then I saw another speck, and chased that. Then another, and this time I was right. It was the raft.

---

2 By *Jack-o'-lantern*, Huck clearly does not mean a Halloween pumpkin. The term had other possible meaning in his time:

a) watchmen's lantern, a shiny glow caused by gases found near swamps or marshes.

b) Saint Elmo's fire, a flamelike glow which sometimes appears on boats, ships, trees, or steeples during stormy weather.

c) large, poisonous mushrooms that glow in the dark.

When I got to it, Jim was sitting there with his head down between his knees, asleep. His right arm was hanging over the steering oar. The other oar was smashed off. And the raft was **littered** up with leaves and branches and dirt. So she'd had a rough time.

I tied the canoe to the raft. Then I laid down under Jim's nose on the raft. I began to yawn, and stretch my fists out against Jim. I says, "Hello, Jim, have I been asleep? Why didn't you stir me up?"

"Goodness gracious, is dat you, Huck? En' you ain't dead—you ain't drownded? You's back again? It's too good for true, honey. It's too good for true.

"Let me look at you, chile. Let me feel you. No, you ain't dead! You's back again, alive en' sound. You's just de same ole Huck. De same ole Huck, thanks to goodness!"

"What's the matter with you, Jim? You been a-drinkin'?"

"Drinkin'? Has I been a-drinkin'? Has I had a chance to be a-drinkin'?"

"Well, then, what makes you talk so wild?"

"How does I talk wild?"

"How?" says I. "Why, ain't you been talking about my coming back, and all that stuff? As if I'd been gone away?"

"Huck—Huck Finn, you look me in de eye. Look me in de eye. Ain't you been gone away?"

"Gone away? Why, what in the nation do you mean? I ain't been gone anywheres. Where would I go to?"

"Well, looky here, boss," says Jim. "There's something wrong, there is. Is I me, or who is I? Is I here, or where is I? Now dat's what I wants to know."

"Well, I think you're here, plain enough. But I think you're a tangle-headed old fool, Jim."

"I is, is I? Well, you answer me dis. Didn't you take out de line in de canoe? Weren't you goin' to make fast to de towhead?"

"No, I didn't," says I. "What towhead? I ain't seen no towhead."

"You ain't seen no towhead? Looky here, didn't de line pull loose? En' didn't de raft go a-hummin' down de river? En' didn't it leave you en' de canoe behind in de fog?"

"What fog?"

"Why, de fog! De fog dat's been around all night. En' didn't you whoop, en' didn't I whoop? En' den we got mixed up in de islands. En' one of us got lost. En' de other one was just as good as lost, 'cause he didn't know where he was.

"En' didn't I bust up against a lot of them islands? En didn't I have a terrible time en' almost git drownded? Now ain't dat so, boss—ain't it so? You answer me dat."

"Well, this is too many for me, Jim. I ain't seen no fog nor no islands. And I ain't seen no troubles nor nothing. I been setting here talking with you all night. Then you went to sleep about ten minutes ago. I reckon I done the same.

"You couldn't have got drunk in that time. So of course you've been dreaming."

"Dad fetch it, how is I goin' to dream all dat in ten minutes?"

"Well, hang it all," says I. "You did dream it. Because there didn't any of it happen."

"But, Huck, it's all just as plain to me as—"

"It don't make no difference how plain it is. There ain't nothing in it. I know, because I've been here all the time."

Jim didn't say nothing for about five minutes. He set there studying over it. Then he says, "Well, den, I reckon I did dream it, Huck. But dog my cats if it ain't de powerfulest dream I ever see. En' I ain't ever had no dream before dat's tired me like dis one."

"Oh, well, that's all right. A dream does tire a body like everything sometimes. But this one was quite some dream. Tell me all about it, Jim."

So Jim went to work. He told me the whole thing right through, just as it happened. Only he painted it up considerable. Then he said he must start in and **interpret** it. Because the dream was sent for a warning.

He said the first towhead stood for a man that would try to do us some good. But the current was another man that would get us away from him.

The whoops was warnings that would come to us every now and then. We had to try hard to make out to understand them. Otherwise, they'd just take us into bad luck, instead of keeping us out of it.

The lot of towheads was troubles we was going to get into. These would be caused by **quarrelsome** people and all kinds of mean folks. But we just had to mind our own business. We mustn't talk back and **aggravate** them.

Then we would pull through and get out of the fog. We'd get into the big clear river. This was the free states. And we wouldn't have no more trouble.

It had clouded up pretty dark just after I got on to the raft. But it was clearing up again now.

"Oh, well, that's all interpreted well enough as far as it goes, Jim," I says. "But what does these things stand for?"

I pointed at the leaves and rubbish on the raft and at the smashed oar. You could see them first-rate now.

Jim looked around at the trash. Then he looked at me, and back at the trash again. He had got the dream fixed so strong in his head, he couldn't seem to shake it loose. And he couldn't get the facts back into its place again right away.

But then he did get the thing straightened around. He looked at me steady without ever smiling, and says, "What do they stand for? I's goin' to tell you. I got all wore out with work, en' with de callin' for you. En' when I went to sleep, my heart was most broke, 'cause you was lost. En' I didn't care no more what become of me en' de raft.

"En' then I wake up en' find you back again, all safe en' sound. En' de tears come. En' I could have got down on my knees en' kiss your foot, I's so thankful.

"En' all you was thinkin' 'bout was how you could make a fool of ole Jim with a lie. Dat truck there is trash. En' trash is what people is dat puts dirt on de head of their friends and makes 'em ashamed."

Then he got up slow and walked to the wigwam. He went in there without saying anything but that. But that was enough. It made me feel mean. I could almost kissed his foot to get him to take it back.

It was fifteen minutes before I could work myself up to go and humble myself to a nigger. But I done it. And I warn't ever sorry for it afterward, neither.

I didn't do him no more mean tricks. And I wouldn't have done that one if I'd have knowed it would make him feel that way.

Chapter 16

The Rattlesnake Skin Does Its Work

VOCABULARY PREVIEW

The following words appear in this chapter. Review the list and get to know the words before you read the chapter.

churning—moving by means of a large paddle wheel
conscience—sense of right and wrong
feverish—nervous; excited
green—unskilled; beginning
nab—grab; seize
obliged—thankful; owning
precious—extremely; very
trembly—shaky; unsteady

We slept most all day, and started out at night. We went a little ways behind a monstrous long raft. It was as long going by as a parade.

She had four sweeps[1] at each end. So we judged she carried as many as thirty men, likely. She had five big wigwams aboard, wide apart. There was an open campfire in the middle, and a tall flagpole at each end.

There was a power of style about her. It *amounted* to something being a raftsman on such a craft as that.

We went drifting down into a big bend. The night clouded up and got hot. The river was very wide and was walled with solid timber on both sides. You couldn't see a break in it hardly ever, or a light.

We talked about Cairo. We wondered whether we would know it when we got to it. I said likely we wouldn't. I had heard say there warn't but about a dozen houses there. Suppose they didn't happen to have them lit up? Then how was we going to know we was passing a town?

1 *Sweeps* are long oars.

Jim said if the two big rivers joined together there, that would show. But I said maybe we might think we was passing the foot of an island. We'd think we was coming into the same old river again.

That disturbed Jim—and me too. So the question was, what to do? I said I'd paddle ashore the first time a light showed. And I'd tell them Pap was behind, coming along with a trading-scow.[2] I'd say he was a **green** hand at the business, and wanted to know how far it was to Cairo.

Jim thought it was a good idea. So we took a smoke on it and waited.

There warn't nothing to do now but to look out sharp for the town. We had to keep from passing it without seeing it. He said he'd be mighty sure to see it. He'd be a free man the minute he seen it. But if he missed it, he'd be in a slave country again. And he'd get no more chance for freedom.

Every little while, he jumps up and says, "There she is?"

But it warn't. It was Jack-o'-lanterns or lightning bugs. So he set down again, and went to watching, same as before.

Jim said it made him all over **trembly** and **feverish** to be so close to freedom. Well, I can tell you, it made me all over trembly and feverish, too, to hear him. I begun to get it through my head that he was most free.

And who was to blame for it? Why, me. I couldn't get that out of my **conscience**, no how nor no way. It got to troubling me so I couldn't rest. I couldn't stay still in one place.

It hadn't ever come home to me before, what this thing was that I was doing. But now it did, and it stayed with me. It scorched me more and more.

I tried to make it out to myself that I warn't to blame. I didn't run Jim off from his rightful owner. But it warn't no use. Conscience up and says, every time, "But you knowed he was running for his freedom. You could have paddled ashore and told somebody."

---

2 A *scow* is a flat-bottomed boat. A *trading-scow* would be similar to a peddler's cart. However, instead of traveling by road, this peddler uses the river as a highway to go from town to town selling goods.

That was so. I couldn't get around that no way. That was where it pinched.

Conscience says to me, "What had poor Miss Watson done to you? How could you see her nigger go off right under your eyes and never say a single word? What did that poor old woman do to you that you could treat her so mean?

"Why, Miss Watson tried to learn you your book. She tried to learn you your manners. She tried to be good to you every way she knowed how. That's what she done."

I got to feeling so mean and so miserable. I most wished I was dead. I fidgeted up and down the raft, abusing myself to myself. Jim was fidgeting up and down past me.

We neither of us could keep still. Once in awhile he danced around and says, "There's Cairo!" It went through me like a shot every time. I thought, what if it was Cairo? I reckoned I would die of miserableness.

Jim talked out loud all the time while I was talking to myself. He was saying what was the first thing he would do when he got to a free state. He would go to saving up money. He would never spend a single cent.

When he got enough, he would buy his wife. She was owned on a farm close to where Miss Watson lived. Then they would both work to buy the two children. If their master wouldn't sell them, they'd get an Abolitionist to go and steal them.

It most froze me to hear such talk. He wouldn't ever dared to talk such talk in his life before. Now he judged he was about free. And just see what a difference it made in him. It was just like the old saying, "Give a nigger an inch and he'll take an ell."[3]

Thinks I, this is what comes of my not thinking. Here was this nigger, which I had as good as helped to run away. And now he comes right out flat-footed and says he would steal his children. And these children belonged to a man I didn't even know. A man that hadn't ever done me no harm.

I was sorry to hear Jim say that. It was such a lowering of him. My conscience got to stirring me up hotter than ever. At last, I says to it, "Let up on me. It ain't too late yet. I'll paddle ashore at the first light and tell."

---

3 An *ell* is an English measure of cloth equal to 45 inches.

I felt easy and happy and light as a feather right off. All my troubles was gone. I went to looking out sharp for a light. I was sort of singing to myself. By and by, one showed, and Jim sings out, "We's safe, Huck, we's safe! Jump up and crack your heels! Dat's de good ole Cairo at last. I just knows it!"

I says, "I'll take the canoe and go and see, Jim. It mightn't be, you know."

He jumped and got the canoe ready. He put his old coat in the bottom for me to set on. Then he give me the paddle. As I shoved off, he says, "Pretty soon, I'll be a-shoutin' for joy. En' I'll say, it's all on accounts of Huck that I's a free man. En' I couldn't ever been free if it hadn't been for Huck.

"Huck done it. Jim won't ever forget you, Huck. You's de best friend Jim's ever had. En' you's de only friend ole Jim's got now."

I was paddling off, all in a sweat to tell on him. But then he says this. It seemed to take all the courage out of me. I went along slow then. I warn't right down certain whether I was glad I started, or whether I warn't.

When I was fifty yards off, Jim says, "There you goes, de ole true Huck. De only white gentleman dat ever kept his promise to ole Jim."

Well, I just felt sick. But I says, I got to do it. I can't get out of it. Right then, along comes a skiff with two men in it with guns. They stopped and I stopped. One of them says, "What's that yonder?"

"A piece of a raft," I says.

"Do you belong on it?"

"Yes, sir."

"Any men on it?"

"Only one, sir."

"Well, there's five niggers run off tonight. They came from up yonder, above the head of the bend. Is your man white or black?"

I didn't answer up promptly. I tried to, but the words wouldn't come. I tried for a second or two to brace up and out with it. But I warn't man enough. I hadn't the guts of a rabbit.

I saw I was weakening. So I just give up trying, and up and says, "He's white."

"I reckon we'll go and see for ourselves."

"I wish you would," says I. "It's Pap that's there. Maybe you'd help me tow the raft ashore where the light is. He's sick—and so is Mam and Mary Ann."

"Oh, the devil! We're in a hurry, boy. But I suppose we've got to. Come, buckle to your paddle, and let's get along."

I buckled to my paddle and they laid to their oars. When we had made a stroke or two, I says, "Pap will be mighty much **obliged** to you, I can tell you. Everybody goes away when I want them to help me tow the raft ashore. I can't do it by myself."

"Well, that's awful mean. Odd, too. Say, boy, what's the matter with your father?"

"It's the—a—the—well, it ain't anything much."

They stopped pulling. It warn't but a mighty little ways to the raft now. One says, "Boy, that's a lie. What is the matter with your pap? Answer up square now, and it'll be the better for you."

"I will, sir," I says. "I will, honest. But don't leave us, please. It's the—the—gentlemen, if you'll only pull ahead. Let me throw you the line. You won't have to come a-near the raft. Please do."

"Set her back, John, set her back!" says one. They backed water. "Keep away, boy. Keep to leeward.[4] Darn it, I just expect the wind has blowed it to us.

"Your pap's got the smallpox, and you know it **precious** well. Why didn't you come out and say so? Do you want to spread it all over?"

"Well," says I, a-blubberin'. "I've told everybody before. They just went away and left us."

"Poor devil, there's something in that," the man says. "We are right down sorry for you. But we—well, hang it, we don't want the smallpox, you see.

"Look here, I'll tell you what to do. Don't you try to land by yourself. You'll smash everything to pieces. Float along down about twenty miles. You'll come to a town on the left-hand side of the river. It will be long after sunup then.

---

4 *Leeward* is away from the wind.

"Go ask for help," the man went on. "Tell them your folks are all down with chills and fever. Don't be a fool again, and let people guess what is the matter.

"Now we're trying to do you a kindness. So you just put twenty miles between us, that's a good boy. It wouldn't do any good to land yonder where the light is. It's only a wood-yard.

"Say, I reckon your father's poor. I'm bound to say he's in pretty hard luck. Here, I'll put a twenty dollar gold piece on this board. You get it when it floats by.

"I feel mighty mean to leave you," the man says. "But my kingdom! It won't do to fool with smallpox, don't you see?"

"Hold on, Parker," says the other man. "Here's a twenty to put on the board for me. Good-bye, boy. You do as Mr. Parker told you, and you'll be all right."

"That's so, my boy. Good-bye, good-bye. If you see any runaway niggers, you get help and **nab** them. You can make some money by it."

"Good-bye, sir," says I. "I won't let no runaway niggers get by me if I can help it."

They went off and I got aboard the raft. I felt bad and low. I knowed very well I had done wrong. And I see it warn't no use for me to try to learn to do right.

A body that don't get started right when he's little ain't got no show. When the pinch comes, there ain't nothing to back him up and keep him to his work. So he gets beat. Then I thought a minute, and says to myself, hold on. Suppose you'd have done right and give Jim up? Would you felt better than what you do now? No, I'd feel bad—I'd feel just the same way I do now.

Well, then, says I, what's the use you learning to do right? It's troublesome to do right and ain't no trouble to do wrong. And the wages is just the same.

I was stuck. I couldn't answer that. So I reckoned I wouldn't bother no more about it. After this, I'd always do whichever come handiest at the time.

I went into the wigwam. Jim warn't there. I looked all around. He warn't anywhere. I says, "Jim!"

"Here I is, Huck. Is dey out of sight yit? Don't talk loud."

He was in the river under the stern oar, with just his nose out. I told him they were out of sight, so he come aboard.

He says, "I was a-listenin' to all de talk, en' I slips into de river. I was goin' to shove for shore if dey come aboard. Then I was goin' to swim to de raft again when dey was gone. But lawsy, how you did fool 'em, Huck!

"Dat was de smartest dodge. I tell you, chile, I expect it saved ole Jim. Ole Jim ain't goin' to forget you for dat, honey."

Then we talked about the money. It was a pretty good raise—twenty dollars apiece. Jim said we could take deck passage[5] on a steamboat now. The money would last us as far as we wanted to go in the free states. He said twenty miles more warn't far for the raft to go. But he wished we was already there.

Towards daybreak, we tied up. Jim was mighty particular about hiding the raft good. Then he worked all day fixing things in bundles. He was getting all ready to quit rafting.

That night about ten, we came in sight of the lights of a town. It was away down in a left-hand bend.

I went off in the canoe to ask about it. Pretty soon, I found a man out in the river with a skiff. He was setting a trotline. I came up and says, "Mister, is that town Cairo?"

"Cairo? No. You must be a blamed fool."

"What town is it, mister?"

"If you want to know, go and find out. Don't stay here botherin' me. Or else in about a half a minute longer, you'll get something you won't want."

I paddled to the raft. Jim was awful disappointed. But I said never mind. Cairo would be the next place, I reckoned.

We passed another town before daylight, and I was going out again. But it was high ground, so I didn't go. No high ground about Cairo, Jim said. I had forgot it.

We laid up for the day on a towhead tolerable close to the left-hand bank. I begun to suspect something. So did Jim. I says, "Maybe we went by Cairo in the fog that night."

---

5 *To take deck passage* is to travel by boat without a cabin or sleeping quarters. Those who took deck passage were the lowest-paying passengers.

He says, "Don't let's talk about it, Huck. Poor niggers can't have no luck. I always expected dat rattlesnake skin warn't done with its work."

"I wish I never saw that snakeskin, Jim. I do wish I never laid eyes on it."

"It ain't your fault, Huck. You didn't know. Don't you blame yourself 'bout it."

When it was daylight, here was the clear Ohio River water inshore, sure enough. And outside was the old regular Muddy![6] So it was all up with Cairo.

We talked it all over. It wouldn't do to take to the shore. We couldn't take the raft up the stream, of course. There warn't no way but to wait for dark. Then we could start back in the canoe and take the chances.

So we slept all day amongst the cottonwood thicket, so as to be fresh for the work. But when we got back to the raft about dark, the canoe was gone!

We didn't say a word for a good while. There warn't anything to say. We both knowed well enough it was some more work of the rattlesnake skin.

So what was the use to talk about it? It would only look like we was finding fault. That would be bound to fetch more bad luck. And keep on fetching it, too, till we knowed enough to keep still.

By and by, we talked about what we better do. We found there warn't but one way. We'd just have to go along down with the raft till we got a chance to buy a canoe to go back in. We warn't going to borrow it when there warn't anybody around, the way Pap would do. That might set people after us.

So we shoved out after dark in the raft.

Maybe you don't believe yet that it's foolishness to handle a snakeskin. Not even after all that snakeskin done for us. You'll believe it now if you read on. You'll see what more it done for us.

---

6 The Mississippi is well known for being muddy. What Huck can see is that the currents of the two rivers have run together. So he knows they have definitely passed Cairo.

The place to buy canoes is off of rafts laying up at shore. But we didn't see no rafts laying up. So we went along for three hours or more. Well, the night got gray and rather thick. This is the next meanest thing to fog. You can't tell the shape of the river, and you can't see no distance.

It got to be very late and still. Then along comes a steamboat up the river. We lit the lantern, and judged she would see it.

Upstream boats didn't generally come close to us. They go out and follow the bars. They hunt for easy water close to the reefs.[7] But nights like this, they bull right up the channel against the whole river.

We could hear her pounding along. But we didn't see her good till she was close. She aimed right for us. Often they will do that and try to see how close they can come without touching. Sometimes the wheel bites off a sweep. Then the pilot sticks his head out and laughs and thinks he's mighty smart.

Well, here she comes. We said she was going to try and shave us. But she didn't seem to be steering off a bit. She was a big one, and she was coming in a hurry, too. She looked like a black cloud with rows of glowworms around it.

All of a sudden, she bulged out, big and scary. She had a long row of wide-open furnace doors shining like red-hot teeth. Her monstrous bows and guards[8] were hanging right over us.

There was a yell at us, and a jingling of bells to stop the engines. We heard a powwow of cussing, and a whistling of steam. Jim went overboard one side and I on the other. Then she come smashing straight through the raft.

I dived—and I aimed to find the bottom, too. For a thirty-foot wheel had got to go over me. I wanted it to have plenty of room. I could always stay under water a minute. This time I reckon I stayed under a minute and a half.

Then I bounced for the top in a hurry, for I was nearly busting. I popped out to my armpits. I blowed the water out of my nose, and puffed a bit.

---

7 A *bar* is a sandbar. A reef is a rocky or sandy ridge near the water's surface.

8 The *bows* refer to the front part of the ship. The *guards* stretch outward from the frame of the boat.

Of course, there was a booming current. And of course, that boat started her engines again ten seconds after she stopped them. They never cared much for raftsmen. So now she was **churning** up the river. She was out of sight in the thick weather, though I could hear her.

I sung out for Jim about a dozen times. But I didn't get any answer. So I grabbed a plank that touched me while I was treading water.[9] I struck out for shore, shoving the plank ahead of me.

But I made out to see that the drift of the current was towards the left-hand shore.[10] That meant that I was in a crossing. So I changed off and went that way.

It was one of these long, slanting, two-mile crossings. So I was a good long time in getting over. I made a safe landing, and clumb up the bank.

I couldn't see but a little ways. But I went poking along over rough ground for a quarter of a mile or more. Then I run across a big, old-fashioned double log house before I noticed it.

I was going to rush by and get away. But a lot of dogs jumped out and went to howling and barking at me. I knowed better than to move another peg.

---

9 *Treading water* is keeping the body upright and the head above water by moving the feet and hands. When treading water, the body remains in one place.

10 The left-hand shore is Kentucky.

Chapter 17

The Grangerfords Take Me In

VOCABULARY PREVIEW

The following words appear in this chapter. Review the list and get to know the words before you read the chapter.

disposition—attitude; mood
fret—worry
obituaries—death notices
outlandish—unusual; bizarre
pry—inspect; examine

In about a minute, somebody spoke out of a window without putting his head out. He says, "Be done, boys! Who's there?"

I says, "It's me."

"Who's me?"

"George Jackson, sir."

"What do you want?"

"I don't want nothing, sir. I only want to go along by. But the dogs won't let me."

"What are you prowling around here this time of night for—hey?"

"I warn't prowling around, sir. I fell overboard off of the steamboat."

"Oh, you did, did you? Strike a light, there, somebody. What did you say your name was?"

"George Jackson, sir. I'm only a boy."

"Look here, if you're telling the truth, you needn't be afraid. Nobody will hurt you. But don't try to budge. Stand right where you are. Wake up Bob and Tom, some of you. Fetch the guns. George Jackson, is there anybody with you?"

"No, sir, nobody."

I heard the people stirring around in the house now. And I saw a light. The man sung out, "Snatch that light away, Betsy, you old fool. Ain't you got any sense? Put it on the floor behind the front door. Bob, if you and Tom are ready, take your places."

"All ready," came two more voices.

"Now, George Jackson, do you know the Shepherdsons?"

"No, sir. I never heard of them."

"Well, that may be so, and it may not. Now, all ready. Step forward, George Jackson. And mind, don't you hurry. Come right slow. If there's anybody with you, let him keep back. If he shows himself, he'll be shot. Come along now," the man went on. "Come slow. Push the door open yourself—just enough to squeeze in, do you hear?"

I didn't hurry. I couldn't if I'd a-wanted to. I took one slow step at a time. There warn't a sound, only I thought I could hear my heart. The dogs were as still as the humans. But they followed a little behind me.

I got to the three log doorsteps. Then I heard them unlocking and unbarring and unbolting. I put my hand on the door and pushed it a little and a little more.

Then somebody said, "There, that's enough. Put your head in." I done it, but I judged they would take it off.

The candle was on the floor. There they all was, looking at me, and me at them. This went on for about a quarter of a minute.

There were three big men with guns pointed at me. That made me wince, I tell you. The oldest was gray and about sixty. The other two were thirty or more. All of them were fine and handsome.

And there was the sweetest old gray-headed lady. Back of her were two young women which I couldn't see right well. The old gentleman says, "There, I reckon it's all right. Come in."

As soon as I was in, the old gentleman locked the door. Then he barred it and bolted it. He told the young men to come in with their guns.

They all went in a big parlor that had a new rag carpet on the floor. They got together in a corner that was out of the range of the front windows. There warn't none on the side.

They held the candle, and took a good look at me. They all said, "Why, he ain't a Shepherdson. No, there ain't any Shepherdson about him."

Then the old man said he hoped I wouldn't mind being searched for arms. He didn't mean no harm by it. It was only to make sure. So he didn't **pry** into my pockets, but only felt outside with his hands. He said it was all right.

He told me to make myself easy and at home, and tell all about myself. But the old lady says, "Why, bless you, Saul, the poor thing's as wet as he can be. And don't you reckon it may be he's hungry?"

"True for you, Rachel—I forgot."

So the old lady says to a nigger woman, "Betsy, you fly around and get him something to eat as quick as you can, poor thing. One of you girls go and wake up Buck and tell him. Oh, here he is himself.

"Buck, take this little stranger and get the wet clothes off from him. Dress him up in some clothes of yours that's dry."

Buck looked about as old as me—thirteen or fourteen or along there. But he was a little bigger than me. He hadn't on anything but a shirt. And his hair was unkept-looking.

He came in yawning and digging one fist into his eyes. He was dragging a gun along with the other one. He says, "Ain't they no Shepherdsons around?"

They said, no, it was a false alarm.

"Well," he says, "if they'd have been some, I reckon I'd have got one."

They all laughed, and Bob says, "Why, Buck, they might have scalped us all, you've been so slow in coming."

"Well, nobody come after me, and it ain't right. I'm always kept down. I don't get no chance."

"Never mind, Buck, my boy," says the old man. "You'll have chance enough, all in good time. Don't you **fret** about that. Go along with you, now. Do as your mother told you."

We got upstairs to his room. He got me a coarse shirt and a roundabout[1] and pants of his. I put them on.

While I was at it, he asked me what my name was. But before I could tell him, he started to tell me about a blue jay and a young rabbit. He had catched them in the woods day before yesterday.

---

1 A *roundabout* is a short, tight jacket, worn by men and boys during the nineteenth century.

Then he asked me where Moses was when the candle went out. I said I didn't know. I hadn't heard about it before, no way.

"Well, guess," he says.

"How am I going to guess?" says I. "I never heard tell of it before."

"But you can guess, can't you? It's just as easy."

"Which candle?" I says.

"Why, any candle," he says.

"I don't know where he was," says I. "Where was he?"

"Why, he was in the dark! That's where he was!"

"Well, if you knowed where he was, what did you ask me for?"

"Why, blame it, it's a riddle, don't you see? Say, how long are you going to stay here? You got to stay always. We can just have booming times. They don't have no school now.

"Do you own a dog? I've got a dog. He'll go in the river and bring out chips that you throw in. Do you like to comb up Sundays, and all that kind of foolishness? You bet I don't, but Ma, she makes me.

"Confound these ole britches! I reckon I'd better put 'em on. But I'd rather not, it's so warm. Are you all ready? All right. Come along, old hoss."[2]

Cold corn pone, cold corn-beef, butter and buttermilk—that is what they had for me down there. And there ain't nothing better that I've ever come across yet.

Buck and his ma and all of them smoked cob pipes. The nigger woman didn't, since she was gone, nor did the two young women. They all smoked and talked, and I eat and talked. The young women had quilts around them. Their hair went down their backs.

They all asked me questions. I told them about Pap and me and all the family. I said we was living on a little farm down at the bottom of Arkansaw.[3]

Then my sister Mary Ann run off and got married. She never was heard of no more. Bill went to hunt them, and he warn't heard of no more. And Tom and Mort died. Then there warn't nobody but just me and Pap left. And he was just trimmed down to nothing, on account of his troubles.

---

2 *Hoss* is a term of familiarity and affection.

3 *Arkansaw* is a misspelling of "Arkansas."

So when he died, I took what was left, because the farm didn't belong to us. I started up the river, deck passage, and fell overboard. That was how I come to be here.

So they said I could have a home there as long as I wanted it. Then it was most daylight, and everybody went to bed. I went to bed with Buck.

Then I waked up in the morning. And drat it all, I had forgot what my name was. So I laid there about an hour trying to think. When Buck waked up, I says, "Can you spell, Buck?"

"Yes," he says.

"I bet you can't spell my name," says I.

"I bet you what you dare I can," he says.

"All right," says I, "go ahead."

"G-e-o-r-g-e J-a-x-o-n. There now," he says.

"Well," says I, "you done it. But I didn't think you could. It ain't no easy name to spell—right off without studying."

I wrote it down, private. Somebody might want me to spell it next. So I wanted to be handy with it. I wanted to be able to rattle it off like I was used to it.

It was a mighty nice family, and a mighty nice house, too. I hadn't seen such a nice house out in the country before. It had so much style.

It didn't have an iron latch on the front door, nor a wooden one with a buckskin string. It had a brass knob to turn, the same as houses in town. There warn't no bed in the parlor, nor a sign of a bed. But heaps of parlors in towns has beds in them.

There was a big fireplace that was bricked on the bottom. The bricks was kept clean and red by pouring water over them. Then they were scrubbed with another brick. Sometimes they wash them over with red water paint, same as they do in town. They call it Spanish-brown.

The fireplace had big brass dog irons that could hold up a sawlog. There was a clock in the middle of the mantelpiece. It had a picture of a town painted on the bottom half of the glass front. It had a round place in the middle of it for the sun. And you could see the pendulum swinging behind it.

It was beautiful to hear that clock tick. Sometimes one of these peddlers came along. They would scour her up and get her in good shape. Then she would start in and strike a hundred and fifty before she got tuckered out. They wouldn't have took any money for her.

Well, there was a big **outlandish** parrot on each side of the clock. They were made of something like chalk, and painted up gaudy. By one of the parrots was a cat made of crockery. There was a crockery dog by the other.

When you pressed down on them, they squeaked. But they didn't open their mouths nor look different nor interested. They squeaked through underneath. There was a couple of big, wild-turkey-wing fans. They were spread out behind those things.

There was a table in the middle of the room. On it was a kind of a lovely crockery basket. It had apples and oranges and peaches and grapes piled up in it. They was much redder and yellower and prettier than real ones is. But they warn't real. You could see where pieces had got chipped off. They showed the white chalk, or whatever it was, underneath.

This table had a cover made out of beautiful oilcloth. It had a red and blue spread-eagle painted on it, and a painted border all around. It come all the way from Philadelphia, they said.

There was some books, too. They were piled up perfectly exact, on each corner of the table. One was a big family Bible full of pictures. One was *Pilgrim's Progress*. It was about a man that left his family, but it didn't say why. I read considerable in it now and then. The statements was interesting, but tough.

Another was *Friendship's Offering*, full of beautiful stuff and poetry. But I didn't read the poetry. Another was *Henry Clay's Speeches*. And another was *Dr. Gunn's Family Medicine*.[4] It told you all about what to do if a body was sick or dead.

There was a hymnbook, and a lot of other books. And there was nice chairs, and perfectly sound, too. They warn't bagged down in the middle and busted, like an old basket.

They had pictures hung on the walls. They were mainly Washingtons and Lafayettes, and battles, and Highland Marys.

4 *Pilgrim's Progress*, by English author John Bunyan, tells the story of Christian's search for the Celestial City. All its characters and places symbolize religious ideas. *Friendship's Offering* was a popular gift book. Henry Clay (1777–1852) was a famous American statesman from Kentucky. He served as Speaker of the House and Secretary of State. Dr. Gunn's book (actually entitled *Domestic Medicine*) was published in 1830.

There was one called *Signing the Declaration*.[5]

There was some pictures that they called crayons. These were made by one of the daughters which was dead. She made these her own self when she was only fifteen years old. They was different from any pictures I ever saw before. They was blacker, mostly, than is common.

One picture was a woman in a slim black dress, belted small under the armpits. She had bulges like a cabbage in the middle of the sleeves. And she wore a large, black, scoop-shovel bonnet with a black veil. She had white, slim ankles crossed about with black tape. She wore very wee black slippers, like a chisel. And she was leaning thoughtfully on a ' tombstone on her right elbow, under a weeping willow. Her other hand hung down her side. It was holding a white handkerchief and a purse. Underneath the picture, it said, "Shall I Never See Thee More Alas."

There was another picture of a young lady. Her hair was all combed up straight to the top of her head. It was knotted there in front of a comb like a chair back. She was crying into a handkerchief. She had a dead bird laying on its back in her other hand with its heels up. Underneath the picture it said, "I Shall Never Hear Thy Sweet Chirrup More Alas."

There was one picture where a young lady was at a window. She was looking up at the moon, and tears were running down her cheeks. She had an open letter in one hand. Black sealing wax[6] showed on one edge of it. She was mashing a locket with a chain attached to it against her mouth. Underneath the picture, it said, "And Art Thou Gone Yes Thou Art Gone Alas."

These was all nice pictures, I reckon. But I didn't somehow seem to take to them. If ever I was down a little, they always gave me the shivers.

Everybody was sorry she died, though. She had laid out a lot more of these pictures to do. A body could see by what she had done what they had lost. But I reckoned that, with her **disposition**, she was having a better time in the graveyard.

---

5 Lafayette (1757–1834) was a French nobleman who became a hero of the American Revolution. Highland Mary was the subject of many poems by Scottish poet Robert Burns (1759–1796). The signing of the American Declaration of Independence was the subject of a famous painting by John Trumbull (1756–1843).

6 Letters of papers were sealed with hot wax. A design was often stamped into the wax.

She was at work on what they said was her greatest picture when she took sick. She wanted to be allowed to live till she got it done. Every day and every night, that was her prayer. But she never got the chance.

It was a picture of a young woman in a long white gown. She was standing on the rail of a bridge, all ready to jump off. Her hair was all down her back. She was looking up to the moon, with the tears running down her face.

She had two arms folded across her breast. And she had two arms stretched out in front, and two more reaching up toward the moon. The idea was to see which pair would look best. Then she could scratch out all the other arms. But, as I was saying, she died before she got her mind made up.

Now they kept this picture over the head of the bed in her room. Every time her birthday come, they hung flowers on it. Other times it was hid with a little curtain. The young woman in the picture had a kind of a nice, sweet face. But there was so many arms. It made her look too spidery, seemed to me.

This young girl kept a scrapbook when she was alive. She used to paste **obituaries** and accidents and cases of patient suffering in it. She got them out of the *Presbyterian Observer.* She wrote poetry after them out of her own head. It was very good poetry.

This is what she wrote about a boy named Stephen Dowling Bots. He fell down a well and was drownded:

Ode[7] To Stephen Dowling Bots, Deceased

And did young Stephen sicken,
And did young Stephen die?
And did the sad hearts thicken,
And did the mourners cry?

No, such was not the fate of
Young Stephen Dowling Bots,
Though sad hearts round him thickened,
'Twas not from sickness' shots.

---

7 An ode is a form of poetry. Some odes, like this one, are funeral songs.

No whooping-cough did rack his frame,
Nor measles drear with spots;
Not these crippled the sacred name
Of Stephen Dowling Bots.

Scorned love struck not with woe
That head of curly knots,
Nor stomach troubles laid him low,
Young Stephen Dowling Bots.

O no. Then list with tearful eye,
Whilst I his fate do tell.
His soul did from this cold world fly
By falling down a well.

They got him out and emptied him;
Alas it was too late;
His spirit was gone for to sport aloft
In the region of the good and great.

Emmeline Grangerford could make poetry like that before she was fourteen. There ain't no telling what she could have done by and by.

Buck said she could rattle off poetry like nothing. She didn't ever have to stop to think. He said she would slap down a line. If she couldn't find anything to rhyme with it, she would just scratch it out. Then she would slap down another one, and go ahead.

She warn't particular. She could write about anything you choose to give her to write about. Just so it was sadful. Every time a man died, or a woman died, or a child died, she would be on hand. And she would come up with her "tribute"[8] before the dead person was cold. She called them tributes.

The neighbors said it was the doctor first, then Emmeline, then the undertaker. The undertaker never got in ahead of

8 A tribute is honor, either written or spoken, given to a dead person. It expresses respect and affection.

Emmeline but once. And then she got stuck on a rhyme for the dead person's name, which was Whistler.

She warn't ever the same after that. She never complained. But she kind of slipped away and did not live long.

Poor thing, many's the time I made myself go up to the little room that used to be hers. I'd get out her poor old scrapbook and read in it. I'd do this when her pictures had been aggravating me and I had soured on her a little. I liked all that family, dead ones and all. I warn't going to let anything come between us.

Poor Emmeline made poetry about all the dead people when she was alive. And now there warn't nobody to make some about her, now she was gone. It didn't seem right. So I tried to sweat out a verse or two myself. But I couldn't seem to make it go somehow.

They kept Emmeline's room trim and nice. All the things was fixed in it just the way she liked to have them when she was alive. Nobody ever slept there. The old lady took care of the room herself, though there was plenty of niggers. She sewed there a good deal and read her Bible there, mostly.

Well, as I was saying about the parlor. There was beautiful curtains on the windows. They were white, with pictures painted on them. These were of castles with vines all down the walls, and cattle coming to drink.

There was a little old piano, too. It had tin pans in it, I reckon. Nothing was ever so lovely as to hear the young ladies play it and sing. They'd sing "The Last Link Is Broken" and play "The Battle of Prague"[9] on it.

The walls of all the rooms was plastered. Most had carpets on the floors. The whole house was whitewashed on the outside.

It was a double house. The big open place between them was roofed and floored. Sometimes the table was set there in the middle of the day. It was a cool, comfortable place.

Nothing couldn't be better. And warn't the cooking good, and just bushels of it, too!

9 "The Last Link Is Broken" is a sentimental tune written by William Clifton around 1840. "The Battle of Prague" was written by Franz Kotswara, a Czech composer, around 1788. It was an overly dramatic piece of music.

Chapter 18

Why Harney Rode Away for His Hat

VOCABULARY PREVIEW

The following words appear in this chapter. Review the list and get to know the words before you read the chapter.

ambush—hidden position in which a person waits to attack
aristocracy—high society; upper class
astonished—surprised; amazed
feud—quarrel; fight
frivolity—foolishness
ransacked—searched
splinters—pieces; fragments

Colonel Grangerford was a gentleman, you see. He was a gentleman all over. So was his family. He was well born, as the saying is. And that's worth as much in a man as it is in a horse, so the Widow Douglas said. And nobody ever denied that she was of the first **aristocracy** in our town. Pap, he always said it, too. But he warn't no more quality than a mudcat[1] himself.

Col. Grangerford was very tall and very slim. He had darkish-paly skin. There was not a sign of red in it lanywheres. He was clean-shaved every morning all over his thin face. And he had the thinnest kind of lips, and the thinnest kind of nostrils.

He had a high nose, and heavy eyebrows, and the blackest kind of eyes. They were sunk so deep back, they seemed like they was looking out of caverns at you, as you might say.

His forehead was high, and his hair was gray and straight and hung to his shoulders. His hands was long and thin. Every day of his life, he put on a clean shirt and a full suit. From head to foot, he was covered with linen so white it hurt your eyes to look at it.

On Sundays he wore a blue tailcoat with brass buttons on it. He carried a reddish-brown wooden cane with a silver head on it.

---

1 A *mudcat* is a kind of Mississippi catfish. Huck has made a good comparison between Pap and a catfish. Both are scavengers who life off of scraps and trash.

There warn't no **frivolity** about him, not a bit. And he warn't ever loud. He was as kind as he could be. You could feel that, you know, and so you had confidence.

Sometimes he smiled, and it was good to see. But sometimes he would straighten himself up like a flagpole. And the lightning would begin to flicker out from under his eyebrows. You wanted to climb a tree first, and find out what the matter was afterwards.

Col. Grangerford didn't ever have to tell anybody to mind their manners. Everybody was always good-mannered where he was. Everybody loved to have him around, too. He was sunshine most always. I mean, he made it seem like good weather.

When he turned into a cloud bank, it was awful dark for half a minute. That was enough. And then nothing would go wrong again for a week.

When him and the old lady come down in the morning, all the family got up out of their chairs. The family give them good day, and didn't set down again till they had set down.

Then Tom and Bob went to the sideboard where the liquor was. They mixed a glass of bitters[2] and handed it to him. He held it in his hand and waited till Tom's and Bob's was mixed.

Then they bowed and said, "Our duty to you, sir, and madam." And the colonel and his wife bowed the least bit in the world, and said thank you.

And so they drank, all three. And Bob and Tom poured a spoonful of water on the sugar and the bit of whisky or apple brandy in the bottom of their glasses. They give it to me and Buck, and we drank to the old people, too.

Bob was the oldest and Tom next. They were tall, beautiful men with very broad shoulders and brown faces. They had long black hair and black eyes. They dressed in white linen from head to foot, like the old gentleman. They wore broad Panama hats.[3]

Then there was Miss Charlotte. She was twenty-five, and tall and proud and grand. But she was as good as she could be when she warn't stirred up. But when she was, she had a look that would make you wilt in your tracks, like her father. She was beautiful.

---

2 *Bitters* is a kind of liquor with bitter herbs.

3 *Panama hats* are white straw hats, commonly worn by Southern gentlemen.

So was her sister, Miss Sophia. But it was a different kind of beautiful. She was gentle and sweet like a dove. And she was only twenty.

Each person had their own nigger to wait on them—Buck too. My nigger had a horribly easy time. I warn't used to having anybody do anything for me. But Buck's was on the jump most of the time.

This was all there was of the family now. There used to be more—three sons. They got killed. And there was Emmeline that died.

The old gentleman owned a lot of farms and over a hundred niggers. Sometimes a stack of people would come there on horseback. They came from ten or fifteen miles around and stayed five or six days.

They would take rides round about and on the river. There would be dances and picnics in the woods daytimes, and balls at the house nights.

These people was mostly kinfolks of the family. The men brought their guns with them. It was a handsome lot of quality, I tell you.

There was another clan[4] of aristocracy around there—five or six families. They were mostly of the name of Shepherdson. They was as high-toned and well born and rich and grand as the tribe of Grangerfords.

The Shepherdsons and the Grangerfords used the same steamboat landing. This was about two miles above our house. Sometimes I went up there with a lot of our folks. And I used to see a lot of the Shepherdsons there on their fine horses.

One day, Buck and me was way out in the woods hunting. We heard a horse coming. We was crossing the road. Buck says, "Quick! Jump for the woods!"

We done it, and then peeped down the woods through the leaves. Pretty soon, a splendid young man came galloping down the road. He rode his horse easy and looked like a soldier. He carried his gun across his saddle. I had seen him before. It was young Harney Shepherdson.

---

4 A *clan* is a group—often a family—that is united by the same interests or characteristics.

I heard Buck's gun go off at my ear. Harney's hat tumbled off from his head. He grabbed his gun and rode straight to the place where we was hid. But we didn't wait. We started through the woods on a run.

The woods warn't thick. So I looked over my shoulder to dodge the bullet. Twice I seen Harney cover Buck with his gun. Then he rode away the way he come. He went to get his hat, I reckon, but I couldn't see. We never stopped running till we got home.

When we told the old gentleman, his eyes blazed a minute. It was pleasure, mainly, I judged. Then his face sort of smoothed down, and he says, kind of gentle, "I don't like that shooting from behind a bush. Why didn't you step into the road, my boy?"

"The Shepherdsons don't, Father. They always take the advantage."

Miss Charlotte, she held her head up like a queen while Buck was telling his tale. Her nostrils spread and her eyes snapped. The two young men looked dark, but never said nothing.

Miss Sophia, she turned pale. But the color come back when she found the man warn't hurt.

Soon, I got Buck down by the corncribs[5] under the trees. We were by ourselves, and I says, "Did you want to kill him, Buck?"

"Well, I bet I did."

"What did he do to you?"

"Him? He never done nothing to me."

"Well, then, what did you want to kill him for?"

"Why, nothing. Only it's on account of the **feud**."

"What's a feud?"

"Why, where was you raised? Don't you know what a feud is?"

"Never heard of it before—tell me about it."

"Well," says Buck, "a feud is this way. A man has a quarrel with another man, and kills him. Then that man's brother kills him. Then the other brothers, on both sides, goes for one another. Then the cousins chip in.

"By and by, everybody's killed off. And there ain't no more

---

5 A *corncrib* is used to store and dry ears of corn.

feud. But it's kind of slow, and takes a long time."

"Has this one been going on long, Buck?"

"Well, I should reckon! It started thirty years ago, or somewheres along there. There was trouble about something. Then there was a lawsuit to settle it. The suit went against one of the men. So he up and shot the man that won the suit—which he would naturally do, of course. Anybody would."

"What was the trouble about, Buck? Land?"

"I reckon maybe—I don't know."

"Well, who done the shooting? Was it a Grangerford or a Shepherdson?"

"Lord, how do I know? It was so long ago."

"Don't anybody know?"

"Oh, yes. Pa knows, I reckon, and some of the other old people. But they don't know now what the row was about in the first place."

"Has there been many killed, Buck?"

"Yes, there's been a right lot of funerals. But they don't always kill. Pa's got a few buckshot in him. But he don't mind it, 'cause he don't weigh much, anyway. Bob's been carved up some with a bowie,[6] and Tom's been hurt once or twice."

"Has anybody been killed this year, Buck?"

"Yes. We got one and they got one. My cousin Bud was fourteen years old. About three months ago, he was riding through the woods on the other side of the river. He didn't have no weapon with him. That was blamed foolishness.

"In a lonesome place, he hears a horse a-comin' behind him. And he sees old Baldy Shepherdson a-comin' after him. He's got his gun in his hand and his white hair a-flyin' in the wind.

"Instead of jumping off and taking to the brush, Bud figured he could outrun him. So they had it, nip and tuck, for five miles or more. The old man was a-gainin' all the time.

"At last, Bud knew it warn't any use. So he stopped and faced around. He wanted to have the bullet holes in front, you know. And the old man he rode up and shot him down. But he didn't git much chance to enjoy his luck. Inside of a week, our folks laid him out."

---

6 A *bowie* is a hunting knife with a long, single-edged blade.

"I reckon that old man was a coward, Buck."

"I reckon he warn't a coward. Not by a blamed sight. There ain't a coward amongst the Shepherdsons—not a one. And there ain't no cowards amongst the Grangerfords, either. Why, that old man kept up his end in a fight one day. He went for half an hour against three Grangerfords. And he come out the winner.

"They was all a-horseback. He got off of his horse and got behind a little woodpile. He kept his horse before him to stop the bullets. But the Grangerfords stayed on their horses and pranced around the old man. They peppered away at him, and he peppered away at them.

"Him and his horse both went home pretty leaky and crippled. But the Grangerfords had to be carried home. And one of 'em was dead, and another died the next day.

"No, sir. If a body's out huntin' for cowards, he don't want to fool away any time amongst them Shepherdsons. They don't breed any of that kind."

Next Sunday, we all went to church, about three miles. Everybody was a-horseback. The men took their guns along, so did Buck. They kept them between their knees or stood them handy against the wall. The Shepherdsons done the same. It was pretty mean preaching—all about brotherly love, and such-like tiresomeness. But everybody said it was a good sermon. They all talked it over going home.

They had a powerful lot to say about faith and good works and free grace and preforeordestination.[7] I don't know what all they said. It did seem to me to be one of the roughest Sundays I had run across yet.

About an hour after dinner, everybody was dozing around. Some were in their chairs and some were in their rooms. It got to be pretty dull. Buck and a dog was stretched out on the grass in the sun. They were sound asleep.

I went up to our room and judged I would take a nap myself. I found that sweet Miss Sophia standing in her door, which was

---

7 *Preforeordestination* is a term that Huck has made up. It is a combination of "foreordination" and "predestination." Both are religious teachings by Calvinists. The teachings express the belief that God has already decided who will go to Heaven and who will be damned.

next to ours. She took me in her room and shut the door very soft.

She asked me if I liked her, and I said I did. And she asked me if I would do something for her and not tell anybody. I said I would.

Then she said she'd forgot her Bible. She'd left it in the seat at church between two other books. Would I slip out quiet and go there and fetch it for her? And would I not say nothing to nobody? I said I would do it.

So I slid out and slipped off up the road. There warn't anybody at the church. There was maybe a hog or two, for there warn't any lock on the door. Hogs like a puncheon floor[8] in summertime because it's cool. If you notice, most folks don't go to church except when they've got to. But a hog is different.

Says I to myself, somethins's up. It ain't natural for a girl to be in such a sweat about a Bible.

So I found the Bible and give it a shake. Out drops a little piece of paper. It had "Half past two" wrote on it with a pencil. I **ransacked** the book, but couldn't find anything else.

I couldn't make anything out of that. So I put the paper in the book again. When I got home and went upstairs, there was Miss Sophia in her door. She was waiting for me.

She pulled me in and shut the door. Then she looked in the Bible till she found the paper. As soon as she read it, she looked glad. And before a body could think, she grabbed me and gave me a squeeze. She said I was the best boy in the world, and not to tell anybody.

She was mighty red in the face for a minute, and her eyes lighted up. It made her powerful pretty. I was a good deal **astonished**. But when I got my breath, I asked her what the paper was about. She asked me if I had read it. I said no. She asked me if I could read writing. I told her, "No, only coarse hand."[9]

Then she said the paper warn't anything but a bookmark to keep her place. She said I might go and play now. I went off down to the river, studying over this thing. Pretty soon I noticed

---

8 A puncheon floor is made from split logs that have been smoothed on top.

9 *Coarse hand* is a type of writing using block letters.

that my nigger was following along behind. When we was out of sight of the house, he looked back and around a second. Then he comes a-runnin', and says, "Master George, come down into de swamp. I'll show you a whole stack of water moccasins."[10]

Thinks I, that's mighty curious. He said that yesterday. He ought to know a body don't love water moccasins enough to go around hunting for them. What is he up to, anyway? So I says, "All right, trot ahead."

I followed a half a mile. Then he struck out over the swamp. We waded ankle-deep as much as another half-mile. We come to a little flat piece of land. It was dry and very thick with trees and bushes and vines. Then he says, "You shove right in there, just a few steps, Master George. There's where dey is. I's seed 'em before. I don't care to see 'em no more."

Then he slopped right along and went away. Pretty soon the trees hid him. I poked into the place a ways. I come to a little open patch as big as a bedroom. It was all hung with vines.

I found a man laying there asleep. And, by jings, it was my old Jim! I waked him up. I reckoned it was going to be a grand surprise to him to see me again. But it warn't. He nearly cried, he was so glad, but he warn't surprised.

Jim said he swum along behind me that night. He heard me yell every time, but didn't dare answer. He didn't want nobody to pick him up and take him into slavery again. Says he, "I got hurt a little, en' couldn't swim fast. So I was a considerable ways behind you towards de last. When you landed, I reckoned I could ketch up with you on de land. I wouldn't have to shout at you.

"But when I see dat house, I begin to go slow. I was off too far to hear what dey say to you. I was 'fraid of de dogs. But when it was all quiet again, I knowed you's in de house. So I struck out for de woods to wait for day.

"Early in de mornin', some of de niggers come along, goin' to de fields. En' dey took me en' showed me dis place. De dogs can't track me here, on accounts of de water. Dey brings me truck to eat every night. En' dey tells me how you's a-gittin' along."

---

10 A *water moccasin* is a poisonous snake found in Southern swamps.

"Why didn't you tell my Jack to fetch me here sooner, Jim?"

"Well, it warn't no use to disturb you, Huck, till we could do somethin'. But we's all right now. I been a-buyin' pots en' pans en' vittles, whenever I got a chance. En' I been a-patchin' up de raft nights, when—"

"What raft, Jim?"

"Our ole raft."

"You mean to say our old raft warn't smashed all to **splinters**?"

"No, she warn't. She was tore up a good deal—one end of her was. But there warn't no great harm done. Only our traps was mos' all lost. We shouldn't have dived so deep en' swum so far under water. If de night hadn't been so dark, en' we warn't so scared, we'd have seed de raft. But we was such pumpkin-heads, as de saying goes.

"But it's just as well we didn't. Now she's all fixed up again, mos' as good as new. En' we's got a new lot of stuff, in de place of what was lost."

"Why, how did you get hold of the raft again, Jim? Did you catch her?"

"How I goin' to catch her when I's out in de woods? No, some of de niggers found her. She was catched on a snag along here in de bend. En' dey hid her in a creek amongst de willows.

"There was a lot of talkin' 'bout which of 'em she belonged to. I come to hear 'bout it pretty soon. So I up en' settles de trouble. I tells 'em she don't belong to none of 'em, but to you en' me.

"I ask 'em if dey goin' to grab a young white gentleman's property, en' git a whipping for it? Den I give 'em ten cents apiece. Dey was mighty well satisfied. Dey wished some more rafts would come along en' make 'em rich again.

"Dey's mighty good to me, these niggers is. Whatever I wants 'em to do for me, I don't have to ask 'em twice, honey. Dat Jack's a good nigger, en' pretty smart."

"Yes, he is. He ain't ever told me you was here. He told me to come, and he'd show me a lot of water moccasins. If anything happens, he ain't mixed up in it. He can say he never seen us together. And it'll be the truth."

I don't want to talk much about the next day. I reckon I'll cut it pretty short. I waked up about dawn. I was a-goin' to turn over and go to sleep again. But then I noticed how still it was. There didn't seem to be anybody stirring. That warn't usual.

Next I noticed that Buck was up and gone. Well, I gets up, a-wonderin', and goes downstairs. There was nobody around, everything as still as a mouse. It was just the same outside.

Thinks I, what does it mean? Down by the woodpile, I come across my Jack. I says, "What's it all about?"

Says he, "Don't you know, Master George?"

"No," says I, "I don't."

"Well, den, Miss Sophia's run off! 'Deed she has. She run off in de night some time. Nobody don't know just when. She run off to get married to dat young Harney Shepherdson, you know. Leastways, so dey expect.

"De family found it out 'bout half an hour ago—maybe a little more. En' I tell you, dey warn't no time lost. Such another hurryin' up of guns en' horses you never see!

"De women folks has gone for to stir up de relations. En' ole Master Saul en' de boys took their guns en' rode up de river road. Dey'll try to catch dat young man. En' dey'll kill him before he can git across de river with Miss Sophia. I reckon there's goin' to be mighty rough times."

"Buck went off without waking me up."

"Well, I reckon he did! Dey warn't goin' to mix you up in it. Master Buck, he loaded up his gun. He swore he's goin' to fetch home a Shepherdson or bust. Well, they'll be plenty of 'em there, I reckon. You bet you he'll fetch one if he gits a chance."

I took up the river road as hard as I could go. By and by, I begin to hear guns a good ways off. Then I came in sight of the log store and the woodpile where the steamboat lands.

I worked along under the trees and brush till I got to a good place. Then I clumb up into the forks of a cottonwood that was out of reach, and I watched. There was a woodpile four foot high a little ways in front of the tree. At first, I was going to hide behind that. But maybe it was luckier I didn't.

There was four or five men prancing around on their horses in the open place before the log store. They were cussing and yelling. They were trying to get at a couple of young chaps that was behind the woodpile alongside of the steamboat landing.

But they couldn't manage it. Every time one of them showed himself on the river side of the woodpile, he got shot at. The two boys was squatting back to back behind the pile. They could watch both ways.

By and by, the men stopped prancing around and yelling. They started riding towards the store. Then up gets one of the boys. He shoots a steady bead over the woodpile. One of the men drops out of his saddle.

All the men jumped off of their horses. They grabbed the hurt one and started to carry him to the store. At that minute, the two boys started on the run.

They got halfway to the tree I was in before the men noticed. Then the men saw them. They jumped on their horses and took out after them.

They gained on the boys, but it didn't do no good. The boys had too good a start. They got to the woodpile that was in front of my tree, and slipped in behind it. They had an advantage on the men again.

One of the boys was Buck. The other was a slim young chap about nineteen years old.

The men ripped around awhile, and then rode away. Soon they was out of sight. I sung out to Buck and told him. He didn't know what to make of my voice coming out of the tree at first. He was awful surprised.

He told me to watch out sharp. I was to let him know when the men come in sight again. He said they was up to some devilment or other. They wouldn't be gone long. I wished I was out of that tree, but I didn't dare come down.

Buck begun to cry and yell. He swore that him and his cousin Joe (that was the other young chap) would make up for this day yet.

He said his father and his two brothers was killed. Two or three of the enemy was too. He said the Shepherdsons laid for them in **ambush**. Buck said his father and brothers ought to have waited for their relations. The Shepherdsons was too strong for them.

I asked him what was become of young Harney and Miss Sophia. He said they'd got across the river and was safe. I was glad of that. But Buck did take on because he didn't manage to kill Harney that day he shot at him. I ain't ever heard anything like it.

All of a sudden, bang! bang! bang! goes three or four guns. The men had slipped around through the woods. They had come in from behind without their horses!

The boys jumped for the river—both of them hurt. They swum down the current. The men run along the bank shooting at them and singing, "Kill them, kill them!"

It made me so sick I most fell out of the tree. I ain't a-goin' to tell all that happened. It would make me sick again if I was to do that. I wished I hadn't ever come ashore that night to see such things. I ain't ever going to forget them. Lots of times I dream about them.

I stayed in the tree till it begun to get dark. I was afraid to come down. Sometimes I heard guns away off in the woods. Twice I saw little gangs of men gallop past the log store with guns. So I reckoned the trouble was still a-goin' on.

I was mighty downhearted. I made up my mind I wouldn't go near that house again. I reckoned I was to blame, somehow.

I judged that that piece of paper had something to do with this. It meant that Miss Sophia was to meet Harney somewheres at half past two and run off. And I judged I ought to have told her father about the paper and the curious way she acted. Then maybe he would have locked her up. This awful mess wouldn't ever have happened.

When I got down out of the tree, I crept down the river-bank a piece. I found the two bodies laying in the edge of the water. I tugged at them till I got them ashore.

Then I covered up their faces and got away as quick as I could. I cried a little when I was covering up Buck's face. He was mighty good to me.

It was just dark now. I never went near the house. I struck through the woods and made for the swamp. Jim warn't on his island. So I tramped off in a hurry for the creek.

I crowded through the willows, red-hot to jump aboard and get out of that awful country. The raft was gone!

My souls, but I was scared! I couldn't get my breath for almost a minute. Then I raised a yell. A voice not twenty-five foot from me says, "Good land! Is dat you, honey? Don't make no noise."

It was Jim's voice. Nothing ever sounded so good before.

I run along the bank a piece and got aboard. Jim, he grabbed me and hugged me, he was so glad to see me.

He says, "Laws bless you, chile. I was right down sure you's dead again. Jack's been here. He say he reckon you's been shot, 'cause you didn't come home no more. So I's just this minute a-startin' de raft down towards de mouth of de creek. I wanted to be all ready to shove out and leave. I was waiting for Jack to come again en' tell me for certain you is dead. Lawsy, I's mighty glad to git you back again, honey."

I says, "All right—that's mighty good. They won't find me. They'll think I've been killed, and floated down the river. There's something up there that will help them think so. So don't you lose no time, Jim. Just shove off for the big water as fast as ever you can."

I never felt easy till the raft was two miles below there and out in the middle of the Mississippi. Then we hung up our signal lantern. We judged that we was free and safe once more.

I hadn't had a bite to eat since yesterday. So Jim, he got out some corn dodgers[11] and buttermilk, and pork and cabbage and greens. There ain't nothing in the world so good when it's cooked right. Whilst I eat my supper, we talked and had a good time.

I was powerful glad to get away from the feuds. So was Jim to get away from the swamp. We said there warn't no home like a raft, after all. Other places do seem so cramped up and smothery, but a raft don't. You feel mighty free and easy and comfortable on a raft.

11 A *corn dodger* is a cake made from corn bread. The dough can be baked, fried, or made into dumplings.

Chapter 19

The Duke and the Dauphin

Come Aboard

VOCABULARY PREVIEW

The following words appear in this chapter. Review the list and get to know the words before you read the chapter.

acknowledge—accept
degraded—lowered in position or rank
exiled—banished; thrown out
forlorn—sad; miserable
frauds—con artists; fakes
huffy—cranky; touchy
paralysis—numbness; loss of feeling

Two or three days and nights went by. I reckon I might say they swum by. They slid by quiet and smooth and lovely.

Here is the way we put in the time. It was a monstrous big river down there, sometimes a mile and a half wide. We run nights, and laid up and hid daytimes.

Soon as night was most gone, we stopped navigating and tied up. This was nearly always in the dead water under a towhead. We cut young cottonwoods and willows, and hid the raft with them. Then we set out the lines. Next we slid into the river and had a swim. This would freshen us up and cool us off. Then we set down on the sandy bottom where the water was about knee-deep, and watched the daylight come.

Not a sound anywheres—perfectly still. Just like the whole world was asleep. Only sometimes the bullfrogs were a-clutterin', maybe. The first thing to see, looking way over the water, was a kind of dull line. That was the woods on the other side. You couldn't make nothing else out.

Then came a pale place in the sky. Then more paleness spreading around. Then the river softened up way off, and warn't black any more, but gray.

You could see little dark spots drifting along ever so far away. They was trading-scows and such things. And there was long black streaks—rafts. Sometimes you could hear a sweep screaking or jumbled-up voices. It was so still, and the sounds come so far.

By and by, you could see a streak on the water. You'd know by the look of the streak that there's a snag there in the swift current. The current breaks on the snag and makes that streak look that way.

You could see the mist curl up off the water. And the east reddens up, and the river. You make out a log cabin in the edge of the woods. It's way on the bank on the other side of the river, being a wood yard, likely. And it's piled by them cheats so you can throw a dog through it anywheres.

Then the nice breeze springs up. It comes fanning you from over there. It's so cool and fresh and sweet to smell, on account of the woods and the flowers. But sometimes it's not that way. Maybe they've left dead fish laying around, gars[1] and such. They do get pretty foul-smelling.

Next you've got the full day. Everything is smiling in the sun, and the songbirds just going at it!

A little smoke couldn't be noticed now. So we would take some fish off of the lines and cook up a hot breakfast. And afterwards, we would watch the lonesomeness of the river. We would kind of lazy along, and by and by, lazy off to sleep.

We'd wake up by and by, and look to see what done it. We'd maybe see a steamboat coughing along upstream. It was far off towards the other side. You couldn't tell nothing about her, only whether she was a stern-wheel or a side-wheel.[2] Then for about an hour, there wouldn't be nothing to hear nor nothing to see, just solid lonesomeness.

---

1 A *gar* is a river fish.

2 A stern-wheel steamboat has a paddle wheel in back. A side-wheel steamboat has wheels on each side.

Next you'd see a raft sliding by, way off yonder. Maybe there'd be a galoot[3] on it chopping. That's what they're most always doing on a raft. You see the ax flash and come down—you don't hear nothing. You see that ax go up again. And by the time it's above the man's head, then you hear the k'chunk! It had took all that time to come over the water.

So we would put in the day, lazying around, listening to the stillness. Once there was a thick fog. The rafts and things that went by was beating tin pans so the steamboats wouldn't run over them. A scow or a raft went by. It was so close we could hear them talking and cussing and laughing. We heard them plain. But we couldn't see no sign of them.

It made you feel crawly. It was like spirits carrying on that way in the air. Jim said he believed it was spirits. But I says, "No. Spirits wouldn't say, 'Dern the dern fog.' "

Soon as it was night, out we shoved. When we got her out to about the middle, we let her alone. We let her float wherever the current wanted her to. Then we lit the pipes, and dangled our legs in the water.

We talked about all kinds of things. We was always naked, day and night, whenever the mosquitoes would let us. The new clothes Buck's folks made for me was too good to be comfortable. Besides, I didn't go much on clothes, nohow.

Sometimes we'd have that whole river all to ourselves for the longest time. Yonder was the banks and the islands, across the water. Maybe there was a spark—which was a candle in a cabin window.

Sometimes on the water you could see a spark or two. It was on a raft or a scow, you know. And maybe you could hear a fiddle or a song coming over from one of them crafts.

It's lovely to live on a raft. We had the sky up there, all speckled with stars. We used to lay on our backs and look up at them. We'd discuss whether they was made or only just happened.

Jim figured they was made, but I figured they happened. I judged it would have took too long to make so many. Jim

3 *Galoot* is a slang word for a big, strong man who is thought to be foolish or stupid.

said the moon could have laid them. Well, that looked kind of reasonable. So I didn't say nothing against it. I've seen a frog lay most as many. So of course it could be done.

We used to watch the stars that fell, too, and see them streak down. Jim guessed they'd got spoiled and was thrown out of the nest.

Once or twice a night, we would see a steamboat slipping along in the dark. Now and then she would belch a whole world of sparks up out of her chimneys. They would rain down in the river and look awful pretty.

Then she would turn a corner. Her lights would wink out and her engine shut off. She would leave the river still again. By and by, her waves would get to us, a long time after she was gone. They would joggle the raft a bit. After that, you wouldn't hear nothing for you couldn't tell how long, except maybe frogs or something.

After midnight, the people on shore went to bed. Then for two or three hours the shores was black. No more sparks in the cabin windows. These sparks was our clock. The first one that showed again meant morning was coming. So we hunted a place to hide and tie up right away.

One morning about daybreak, I found a canoe. I got in it and crossed over a chute[4] to the main shore. It was only two hundred yards. Then I paddled about a mile up a creek amongst the cypress woods. I wanted to see if I could find some berries.

I was just passing a place where a kind of a cow path crossed the creek. Then here comes a couple of men tearing up the path. They were going as fast as they could foot it.

I thought I was a goner. For whenever anybody was after anybody, I judged it was me—or maybe Jim. I was about to dig out from there in a hurry. But they was pretty close to me then.

They sung out and begged me to save their lives. Said they hadn't been doing nothing, and was being chased for it. They said there was men and dogs a-comin'. They wanted to jump right in. But I says, "Don't you do it. I don't hear the dogs and horses yet. You've got time to crowd down through the brush

---

4 A *chute* is a rapid or a place in the river where the current is swift.

and get up the creek a little ways. Then you take to the water and wade down to me and get in. That will throw the dogs off the scent."

They done it, and soon they was aboard. Then I lit out for our towhead. In about five or ten minutes, we heard the dogs and the men way off, shouting. We heard them come along towards the creek. But we couldn't see them.

They seemed to stop and fool around awhile. As we got further and further away all the time, we couldn't hardly hear them at all.

Soon we had left a mile of woods behind us and struck the river. Everything was quiet. We paddled over to the towhead and hid in the cottonwoods and was safe.

One of these fellows was about seventy or upwards. He had a bald head and very gray whiskers. He had an old battered-up slouch hat on, and a greasy, blue woolen shirt. And he had ragged old blue jeans britches stuffed into his boot tops, and home-knit suspenders—no, he only had one.

He had an old long-tailed blue jeans coat with slick brass buttons. It was flung over his arm. Both men had big, fat, ratty-looking carpetbags.

The other fellow was about thirty. He was dressed about as ornery. After breakfast, we all laid off and talked. The first thing that come out was that these chaps didn't know one another.

"What got you into trouble?" says the baldhead to the other chap.

"Well, I'd been selling an article to take the tartar off the teeth. And it does take it off, too, and generally the outer layer of the teeth along with it. But I stayed about one night longer than I ought to.

"I was just in the act of sliding out. Then I ran across you on the trail this side of town. You told me they were coming, and begged me to help you to get off. So I told you I was expecting trouble myself, and would scatter out with you. That's my whole story—what's yours?"

"Well, I'd been a-runnin' a little temperance revival there 'bout a week. I was the pet of the women folks, big and little. I was makin' it mighty warm for the rummies, I tell you. And I was takin' as much as five or six dollars a night. I got ten cents a head, children and niggers free.

"Business was a-growin' all the time. Then somehow or another a little report got around last night. They said I had a way of puttin' in my time with a private jug on the sly.

"A nigger woke me up this mornin'. He told me the people was gatherin' on the quiet with their dogs and horses. They'd be along pretty soon and give me 'bout half an hour's start.

"Then they would run me down if they could. And if they got me they'd tar and feather me and ride me on a rail, sure.[5] I didn't wait for no breakfast—I warn't hungry."

"Old man," said the young one, "I reckon we might double-team it together. What do you think?"

"I ain't against it. What's your line—mainly?"

"Jour[6] printer by trade. Do a little in patent medicines. Theater actor—tragedy, you know. Take a turn to mesmerism and phrenology[7] when there's a chance. Teach singing-geography school for a change. Sling a lecture sometimes. Oh, I do lots of things—most anything that comes handy, so it ain't work. What's your game?"

"I've done considerable in the doctoring way in my time. Laying on of hands is my best game. I use it for cancer and **paralysis**, and such things.

"And I can tell a fortune pretty good. But only when I've got somebody along to find out the facts for me. Preachin's my line, too, and workin' camp meetings, and missionaryin' around."

Nobody never said anything for a while. Then the young man heaves a sigh and says, "Alas!"

"What are you alassin' about?" says the baldhead.

"To think I should have lived to be leading such a life, and be **degraded** down into such company." And he begun to wipe the corner of his eye with a rag.

---

5 Angry mobs used to tar and feather people. The victim would be tied to a rail and then covered with hot tar and feathers. This punishment was extremely painful and the victim often died.

6 *Jour* is short for "journeyman," a person trained in a craft or trade. Journeymen usually worked by the day or by the job, and then they would move on to another job.

7 *Mesmerism* is hypnotism. The name comes from Anton Mesmer (1734–1815), an Austrian doctor. People who practiced phrenology claimed to read personality and mental abilities from the shape of skulls.

"Dern your skin. Ain't the company good enough for you?" says the baldhead, pretty pert and uppish.

"Yes, it is good enough for me. It's as good as I deserve. For who fetched me so low when I was so high? I did myself. I don't blame you, gentlemen. Far from it. I don't blame anybody. I deserve it all.

"Let the cold world do its worst. One thing I know—there's a grave somewhere for me. The world may go on just as it's always done. It can take everything from me—loved ones, property, everything. But it can't take that.

"Someday I'll lie down in that grave and forget it all. And my poor broken heart will be at rest." He went on a-wipin'.

"Drat your poor broken heart," says the baldhead. "What are you heaving your poor broken heart at us for? We ain't done nothing."

"No, I know you haven't. I ain't blaming you, gentlemen. I brought myself down—yes, I did it myself. It's right I should suffer—perfectly right. I don't make any moan."

"Brought you down from where? Where was you brought down from?"

"Ah, you would not believe me. The world never believes—let it pass. 'Tis no matter. The secret of my birth—"

"The secret of your birth! Do you mean to say—"

"Gentlemen," says the young man, very solemn, "I will reveal it to you. For I feel I may have confidence in you. By rights I am a duke!"

Jim's eyes bugged out when he heard that. I reckon mine did, too. Then the baldhead says, "No! You can't mean it?"

"Yes. My great-grandfather was the eldest son of the Duke of Bridgewater. He fled to this country about the end of the last century. He came to breathe the pure air of freedom.

"He married here, and died, leaving a son. His own father died about the same time. The second son of the late duke seized the titles and estates. The infant real duke was ignored.

"I am the lineal descendant[8] of that infant. I am the rightful Duke of Bridgewater. And here am I, **forlorn**, torn from my high position. Hunted of men, despised by the cold world, ragged,

---

8 A *lineal descendant* is a child, grandchild, great-grandchild, etc., of someone.

worn, and heartbroken. And I am degraded to the friendship of criminals on a raft!"

Jim pitied him ever so much, and so did I. We tried to comfort him. But he said it warn't much use, 'cause he couldn't be much comforted. He said if we was of a mind to **acknowledge** him, that would do him more good than most anything else. So we said we would, if he would tell us how.

He said we ought to bow when we spoke to him. We should say "Your Grace," or "My Lord," or "Your Lordship." And he wouldn't mind it if we called him plain "Bridgewater." That, he said, was a title anyway, and not a name. One of us ought to wait on him at dinner, and do any little thing for him he wanted done.

Well, that was all easy, so we done it. All through dinner, Jim stood around and waited on him. He says, "Will your Grace have some of dis or some of dat?" and so on. A body could see it was mighty pleasing to him.

But the old man got pretty silent by and by. He didn't have much to say. And he didn't look pretty comfortable. Too much petting was going on around that duke. He seemed to have something on his mind.

So, along in the afternoon, the old man says, "Looky here, Bilgewater,"[9] he says. "I'm awfully sorry for you. But you ain't the only person that's had troubles like that."

"No?"

"No, you ain't. You ain't the only person that's been snaked down wrongfully out of a high place."

"Alas!"

"No, you ain't the only person that's had a secret of his birth." And, by jingo, he begins to cry.

"Hold! What do you mean?"

"Bilgewater, can I trust you?" says the old man, still sort of sobbing.

"To the bitter death!" He took the old man by the hand and squeezed it. He says, "That secret of your being: speak!"

"Bilgewater, I am the late Dauphin!"

---

9 *Bilge water* is old, foul water that gathers in the lower part of a ship. Using this made-up name shows Twain's humor, as well as suggests the duke's foul or dirty character.

You bet you, Jim and me stared this time. Then the duke says, "You are what?"

"Yes, my friend, it is too true. Your eyes is lookin' at this very moment on the poor disappeared Dauphin. I am Louie the Seventeen, son of Louie the Sixteen and Marry Antoinette."[10]

"You! At your age! No! You mean you're the late Charlemagne. You must be six or seven hundred years old, at the very least."[11]

"Trouble has done it, Bilgewater, trouble has done it. Trouble has brung these gray hairs and this premature balditude.[12] Yes, gentlemen. Look what you see before you, in blue jeans and misery. The wanderin', **exiled**, trampled-on, and sufferin' rightful King of France."

Well, he cried and took on so. Me and Jim didn't know hardly what to do. We was so sorry. And we was so glad and proud we'd got him with us, too. So we set in, like we done before with the duke, and tried to comfort him.

But he said it warn't no use. Nothing but to be dead and done with it all could do him any good. But he said it often made him feel easier and better for a while if people treated him according to his rights.

They could get down on one knee and speak to him, and always call him "Your Majesty." And they could wait on him first at meals, and not set down in his presence till he asked them.

So Jim and me set to majestying him. We did this and that and the other for him. We stood up till he told us we might set down. This done him heaps of good, and so he got cheerful and comfortable.

But the duke kind of soured on him. He didn't look a bit satisfied with how things was going. Still, the king acted real friendly towards him. He said the duke's great grandfather and all the other Dukes of Bilgewater was a good deal thought of by his father. They was allowed to come to the palace considerable.

But the duke stayed **huffy** a good while. By and by, the king

10 The Dauphin means Marie Antoinette, Queen of France from 1775–1793.

11 Charlemagne was emperor of the Western Roman Empire in the early ninth century. The duke is making fun of the Dauphin, claiming he looks too old to be the Dauphin.

12 *Balditude* is not a real word. The Dauphin is creating a word to make reference to his balding head.

says, "Like as not we got to be together a blamed long time on this here raft, Bilgewater. So what's the use of your bein' sour? It'll only make things uncomfortable.

"It ain't my fault I warn't born a duke. And it ain't your fault you warn't born a king. So what's the use to worry? Make the best of things the way you find 'em, says I—that's my motto.

"This ain't no bad thing that we've struck here—plenty grub and an easy life. Come, give us your hand, duke, and let's all be friends."

The duke done it, and Jim and me was pretty glad to see it. It took away all the uncomfortableness and we felt mighty good over it.

It would have been a miserable business to have any unfriendliness on the raft. We wanted everybody to be satisfied, and feel right and kind towards the others. That's what you want above all things on a raft.

It didn't take me long to make up my mind that these liars warn't no kings nor dukes at all. They was just low-down humbugs and **frauds**. But I never said nothing, never let on. I kept it to myself.

It's the best way. Then you don't have no quarrels, and don't get into no trouble. If they wanted us to call them kings and dukes, I hadn't no objections. As long as it would keep peace in the family. It warn't no use to tell Jim, so I didn't tell him.

I didn't learn much out of Pap. But I did learn the best way to get along with his kind of people is to let them have their own way.

Chapter 20

What Royalty Did to Parkville

VOCABULARY PREVIEW

The following words appear in this chapter. Review the list and get to know the words before you read the chapter.

benefactors—helpers; supporters
campaign—plot; plan
oppression—cruelty; unfair treatment
rousing—lively; spirited

They asked us considerable many questions. They wanted to know why we covered up the raft that way. And they wanted to know why we laid by in the daytime instead of running. Was Jim a runaway nigger? Says I, "Goodness sakes! Would a runaway nigger run south?"

No, they figured he wouldn't. I had to account for things some way, so I says, "My folks was living in Pike County, in Missouri. I was born there. They all died off but me and Pa and my brother, Ike. Pa, he figured he'd break up and go down and live with Uncle Ben. He's got a little one-horse place on the river, forty-four miles below Orleans.

"Pa was pretty poor, and had some debts. So when he squared up, there warn't nothing left but sixteen dollars and our nigger, Jim. That warn't enough to take us fourteen hundred miles, deck passage nor no other way.

"Well, when the river rose, Pa had a streak of luck one day. He catched this piece of a raft. So we reckoned we'd go down to Orleans on it. Only Pa's luck didn't hold out.

"A steamboat run over the forward corner of the raft one night. We all went overboard and dove under the wheel. Jim and me come up all right. But Pa was drunk, and Ike was only four years old. So they never come up no more.

"Well, for the next day or two we had considerable trouble. People was always coming out in skiffs and trying to take Jim away from me. They said they believed he was a runaway nigger. We don't run daytimes no more now. Nights they don't bother us."

The duke says, "Leave me alone to figure out a way so we can run in the daytime if we want to. I'll think the thing over and invent a plan that will fix it. We'll let it alone for today. Because of course, we don't want to go by that town yonder in daylight. It mightn't be healthy."

Towards night it begun to darken up and look like rain. The heat lightning was squirting around low down in the sky. The leaves was beginning to shiver. It was going to be pretty ugly. It was easy to see that.

So the duke and the king went to looking over our wigwam. They wanted to see what the beds was like. My bed was a straw tick.[1] It was better than Jim's, which was a cornshuck tick.

There's always cobs around about in a shuck tick. They poke into you and hurt. When you roll over, the dry shucks sound like you was rolling over in a pile of dead leaves. It makes such a rustle that you wake up.

Well, the duke said he would take my bed. But the king allowed he wouldn't. He says, "I should have reckoned the difference in rank would have suggested different to you. A cornshuck bed ain't just fittin' for me to sleep on. Your Grace will take the shuck bed yourself."

Jim and me was in a sweat again for a minute. We were afraid there was going to be some more trouble amongst them.

We was pretty glad when the duke says, 'Tis my fate. I shall always be ground into the dirt under the iron heel of **oppression**. Bad luck has broken my once proud spirit.

"I yield, I submit. 'Tis my fate. I am alone in the world—let me suffer. I can bear it."

We got away as soon as it was good and dark. The king told us to head well out towards the middle of the river. He said not to show a light till we got a long ways below the town.

We come in sight of the little bunch of lights by and by. That was the town, you know. We slid by, about a half a mile out, all

---

1 A *tick* is a lightweight mattress.

right. When we got three-quarters of a mile below, we hoisted up our signal lantern.

About ten o'clock, it come on to rain and blow and thunder and lightning like everything. So the king told us to both stay on watch till the weather got better. Then him and the duke crawled into the wigwam and turned in for the night.

It was my watch below till twelve. But I wouldn't have turned in anyway if I'd had a bed. A body don't see such a storm as that every day in the week. Not by a long sight.

My souls, how the wind did scream along! And every second or two, there'd come a glare that lit up the whitecaps for a half a mile around. You'd see the islands looking dusty through the rain. The trees would show, thrashing around in the wind.

Then comes a h-whack!—bum! bum! bumble-umble-umbum-bum-bum-bum. And the thunder would go rumbling and grumbling away, and quit. Then rip comes another flash and another powerful boom.

The waves most washed me off the raft sometimes. But I hadn't any clothes on and didn't mind. We didn't have no trouble about snags. The lightning was glaring and flittering around constant. We could see them plenty soon enough. Then we'd throw her head this way or that and miss them.

I had the middle watch, you know, but I was pretty sleepy by that time. So Jim, he said he would stand the first half of it for me. He was always mighty good that way, Jim was.

I crawled into the wigwam. But the king and the duke had their legs sprawled around. There warn't no room for me. So I laid outside. I didn't mind the rain because it was warm. And the waves warn't running so high now.

About two, they come up again, though. Jim was going to call me, but he changed his mind. He reckoned they warn't high enough yet to do any harm.

But he was mistaken about that. Pretty soon, all of a sudden along comes a regular ripper and washed me overboard. It most killed Jim a-laughin'. He was the easiest nigger to laugh that ever was, anyway.

After that I took the watch. Jim, he laid down and snored away. By and by, the storm let up for good and all. The first cabin light that showed, I woke him up. We slid the raft into hiding quarters for the day.

The king got out an old ratty deck of cards after breakfast. Him and the duke played seven-up awhile, five cents a game. Then they got tired of it. So they decided they would "lay out a **campaign**," as they called it.

The duke went down into his carpetbag. He fetched up a lot of little printed bills and read them out loud.

One bill said, "The celebrated Dr. Armand de Montalban, of Paris," would "lecture on the Science of Phrenology." It gave such and such a place, on the blank day of blank, at ten cents admission. He would "furnish charts of character at twenty-five cents apiece." The duke said that was him.

In another bill he was the "famous Shakespearian[2] tragedian, Garrick the Younger, of Drury Lane, London."

In other bills, he had a lot of other names. He had done other wonderful things. He did things like find water and gold with a "divining rod,"[3] "getting rid of witch spells," and so on.

By and by, he says, "But the histrionic muse is the darling. Have you ever trod the boards,[4] Royalty?"

"No," says the king.

"You shall, then, before you're three days older," says , the duke. "The first good town we come to, we'll hire a hall. We'll do the swordfight in Richard III and the balcony scene in Romeo and Juliet. How does that strike you?"

"I'm in for anything that will pay, Bilgewater. And I'm in up to the hub. But you see, I don't know nothin' about play-actin'. I ain't ever seen much of it. I was too small when Pap used to have 'em at the palace. Do you reckon you can learn me?"

"Easy!"

"All right. I'm just a-freezin' for something fresh, anyway. Let's start right away."

---

2 *Shakespearian* is an alternate spelling of "Shakespearean."

3 A *divining rod* is a forked stick used for finding underground water. It supposedly bends downward when held over water.

4 *Histrionic* means "dramatic" or "theatrical." A *muse* is a goddess of artistic inspiration. *To trod the boards* means "perform on stage."

So the duke told him all about who Romeo was and who Juliet was. He said he was used to being Romeo. So the king could be Juliet.

"But Juliet's such a young gal, duke. My peeled head and my white whiskers is goin' to look uncommon odd on her, maybe."

"No, don't you worry. These country jakes won't ever think of that. Besides, you know, you'll be in costume. That makes all the difference in the world."

The duke says, "Juliet's in a balcony, enjoying the moonlight before she goes to bed. She's got on her nightgown and her ruffled nightcap. Here are the costumes for the parts."

He got out two or three curtain-calico suits. He said these was old-fashioned armor for Richard III and the other chap. And there was a long white cotton nightshirt and a ruffled nightcap to match.

The king was satisfied. So the duke got out his book and read the parts over in the most splendid, spread-eagle way.[5] He pranced around and acted at the same time. He showed how it had got to be done. Then he give the book to the king and told him to get his part by heart.

There was a little one-horse town about three miles down the bend. After dinner, the duke said he had figured out an idea. He knew how to run in daylight without it being dangersome[6] for Jim. So he said he would go down to the town and fix that thing.

The king said he would go, too, and see if he couldn't strike something. We was out of coffee, so Jim said I better go along with them in the canoe and get some.

When we got there, there warn't nobody stirring. The streets were empty, and perfectly dead and still, like Sunday.

We found a sick nigger sunning himself in a back yard. He said everybody that warn't too young or too sick or too old was gone to camp meeting. It was about two miles back in the woods.

The king got the directions. He said he'd go and work that camp meeting for all it was worth. And he said I might go, too.

---

5 *In a spread-eagle way* means the duke is reciting the lines "in an overdone manner."

6 By *dangersome* Huck means "dangerous."

The duke said what he was after was a printing office. We found it. It was a little bit of a business, up over a carpenter shop. The carpenters and printers had all gone to the meeting. They'd left the doors unlocked.

It was a dirty, littered-up place. It had ink marks and handbills with pictures of horses and runaway niggers on them, all over the walls. The duke shed his coat and said he was all right now. So me and the king lit out for the camp meeting.

We got there in about a half an hour, fairly dripping. It was a most awful hot day. There was as much as a thousand people there from twenty miles around.

The woods was full of teams and wagons, hitched everywheres. They was feeding out of the wagon troughs and stomping to keep off the flies.

There was sheds made out of poles and roofed over with branches. They had lemonade and gingerbread to sell. And there was piles of watermelons and green corn and suchlike truck.

The preaching was going on under the same kinds of sheds. Only these sheds was bigger and held crowds of people. The benches was made out of outside slabs of logs. They had holes bored in the round side to drive sticks into for legs. They didn't have no backs.

The preachers had high platforms to stand on at one end of the sheds. The women had on sunbonnets. Some had linsey-woolsey frocks, some gingham[7] ones. A few of the young ones had on calico.

Some of the young men was barefooted. Some of the children didn't have on any clothes but just a linen shirt. Some of the old women was knitting. And some of the young folks was courting on the sly.

The first shed we come to, the preacher was singing out a hymn. He sang out two lines and everybody sung it. It was kind of grand to hear it. There was so many of them, and they done it in such a **rousing** way. Then he sang out two more for them to sing—and so on.

---

7 *Linsey-woolsey* is a cloth woven from wool and linen. Gingham is dyed cotton fabric, usually with checked or striped patterns.

The people woke up more and more, and sung louder and louder. Towards the end, some begun to groan, and some begun to shout. Then the preacher begun to preach. He begun in earnest, too. He went weaving first to one side of the platform and then the other.

Then he leaned down over the front of it. His arms and his body was going all the time. He shouted his words out with all his might. Every now and then, he would hold up his Bible and spread it open.

He would kind of pass it around this way and that, shouting, "It's the brazen serpent in the wilderness! Look upon it and live!"

And the people would shout out, "Glory!—A-a-men!"

And so he went on. And the people kept groaning and crying and saying amen.

"Oh, come to the mourners' bench![8] Come, black with sin! (amen!) Come, sick and sore! (amen!) Come, lame and crippled and blind! (amen!) Come, poor and needy, sunk in shame (a-a-men!) Come, all that's worn and soiled and suffering!

"Come with a broken spirit! Come with a sorrowful heart! Come in your rags and sin and dirt! The waters that cleanse is free! The door of heaven stands open! Oh, enter in and be at rest!" (a-a-men! glory, glory hallelujah!)

And so on. You couldn't make out what the preacher said anymore. There was too much shouting and crying. Folks got up everywheres in the crowd. They worked their way just by main strength to the mourners' bench. Tears was running down their faces.

Finally, all the mourners got up there to the front benches in a crowd. They sung and shouted and flung themselves down on the straw. They was just crazy and wild.

Well, the first I knowed, the king got a-goin'. You could hear him over everybody. Next, he went a-chargin' up onto the platform. The preacher, he begged him to speak to the people. And he done it.

---

8 At a revival meeting, mourners are those who repent in public. The mourners' bench is where they wait to make their public confession.

He told them he was a pirate. He'd been a pirate for thirty years out in the Indian Ocean. His crew was thinned out considerable last spring in a fight. He was home now to take out some fresh men.

And thanks to goodness, he'd been robbed last night. He was put ashore off a steamboat without a cent. He was glad of it. It was the blessedest thing that ever happened to him. He was a changed man now, and happy for the first time in his life.

Poor as he was, he was going to start right off and work his way back to the Indian Ocean. He would put in the rest of his life there, trying to turn the pirates into the true path.

He knew he could do it better than anybody else. He knew all the pirate crews in that ocean. It would take him a long time to get there without money. But he would get there anyway.

Every time he convinced a pirate, he would say to him, "Don't you thank me, don't you give me no credit. It all belongs to them dear people in Pokeville camp meeting. They are natural brothers and **benefactors** of the race. And to that dear preacher there, the truest friend a pirate ever had!"

And then he busted into tears, and so did everybody. Then somebody sings out, "Take up a collection for him, take up a collection!"

Well, half a dozen made a jump to do it, but somebody sings out, "Let him pass the hat around!" Then everybody said it, the preacher too.

So the king went all through the crowd with his hat, swabbing his eyes. He blessed the people and praised them. He thanked them for being so good to the poor pirates way off there.

Every little while, the prettiest kind of girls came up. They had tears running down their cheeks. They would up and ask him, would he let them kiss him for to remember him by? And he always done it. Some of them he hugged and kissed as many as five or six times.

He was invited to stay a week. Everybody wanted him to live in their houses. They said they'd think it was an honor.

But he said that as this was the last day of the camp meeting, he couldn't do no good. Besides, he was in a sweat to get to the Indian Ocean right off. He wanted to go to work on the pirates.

When we got back to the raft, he counted up and found he had collected eighty-seven dollars and seventy-five cents. And he had fetched away a three-gallon jug of whisky, too. He had found that under a wagon when he was starting home through the woods.

The king said, take it all around, it was better than any day he'd ever put in in the missionarying line. He said it warn't no use talking, unbelievers don't amount to shucks. Pirates are the thing to work a camp meeting with.

The duke was thinking he'd been doing pretty well. But now the king had come to show up. After that he didn't think so much.

The duke had set up and printed off two little jobs for farmers in that printing office—horse bills. And he took the money, four dollars. And he got in ten dollars' worth of advertisements for the paper. He said he would put them in for four dollars if they would pay in advance. So they done it.

The price of the paper was two dollars a year. But he took in three subscriptions for half a dollar apiece on condition of them paying him in advance.

They were going to pay him in cordwood and onions as usual. But he said he had just bought the business. And he had knocked down the price as low as he could afford it. Now he was going to run it for cash.

He set up a little piece of poetry. He made it himself, out of his head. It was three verses, kind of sweet and sad-dish. The name of it was, "Yes, crush, cold world, this breaking heart." He left that all set up and ready to print in the paper. He didn't charge nothing for it.

Well, he took in nine dollars and a half. He said he'd done a pretty square day's work for it.

Then he showed us another little job he'd printed. He hadn't charged for it, because it was for us. It had a picture of a runaway nigger. He had a bundle on a stick over his shoulder. "$200 reward" was written under it.

The reading was all about Jim. It just described him to a dot. It said he run away from St. Jacques' plantation, forty miles below New Orleans. He had run away last winter, and likely went north. Whoever would catch him and send him back could have the reward and the expenses.

"Now," says the duke, "after tonight, we can run in the daytime if we want to. Whenever we see anybody coming, we can tie Jim hand and foot with a rope. Then we'll lay him in the wigwam. We'll show this handbill and say we captured him up the river.

"We'll say we're too poor to travel on a steamboat. So we got this little raft on credit from our friends. We are going down to get the reward.

"Handcuffs and chains would look still better on Jim. But it wouldn't go well with the story of us being so poor. Too much like jewelry. Ropes are the correct thing. We must preserve the unities,[9] as we say on the boards."

We all said the duke was pretty smart. There couldn't be no trouble about running daytimes. We judged we could make miles that night. We reckoned the duke's work in the printing office would make a powwow in that little town. We wanted to be out of reach before it happened. Then we could move right along if we wanted to.

We laid low and kept still, and never shoved out till nearly ten o'clock. Then we slid by, pretty wide away from the town. We didn't raise our lantern till we was clear out of sight of it.

When Jim called me to take the watch at four in the morning, he says, "Huck, does you reckon we goin' to run across any more kings on dis trip?"

"No," I says. "I reckon not."

"Well," says he, "dat's all right, den. I don't mind one or two kings, but dat's enough. Dis one's powerful drunk, en' de duke ain't much better."

I found Jim had been trying to get the king to talk French. He wanted to hear what it was like. But the king said he had been in this country too long. He had so much trouble here, he'd forgot it.

---

9 Aristotle, an ancient Greek thinker, developed the idea of the unities. He said that a play should be unified in time, place, and action. Of course, this has nothing to do with the question of how Jim should be tied. Perhaps *verisimilitude* is the word the duke is actually looking for. This means "the appearance of being real or believable."

Chapter 21

An Arkansaw Difficulty

VOCABULARY PREVIEW

The following words appear in this chapter. Review the list and get to know the words before you read the chapter.

bellow—yell; cry out
encores—repeat performances
hoist—raise; lift
rave—storm; explode
sarcastic—mocking; insulting
swindled—cheated

It was after sunup now, but we went right on and didn't tie up. The king and the duke turned out by and by. They looked pretty rusty. But they jumped overboard and took a swim. That livened them up a good deal.

After breakfast, the king, he took a seat on the corner of the raft. He pulled off his boots and rolled up his britches. Then he let his legs dangle in the water, so as to be comfortable.

He lit his pipe, and went into getting his *Romeo and Juliet* by heart. Soon he had got it pretty good. Then him and the duke begun to practice it together.

The duke had to learn him over and over again how to say every speech. He made him sigh, and put his hand on his heart. After a while, he said he done it pretty well.

"Only," he says, "you mustn't **bellow** out *Romeo!* that way, like a bull. You must say it soft and sick and wiltingly,—R-o-o-meo! That is the idea. Juliet's a dear sweet little child of a girl, you know. She doesn't bray like a jackass."

Well, next they got out a couple of long swords. The duke had made these out of oak wood strips. Then they begun to practice the swordfight. The duke called himself Richard III. The way they laid on and pranced around the raft was grand to see.

But by and by, the king tripped and fell overboard. After that, they took a rest. They had a talk about all kinds of adventures they'd had in other times along the river. After dinner, the duke says, "Well, Capet,[1] we'll want to make this a first-class show, you know. So I guess we'll add a little more to it. We want a little something to answer **encores** with, anyway."

"What's encores, Bilgewater?"

The duke told him, and then says, "I'll answer by doing the Highland fling or the sailor's hornpipe.[2] And you—well, let me see. Oh, I've got it. You can do Hamlet's soliloquy."[3]

"Hamlet's which?"

"Hamlet's soliloquy. You know, the most celebrated thing in Shakespeare. Ah, it's superb, superb! Always brings down the house.

"I haven't got it in the book—I've only got one volume. But I reckon I can piece it out from memory. I'll just walk up and down a minute. Let's see if I can call it back from memory's storage places."

So he went to marching up and down, thinking. He'd frown horrible every now and then. Then he would **hoist** up his eyebrows.

Next he would squeeze his hand on his forehead. He'd stagger back and kind of moan. Next he would sigh, and next he'd let on to drop a tear. It was beautiful to see him.

By and by he got it. He told us to give attention.

Then he strikes a most noble attitude. He shoves one leg forwards, and stretches his arms way up. His head is tilted back, looking up at the sky. Then he begins to rip and **rave** and grit his teeth. After that, all through his speech, he howled, and spread around, and swelled up his chest.

It just knocked the spots out of any acting *I* ever saw before.

---

1 Capet was the family name of a long line of French kings who ruled from 987–1328. The duke has made a mistake. He probably means Capulet, Juliet's family name in *Romeo and Juliet.*

2 The *Highland fling* and the *sailor's hornpipe* are Scottish and British folk dances. They both demand grace and energy.

3 A *soliloquy* is a character's speech that reveals thoughts and ideas that are in the character's mind. It is delivered while the character is alone on stage. Hamlet's soliloquy is the famous "To Be or Not To Be" speech.

This was the speech. I learned it, easy enough, while he was learning it to the king:[4]

To be, or not to be; that is the bare dagger
That makes misery of so long life,
For who would burdens bear, till Birnam Wood do come to Dunsinane.
But that the fear of something after death
Murders the innocent sleep, Great nature's second course,
And makes us rather sling the arrows of outrageous fortune
Then fly to others that we know not of.
There's the respect must give us pause:
Wake Duncan with thy knocking! I would thou could;
For who would bear the whips and scorns of time,
The oppressor's wrong, the proud man's contempt,
The law's delay, and the final blow which his pangs might take,
In the dead waste and middle of the night, when churchyards yawn
In their usual suits of solemn black,
But that the undiscovered country from whose journey no traveler returns,
Breathes forth sickness on the world,
And thus the native hue of resolution, like the poor cat in the old saying,
Is sicklied o'er with care.
And all the clouds that lowered o'er our housetops,
With this regard their currents turn twisted,
And lose the name of action.
'Tis a consummation sincerely to be wished. But soft you, the fair Ophelia:
Open not thy ponderous and marble jaws,
But get thee to a nunnery—go!

---

4 Much of the following speech is drawn from Hamlet's famous soliloquy in *Hamlet* Act III, Scene i. But phrases have been changed or switched around so it makes little sense. Also included are bits from *Richard III*, *Macbeth*, and other parts of *Hamlet*. The duke (who doesn't seem to know Shakespeare very well himself) figures his audience will never know the difference.

Well, the old man, he liked the speech. He mighty soon got it so he could do it first rate. It seemed like he was just born for it. In his excitement, he used his hands to help him speak. It was perfectly lovely the way he would rip and tear and rear up behind when he was speaking.

The first chance we got, the duke had some show bills printed. After that, we floated along for two or three days. And the raft was a most uncommon lively place. There warn't nothing but sword fighting and rehearsing—as the duke called it—going on all the time.

One morning, we was pretty well down the state of Arkansaw. We come in sight of a little one-horse town in a big bend. So we tied up about three-quarters of a mile above it in the mouth of a creek, which was shut in like a tunnel by the cypress trees.

All of us but Jim took the canoe. We went down there to see if there was any chance in that place for our show.

We struck it mighty lucky. There was going to be a circus there that afternoon. The country people was already beginning to come in. They was in all kinds of old shackly[5] wagons and on horses.

The circus would leave before night. So our show would have a pretty good chance. The duke, he hired the courthouse, and we went around and stuck up our bills. They read like this:

Shaksperean[6] Revival!!!
Wonderful Attraction For One Night Only!
The world famous tragedians,
David Garrick the younger, of Drury Lane Theatre,
London, and Edmund Kean the elder,[7]
of the Royal Haymarket Theatre,
Whitechapel, Pudding Lane, Piccadilly, London,
and the
Royal Continental Theatres, in their sublime

5 By *shackly* Huck either means "shaky," or he is making a word from "shack." At any rate, he is suggesting that the wagons are run-down and in need of repair.

6 *Shaksperean* is another alternate spelling of "Shakespearean."

7 David Garrick (1717–1779) and Edmund Kean (1787–1833) were famous Shakespearean actors.

Shaksperean Spectacle entitled
THE BALCONY SCENE
in ROMEO AND JULIET!!!
Romeo..Mr. Garrick
Juliet..Mr. Kean
Assisted by the whole strength of the company!
New costumes, new scenery, new appointments!
Also:
The thrilling, masterly, and blood-curdling
Broad-sword conflict
In RICHARD III!!!
Richard III......................................Mr. Garrick
Richmond...Mr. Kean
Also: (by special request)
Hamlet's Undying Soliloquy!!
By the Famous Kean!
Done by him 300 nights in a row in Paris!
For One Night Only,
On account of important European engagements!
Admission 25 cents; children and servants, 10 cents.

Then we went loafing around town. The stores and houses was most all old, shackly, dried-up frame outfits that hadn't ever been painted. They was set up three or four foot above ground on stilts. This put them out of reach of the water when the river overflowed.

The houses had little gardens around them. But they didn't seem to raise hardly anything in them but jimsonweeds and sunflowers and ash piles. And they had old curled-up boots and shoes, and pieces of bottles, and rags, and played-out tinware.

The fences was made of different kinds of boards, nailed on at different times. They leaned every which way. The gates didn't generally have but one hinge—a leather one. Some of the fences had been whitewashed[8] some time or another. But the duke said it was in Columbus' time, like enough. There was generally hogs in the garden, and people driving them out.

---

8 *Whitewash* is a liquid—usually made from lime and water—used to whiten a surface.

All the stores was along one street. They had white domestic awnings[9] in front. The country people hitched their horses to the awning posts.

There was empty drygoods[10] boxes under the awnings. Loafers sat around on them all day long. They whittled them with their Barlow knives and chawed[11] tobacco. They gaped and yawned and stretched—a mighty ornery lot.

They generally had on yellow straw hats as wide as an umbrella. But they didn't wear no coats nor waistcoats. They called one another Bill, and Buck, and Hank, and Joe, and Andy. They talked lazy and drawly, and used considerable many cusswords.

There was as many as one loafer leaning up against every awning post. He most always had his hands in his britches pockets. He only took them out to lend a chaw of tobacco or scratch. What a body was hearing amongst them all the time was, "Give me a chaw of tobacco, Hank."

"Can't. I ain't got but one chaw left. Ask Bill."

Maybe Bill, he gives him a chaw. Maybe he lies and says he ain't got none. Some of them kinds of loafers never has a cent in the world, nor a chaw of tobacco of their own. They get all their chawing by borrowing.

They say to a fellow, "I wish you'd lend me a chaw, Jack. I just this minute give Ben Thompson the last chaw I had."

This is a lie pretty much every time. It don't fool nobody but a stranger.

But Jack ain't no stranger, so he says, "*You* give him a chaw, did you? So did your sister's cat's grandmother. You pay me back the chaws you's already borrowed off of me, Lafe Buckner. Then I'll loan you one or two ton of it. I won't charge you no back interest, neither."

"Well, I *did* pay you back some of it once."

"Yes, you did. About six chaws. You borrowed store tobacco from me and paid back with cheap tobacco."

---

9 Domestic awnings are made from rough canvas. They are hung over doors and windows to provide protection from the sun.

10 *Drygoods* are textiles or ready-to-wear clothing, not hardware or groceries.

11 *Chaw* is slang for "chew."

Store tobacco is flat black plug. But these fellows mostly chaws the natural leaf twisted. When they borrow a chaw, they don't generally cut it off with a knife. They set the plug in between their teeth. Then they gnaw it with their teeth and tug at the plug with their hands till they get it in two.

Then sometimes, the one that owns the tobacco looks mournful at it when it's handed back, and says, **sarcastic,** "Here, give me the *chaw,* and you take the *plug.*"

All the streets and lanes was just mud. They warn't nothing else *but* mud. This mud was as black as tar and near about a foot deep in some places. It was two or three inches deep in *all* the places.

The hogs loafed and grunted around everywheres. You'd see a muddy sow and a litter of pigs lazying along the street. And she'd whollop herself right down in the way. Folks had to walk around her. She'd stretch out and shut her eyes and wave her ears whilst the pigs was milking her. She'd look as happy as if she was on salary.

And pretty soon, you'd hear a loafer sing out, "Hi! *so* boy! Sick him, Tige!"

And away the sow would go, squealing most horrible. She'd have a dog or two swinging to each ear, and three or four dozen more a-comin'. Then you would see all the loafers get up and watch the thing out of sight. They'd laugh at the fun and look grateful for the noise.

Then they'd settle back again till there was a dogfight. There couldn't anything wake them up all over, and make them happy all over, like a dogfight. Only thing better than a dogfight might be someone putting turpentine on a stray dog and setting fire to him. Or someone tying a tin pan to his tail and seeing him run himself to death.

On the riverfront, some of the houses was sticking out over the bank. They was bowed and bent, and about ready to tumble in. The people had moved out of them. The bank was caved away under one corner of some others. That corner was hanging over. People lived in them yet, but it was dangersome.

Sometimes a strip of land as wide as a house caves in at a time. Sometimes a belt of land a quarter of a mile deep will start in. It will cave along and cave along till it all caves into the river in one summer. Such a town as that has to be always moving back, and back, and back. The river's always gnawing at it.

It got nearer to noon. The wagons and horses got thicker and thicker in the streets. More kept coming all the time. Families brought their dinners with them from the country, and eat them in the wagons. There was considerable whisky drinking going on. And I seen three fights. By and by, somebody sings out, "Here comes old Boggs! In from the country for his little old monthly drunk. Here he comes, boys!"

All the loafers looked glad. I reckoned they was used to having fun out of Boggs. One of them says, "Wonder who he's a-goin' to chaw up this time. If he'd a-chawed up all the men he's been a-goin' to chaw up in the last twenty years, he'd have a considerable reputation now."

Another one says, "I wish old Boggs would threaten me. Then I'd know I warn't goin' to die for a thousand years."

Boggs comes a-tearin' along on his horse. He was whooping and yelling like an Injun, and singing out, "Clear the track, there. I'm on the warpath. And the price of coffins is a-goin' to raise."

He was drunk, and weaving about in his saddle. He was over fifty years old, and had a very red face. Everybody yelled at him and laughed at him. They sassed at him and he sassed back.

He said he'd attend to them and lay them out in regular turns. But he couldn't wait now. He'd come to town to kill old Colonel Sherburn. And his motto was, "Meat first, and dessert afterwards."

He saw me, and rode up and says, "Where'd you come from, boy? You prepared to die?"

Then he rode on. I was scared, but a man says, "He don't mean nothing. He's always a-carryin' on like that when he's drunk. He's the best-naturedest old fool in Arkansaw. He never hurt nobody, drunk nor sober."

Boggs rode up before the biggest store in town. He bent his head down so he could see under the curtain of the awning and yells, "Come out here, Sherburn! Come out and meet the man you've **swindled.** You're the hound I'm after. And I'm a-goin' to have you, too!"

And so he went on, calling Sherburn everything he could lay his tongue to. And the whole street packed with people listening and laughing and going on.

By and by, a proud-looking man about fifty-five steps out of the store. He was by far the best-dressed man in that town. The crowd drops back on each side to let him come.

He says to Boggs, mighty calm and slow—he says, "I'm tired of this, but I'll put up with it till one o'clock. Till one o'clock, mind—no longer. Don't you open your mouth against me even once after that time. If you do, you can't travel so far but I will find you."

Then he turns and goes in. The crowd looked mighty sober. Nobody stirred, and there warn't no more laughing. Boggs rode off, insulting Sherburn as loud as he could yell, all down the street.

Pretty soon, back he comes and stops before the store, i still keeping it up. Some men crowded around him and tried to get him to shut up. But he wouldn't. They told him it would be one o'clock in about fifteen minutes. So he *must* go home—he must go right away. But it didn't do no good.

He cussed away with all his might. He throwed his hat down in the mud and rode over it. Pretty soon, away he went a-ragin' down the street again. His gray hair was a-flyin'.

Everybody that could get a chance at him tried their best to coax him off of his horse. Then they could lock him up and get him sober. But it warn't no use. Up the street he would tear again, and give Sherburn another cussing.

By and by, somebody says, "Go for his daughter! Quick, go for his daughter. Sometimes he'll listen to her. If anybody can bring him around, she can."

So somebody started on a run.

I walked down the street a ways and stopped. In about five or ten minutes, here comes Boggs again, but not on his horse. He was a-reelin' across the street towards me, bareheaded. He had a friend on both sides of him. They had ahold of his arms and were hurrying him along.

He was quiet, and looked uneasy. He warn't hanging back any, but was doing some of the hurrying himself.

Somebody sings out, "Boggs!"

I looked over there to see who said it. It was that Colonel Sherburn. He was standing perfectly still in the street and had a pistol raised in his right hand. He wasn't aiming it, but held it out with the barrel tilted up towards the sky.

The same second, I saw a young girl coming on the run. She had two men with her. Boggs and the men turned round to see who called him. When they saw the pistol, the men jumped to one side. The pistol barrel come down slow and steady to a level—both barrels cocked.

Boggs throws up both of his hands and says, "O Lord, don't shoot!"

Bang! goes the first shot. Boggs staggers back, clawing at the air. Bang! goes the second one. And he tumbles backwards onto the ground, heavy and solid, with his arms spread out.

That young girl screamed out and comes rushing. Down she throws herself on her father, crying and saying, "Oh, he's killed him, he's killed him!"

The crowd closed up around them. They shouldered and jammed one another with their necks stretched, trying to see. People on the inside tried to shove them back, shouting, "Back, back! Give him air, give him air!"

Colonel Sherburn, he tossed his pistol onto the ground. Then he turned around on his heels and walked off.

They took Boggs to a little drug store. The crowd was pressing around just the same, and the whole town was following. I rushed and got a good place at the window. There I was close to him and could see in.

They laid him on the floor and put one large Bible under his head. They opened another one and spread it on his breast. But they tore open his shirt first. I seen where one of the bullets went in.

He made about a dozen long gasps. His breast lifted the Bible up when he drawed in his breath. And it let it down again when he breathed it out. After that, he laid still. He was dead.

Then they pulled his daughter away from him and took her off. She was screaming and crying. She was about sixteen, and very sweet and gentle looking. But she was awful pale and scared.

Well, pretty soon the whole town was there. They squirmed and pressed and pushed and shoved. They wanted to get at the window and have a look.

But people that had the places wouldn't give them up. And folks behind them was saying all the time, "Say, now, you've looked enough, you fellows. It ain't right and it ain't fair for you to stay there all the time. Give somebody else a chance. Other folks has their rights as well as you."

There was considerable talking back, so I slid out. I thought maybe there was going to be trouble.

The streets was full, and everybody was excited. Everybody that seen the shooting was telling how it happened. There was a big crowd packed around each one of these fellows. They stretched their necks and listened.

One of the fellows was a long, lanky man. He had long hair and a big white fur stovepipe hat on the back of his head, and a crooked-handled cane. He marked out the places on the ground where Boggs stood and where Sherburn stood. The people followed him around from one place to the other. They watched everything he done, bobbing their heads to show they understood.

They stooped a little and rested their hands on their thighs.

They watched him mark the places on the ground with his cane. Then he stood up straight and stiff where Sherburn had stood. He frowned and pulled his hatbrim down over his eyes.

He sung out, "Boggs!" Then he fetched his cane down slow to a level. He says "Bang!" and staggered backwards. He says "Bang!" again, and fell down flat on his back.

The people that had seen the thing said he done it perfect. Said it was just exactly the way it happened. Then as much as a dozen people got out their bottles and treated him.

Well, by and by, somebody said Sherburn ought to be lynched. In about a minute, everybody was saying it. So away they went, mad and yelling. They snatched down every clothesline they come to to do the hanging with.

Chapter 22

Why the Lynching Bee Failed

VOCABULARY PREVIEW

The following words appear in this chapter. Review the list and get to know the words before you read the chapter.

acquit—find not guilty in a court of law
bully—well done; great
deliberate—steady; balanced

They swarmed up towards Sherburn's house, a-whoopin' and ragin' like Injuns. Everything had to clear the way or get run over and tromped to mush. It was awful to see.

Children was heeling it ahead of the mob. They was screaming and trying to get out of the way. Every window along the road was full of women's heads. There was nigger boys in every tree, and boys and girls looking over every fence.

They would let the mob get nearly to them. Then they would break and skaddle back out of reach. Lots of the women and girls was crying and taking on. They was scared most to death.

They swarmed up in front of Sherburn's fence as thick as they could jam together. You couldn't hear yourself think for the noise. It was a little twenty-foot yard. Some sung out, "Tear down the fence! Tear down the fence!"

There was a racket of ripping and tearing and smashing. Then down she goes. The front wall of the crowd began to roll in like a wave.

Just then, Sherburn steps out onto the roof of his little front porch. He has a double-barrel gun in his hand. He takes his stand, perfectly calm and deliberate, not saying a word. The racket stopped, and the wave sucked back.

Sherburn never said a word. He just stood there, looking down. The stillness was awful creepy and uncomfortable. Sherburn run his eyes slow along the crowd. Wherever it struck, the people tried a little to outgaze him. But they couldn't. They dropped their eyes and looked sneaky.

Then pretty soon, Sherburn sort of laughed—but not the pleasant kind. It's the kind that makes you feel like when you are eating bread that's got sand in it.

Then he says, slow and scornful, "The idea of *you* lynching anybody! It's amusing. The idea of you thinking you had pluck enough to lynch a *man!*

"So, you're brave enough to tar and feather poor, friendless, castout women that come along here. Did that make you think you had grit enough to lay your hands on a *man?*

"Why, a *man's* safe in the hands of ten thousand of your kind. As long as it's daytime and you're not behind him.

"Do I know you? I know you clear through. I was born and raised in the South, and I've lived in the North. So I know the average all around.

"The average man's a coward. In the North, he lets anybody walk over him that wants to. Then he goes home and prays for a humble spirit to bear it. In the South, one man, all by himself, has stopped a stage full of men in the daytime. He robbed the lot.

"Your newspapers call you a brave people so much. So you think you *are* braver than any other people. But you're just *as* brave, and no braver.

"Why don't your juries hang murderers? Because they're afraid the man's friends will shoot them in the back, in the dark. And it's just what they *would* do.

"So they always **acquit**. Then a man goes in the night, with a hundred masked cowards at his back. And they lynch the rascal.

"Your mistake is that you didn't bring a man with you. That's one mistake. The other is that you didn't come in the dark and fetch your masks. You brought *part* of a man—Buck Harkness, there. And if you hadn't had him to start you, you'd have taken it out in talk.

"You didn't want to come. The average man don't like trouble and danger. *You* don't like trouble and danger. But then only half a man—like Buck Harkness, there—shouts 'Lynch him! Lynch him!' And you're afraid to back down. You're afraid you'll be found out to be what you are—*cowards.*

"And so you raise a yell. And you hang yourselves onto that half-a-man's coattail. You come raging up here, swearing what big things you're going to do.

"The sorriest thing out is a mob. That's what an army is—a mob. They don't fight with courage that's born in them. They fight with courage that's borrowed from their mass, and from their officers. But a mob without any *man* at the head of it is *beneath* pitiful.

"Now the thing for *you* to do is to droop your tails and go home and crawl in a hole. If any real lynching's going to be done, it will be done in the dark, Southern fashion. And when they come, they'll bring their masks, and fetch a *man* along. Now *leave*—and take your half-a-man with you."

He tossed his gun up across his left arm and cocked it when he said this. The crowd washed back sudden. Then it broke all apart, tearing off every which way. Buck Harkness heeled it after them, looking tolerable cheap. I could have stayed if I wanted to, but I didn't want to.

I went to the circus and loafed around the back side till the watchman went by. Then I dived in under the tent.

I had my twenty-dollar gold piece and some other money. But I reckoned I better save it. There ain't no telling how' soon you are going to need it, especially being away from home and amongst strangers. You can't be too careful. I ain't opposed to spending money on circuses when there ain't no other way. But there ain't no use in *wasting* it on them.

It was a real **bully** circus. It was the splendidest sight that ever was when they all come riding in. They came two and two, and gentleman and lady, side by side.

The men were just in their drawers and undershirts, and no shoes nor stirrups. They rested their hands on their thighs easy and comfortable. There must have been twenty of them.

Every lady had a lovely appearance, and was perfectly beautiful. They looked just like a gang of real sure-enough queens. They were dressed in clothes that cost millions of dollars, and just littered with diamonds. It was a powerful fine sight. I never saw anything so lovely.

And then, one by one, they got up and stood. They went a-weavin' around the ring so gentle and wavy and graceful.

The men looked ever so tall and airy and straight. Their heads bobbed and skimmed along, way up there under the tent roof. Every lady's rose-leafy dress flapped soft and silky around her hips. She looked like the most loveliest sun umbrella.

And then faster and faster they went. All of them danced, first one foot out in the air and then the other. The horses leaned more and more. And the ringmaster went round and round the center pole. He cracked his whip and shouted, "Hi!—hi!" And the clown cracked jokes behind him.

By and by, all hands dropped the reins. Every lady put her knuckles on her hips and every gentleman folded his arms. Then how the horses did lean over and move along!

And so, one after the other, they all skipped off into the ring. They made the sweetest bows I ever saw. Then they scampered out. Everybody clapped their hands and went just about wild.

Well, all through the circus they done the most astonishing things. And all the time that clown carried on so it most killed the people. The ringmaster couldn't ever say a word to him but he was back at him quick as a wink.

That clown said the funniest things a body ever said. And how *could* he ever think of so many of them, and so sudden and so pat? That was what I couldn't no way understand. Why, I couldn't have thought of them in a year.

And by and by, a drunken man tried to get into the ring. He said he wanted to ride. He said he could ride as well as anybody that ever was. They argued and tried to keep him out, but he wouldn't listen. The whole show come to a standstill.

Then the people begun to holler at him and make fun of him. That made him mad, and he begun to rip and tear. That stirred up the people. A lot of men begun to pile down off of the benches, and swarm toward the ring. They said, "Knock him down! Throw him out!" One or two women begun to scream.

So then the ringmaster made a little speech. He said he hoped there wouldn't be no disturbance. If the man would promise he wouldn't make no more trouble, he would let him ride. But only if he thought he could stay on the horse.

So everybody laughed and said all right, and the man got on. The minute he was on, the horse begun to rip and tear and jump and prance around. Two circus men were hanging on to the horse's sides, trying to hold him. And the drunken man hung on to the horse's neck.

The drunken man's heels flew in the air every jump. The whole crowd of people were standing up shouting and laughing till tears rolled down. And at last, sure enough, all the circus men could do, the horse broke loose. Away he went like the very nation, 'round and 'round the ring.

That drunkard was laying down on him and hanging on to his neck. First one leg hung most to the ground on one side. Then the other one on the other side. The people was just crazy.

It warn't funny to me, though. I was all of a tremble to see his danger. But pretty soon, he struggled up onto the saddle and grabbed the bridle. He was a-reelin' this way and that.

The next minute, he sprung up and dropped the bridle and stood! And the horse was a-goin' like a house afire, too. He just stood up there. He sailed around as easy and comfortable as if he warn't ever drunk in his life.

Then he begun to pull off his clothes and sling them. He shed them so thick, they kind of clogged up the air.

Altogether, he shed seventeen suits.

Then there he was, slim and handsome. And he was dressed the gaudiest and prettiest you ever saw. He lit into that horse with his whip and made him fairly hum.

Finally, he skipped off. He made his bow and danced off to the dressing room. Everybody just a-howled with pleasure and surprise.

Then the ringmaster saw how he had been fooled. He *was* the sickest ringmaster you ever saw, I reckon. Why, it was one of his own men! That performer had got up that joke all out of his own head. And he never let on to nobody.

Well, I felt sheepish enough to be took in so. But I wouldn't have been in that ringmaster's place, not for a thousand dollars.

I don't know, there may be bullier circuses than what that one was, but I never struck them yet. Anyways, it was plenty good enough for *me.* And wherever I run across it, it can have all of *my* business every time.

Well, that night we had *our* show. But there warn't only about twelve people there—just enough to pay expenses. They laughed all the time, and that made the duke mad. Everybody left, anyway, before the show was over. There was but one boy left, and he was asleep.

So the duke said these Arkansaw lunkheads couldn't come up to Shakespeare. What they wanted was low comedy.[1] Or maybe something rather worse than low comedy, he reckoned.

He said he could suit their style. So next morning, he got some big sheets of wrapping paper and some black paint. He drawed off some handbills, and stuck them up all over the village. The bills said:

AT THE COURT HOUSE!
FOR 3 NIGHTS ONLY!
The World-Famous Tragedians
DAVID GARRICK THE YOUNGER!
AND
EDMUND KEAN THE ELDER!
Of the London and Continental
Theatres,
In their Thrilling Tragedy of
THE KING'S CAMELEOPARD,[2]
OR
THE ROYAL NONESUCH!!![3]

Admission 50 cents.

Then at the bottom was the biggest line of all, which said:

LADIES AND CHILDREN NOT ADMITTED

"There," says he, "if that line don't fetch them, I don't know Arkansaw!"

---

1 Low comedy is based on slapstick or silly actions. It is the opposite of high comedy, which uses more spoken humor.

2 A *cameleopard* could be a giraffe or a purely imaginary animal.

3 *Nonesuch* means "a person or thing that has no equal."

Chapter 23 (Summary)

The Orneriness of Kings

The king and duke practiced for hours on their new show. Then for two nights they entertained a full house with a short, vulgar show. But the townspeople soon figured out that they were getting cheated. So on the third night, they arrived with rotten eggs and cabbages to give the king and duke their due.

But the two rascals had seen this coming. While the audience was busy getting seated, the duke and Huck sneaked back to the raft. Huck worried about leaving the king to reckon with the audience. Back at the raft, Huck found his fears were unnecessary. The crafty king had never even left the raft.

Later that night, Huck and Jim had a long talk about kings and dukes in general. Huck recited a wild, nonsense history of European royalty. He told Jim that the king and duke weren't that awful when compared to others of royal birth.

Jim took Huck's turn at watch so Huck could sleep. Later Jim talked about his family. He related a touching story about his daughter who went deaf and dumb after coming down with scarlet fever. Huck was amazed that Jim seemed to care for his family as much as white people did for theirs. Huck decided that Jim was "a mighty good nigger."

Chapter 24 (Summary)

The King Turns Parson

The next day the runaways hid the raft. They noticed that their stopping point was between two villages, one on either side of the river. At once the king and duke tried to come up with a plan for "working the towns."

While the duke went to scout out one village, the king and Huck started over to the other. On the way, the king and Huck ran into one of the townspeople. He told them the story of Peter Wilks, a wealthy villager who had just died. The town was now waiting for word from the dead man's heirs, his two brothers from England. Word had spread that several thousand dollars were hidden away for the brothers.

Luck struck again for the king and duke. The two frauds happened to be about the same age as the Englishmen. However, the younger brother was deaf and dumb.

After collecting all the information he could about the dead man and the town, the king scurried back to the duke. When the duke heard the king's story, he agreed to play the deaf and dumb brother.

The duke practiced "sign language," and the king tried out his English accent. Then they and Huck hailed a river-boat and rode to the town. When the king asked some townspeople for Peter Wilks' address, the townspeople at once supposed that he and the duke were the heirs from England. Upon hearing of Wilks' death, the king and duke put on a big show of blubbering and going to pieces. Their phony behavior made Huck ashamed of the human race.

Chapter 25 (Summary)

All Full of Tears and Flapdoodle

News spread quickly that the heirs from England, Harvey and William Wilks, had arrived. People came rushing from all directions to see them and lead them to Peter Wilks' house.

When they got there, the king and duke were introduced to the dead man's three nieces: Mary Jane, Joanna, and Susan. Everyone burst into tears of joy at seeing the relatives meet at last.

After staring at the dead body and blubbering some more, the king read the letter Wilks left behind. The letter detailed what Wilks' relatives would inherit. It turned out he left the house and three thousand dollars to the girls. To Harvey and William, he left the rest of his property, including land, houses, and six thousand dollars cash. According to the letter, the brothers' money was hidden in the cellar.

The two frauds went to get the money. Then, to make things seem even more on the up and up, they decided to give it to the girls. At hearing this, the girls and everyone else in the house sobbed for joy again. They all declared how good Harvey and his brother were. But Huck, who was playing the English brothers' servant in this game, had his doubts. He knew the girls wouldn't have that money for long if the two rascals had their way.

In the midst of the excitement, Dr. Robinson, Peter Wilks' doctor, showed up. He laughed in the king's face and called him a fraud whose English accent was the worst he had ever heard. The people were shocked and tried to set the doctor straight. But he insisted that the king and duke were not Peter Wilks' true brothers.

Mary Jane, the oldest of the girls, refused to listen to anything Dr. Robinson said. To prove her trust in her "uncles," she gave all the money back to the king and told him to invest it for her.

Chapter 26 (Summary)

I Steal the King's Plunder

After dinner that evening, Huck and Joanna sat in the kitchen and talked. Joanna asked many probing questions about life in England. Huck's answers were so wild and mixed up that Joanna didn't believe him. She accused Huck of lying just as Mary Jane and Susan walked in. They scolded Joanna for being rude and made her apologize to Huck. The girls were so nice to him that Huck felt almost like part of the family.

After this, Huck felt terrible about the king and duke's plan to cheat the girls. He decided to steal the bag of money from the king and hide it. Then later when he had escaped, he would write Mary Jane a letter that told her where the money was.

Huck quickly set his plan in motion. He found the money in the king's room and swiped it. Then that night, when everyone was asleep, he slipped downstairs to find a hiding place for the bag.

Chapter 27 (Summary)

Dead Peter Has His Gold

When Huck got downstairs with the money, he was startled to hear Mary Jane coming down the stairs. In his panic, he put the bag in the first place he saw—the coffin. Then he sneaked back upstairs.

The next day at the funeral, the coffin was sealed shut before Huck could retrieve the money. So Huck decided he wouldn't write to Mary Jane about the money after all. He felt that he had made the whole situation worse than it was.

Meanwhile, the king and duke kept up their fraud. The king told everyone that he and "William" planned to stay in town for a few more days to sell the estate. Then they would return to England and take the girls with them. The girls were wild with joy. But their happiness turned to grief when the king broke up a slave family by selling a mother and her sons to different traders.

The day after the funeral, the king and duke discovered that the bag of money was gone. They questioned Huck, and he told them that he had seen some slaves in the room where the money was. As Huck hoped, the king and duke assumed the slaves had the cash. But the slaves had already been sold, and there was nothing the two men could do about it. The angry king and duke left Huck, cussing each other out.

Chapter 28 (Summary)

Overreaching Don't Pay

The next morning, Huck passed Mary Jane's room and found her crying over the slaves' fate. Because Huck felt sorry for her, he decided to tell her the truth about the king and duke.

As Mary Jane heard Huck's account of the frauds' doings, her eyes blazed in anger. She was all for tarring and feathering the two rascals right away.

But Huck was worried about Jim's safety. So he thought of a way to expose the king and duke and still allow Jim and himself to escape.

However, Huck didn't tell Mary Jane about his plan. Instead, he asked her to go visit friends for the day. He said that when she returned that evening, she was to wait for him until eleven o'clock. If he hadn't shown up by then, Mary Jane was to blow the whistle on the frauds.

Mary Jane agreed to do this and left immediately. To explain her absence to the family, Huck told them another one of his wild fibs.

Late that afternoon a steamboat landed. And with the boat came a surprise: two more men who claimed to be Peter Wilks' brothers!

Chapter 29 (Summary)

I Light Out in the Storm

The king and duke's luck held out for a little longer. At the sight of the new heirs, many of the townspeople gathered around the king to show their support. And the newcomers' luggage had been delayed, so they couldn't prove who they were.

Soon the townspeople began to question the four men, trying to trap the false heirs. But the questions went nowhere. At last the men were called on to produce samples of their handwriting. But the new "William" was unable to write because of a broken arm. And the handwriting of the other three did not match that found in letters from the Wilks brothers.

Then a question arose of a certain tattoo on the dead man's breast. To find out who was telling the truth, the townspeople—with the four "heirs" and Huck in their grip—marched to the graveyard to look at the body. As they dug up the coffin, a storm rolled in. Finally the coffin was opened. In a flash of lightning, the lost bag of gold was shown on Peter Wilks' breast.

In the excitement that followed, Huck broke free and made a wild dash for the raft. He and Jim had a brief reunion and then cut the raft loose. They danced for joy at the thought of being free of the two rascals. But their joy turned to misery when they glanced up the river and saw the king and duke rowing toward them.

Chapter 30 (Summary)

The Gold Saves the Thieves

At first the king and duke were furious with Huck for leaving them with the angry mob. But then the two began accusing each other of trying to keep the money for himself. The duke almost strangled the king until the king admitted hiding the bag in the coffin. This false confession greatly relieved Huck.

After cussing each other out some more, the two men turned to the bottle for comfort. And before long they were once again the best of friends.

Chapter 31

You Can't Pray a Lie

VOCABULARY PREVIEW

The following words appear in this chapter. Review the list and get to know the words before you read the chapter.

bogus—fake; counterfeit
confidential—secret; private
deviltry—mischief; foul play
disgraced—shamed; dishonored
scoundrels—villains; good-for-nothings
shabby—run-down; untidy
shirk—avoid; sneak off from

We didn't dare stop again at any town for days and days. We kept right along down the river. We was down South in the warm weather now, and a mighty long ways from home.

We begun to come to trees with Spanish moss on them. It hung down from the limbs like long, gray beards. It was the first I ever saw it growing. It made the woods look solemn and dismal. So now the frauds reckoned they was out of danger. They begun to work the villages again.

First, they done a lecture on temperance. But they didn't make enough for them both to get drunk on. Then in another village they started a dancing school. But they didn't know no more how to dance than a kangaroo does. So the first prance they made, the general public jumped in and pranced them out of town.

Another time, they tried to go at yellocution.[1] But they didn't yellocute long. The audience got up and give them a solid good cussing. And they made them skip out.

1 By *yellocution*, Huck means "elocution," the art of effective public speaking.

They tackled missionarying, and mesmerizing, and doctoring, and telling fortunes. A little of everything. But they couldn't seem to have no luck.

So at last they got just about dead broke. They laid around the raft as she floated along, thinking and thinking. They never said nothing, by the half a day at a time. They was dreadful blue and desperate.

At last, they took a change. They begun to lay their heads together in the wigwam. They talked low and **confidential** two or three hours at a time.

Jim and me got uneasy. We didn't like the look of it. We judged they was studying up some kind of worse **deviltry** than ever. We turned it over and over. At last we made up our minds they was going to break into somebody's house or store. Or they was going into the counterfeit-money business or something.

So then we was pretty scared. We made up an agreement. We wouldn't have nothing in the world to do with such actions. If we ever got the least chance, we would give them the cold shake. We would clear out and leave them behind.

Well, early one morning, we hid the raft in a good, safe place. It was about two miles below a little bit of a **shabby** village named Pikesville.

The king, he went ashore. He told us all to stay hid whilst he went up to town. He was going to smell around to see if anybody had got any wind of the "Royal Nonesuch" there yet.

House to rob, you *mean,* says I to myself. And when you get through robbing it, you'll come back here. You'll wonder what has become of me and Jim and the raft. You'll have to take it out in wondering.

And the king said if he warn't back by midday, the duke and me would know it was all right. Then we was to come along.

So we stayed where we was. The duke, he fretted and sweated around. He was in a mighty sour way. He scolded us for everything. We couldn't seem to do nothing right.

He found fault with every little thing.

Something was a-brewin', sure. I was good and glad when midday come and no king. We could have a change, anyway. And maybe we'd have a chance for *the* change on top of it. So me and the duke went up to the village. We hunted around there for the king.

By and by, we found him in the back room of a little low doggery,[2] very drunk. A lot of loafers were bully-ragging him for sport. He was a-cussin' and a-threatenin' with all his might. He was so drunk he couldn't walk, and couldn't do nothing to them.

The duke begun to abuse him for an old fool. The king begun to sass back. In a minute they was fairly at it. I lit out and shook the reefs out of my hind legs.[3] I spun down the river road like a deer. For I saw our chance. I made up my mind that it would be a long day before they ever saw me and Jim again.

I got down there all out of breath but loaded up with joy. I sung out, "Set her loose, Jim. We're all right now!"

But there warn't no answer. Nobody come out of the wigwam. Jim was gone! I set up a shout—and then another—and then another one. I run this way and that in the woods, whooping and screeching. But it warn't no use-old Jim was gone.

Then I set down and cried. I couldn't help it. But I couldn't set still long. Pretty soon I went out on the road, trying to think what I better do.

I run across a boy walking. I asked him if he'd seen a strange nigger dressed so and so.

He says, "Yes."

"Whereabouts?" says I.

"Down to Silas Phelps' place, two miles below here. He's a runaway nigger, and they've got him. Was you looking for him?"

---

2 A *doggery* is a cheap saloon.

3 A *reef* is a dangerous obstacle. What Huck means here is that he didn't waste any time getting rid of the king and duke.

"You bet I ain't! I run across him in the woods about an hour or two ago. He said if I hollered, he'd cut my livers out. He told me to lay down and stay where I was. I done it. Been there ever since, afeard to come out."

"Well," he says, "you needn't be afeard no more. They've got him. He run off from down South, somewheres."

"It's a good job they got him."

"Well, I *reckon!* There's two hundred dollars' reward on him. It's like picking up money out of the road."

"Yes, it is. And I could have had it if I'd been big enough. I saw him *first.* Who nailed him?"

"It was an old fellow—a stranger. And he sold out his chance in him for forty dollars. He's got to go up the river and can't wait. Think of that, now! You bet *I'd* wait, if it was seven years."

"That's me, every time," says I. "But maybe his chance ain't worth no more than that, if he'd sell it so cheap. Maybe there's something ain't straight about it."

"But it is, though—straight as a string. I saw the handbill myself. It tells all about him, to a dot. It paints him like a picture, and tells the plantation he's from, below New Orleans.

"No-sirree-bob, they ain't no trouble about *that* deal, you bet you. Say, give me a chaw of tobacco, won't you?"

I didn't have none, so he left. I went to the raft, and set down in the wigwam to think. But I couldn't come to nothing. I thought till I wore my head sore. But I couldn't see no way out of the trouble.

After all this long journey, and after all we'd done for them **scoundrels**, here it was all come to nothing. Everything was all busted up and ruined. How could they have the heart to serve Jim such a trick as that? They'd make him a slave again all his life, and amongst strangers, too, for forty dollars.

Once I said to myself, it would be a thousand times better for Jim to be a slave at home, where his family was. At least as long as he'd got to be a slave. So I'd better write a letter to Tom Sawyer. I'd tell him to tell Miss Watson where he was.

But I soon give up that notion for two things. She'd be mad and disgusted at his rascality and ungratefulness for leaving her. So she'd sell him straight down the river again. If she didn't, everybody naturally despises an ungrateful nigger. They'd make Jim feel it all the time. He'd feel ornery and **disgraced**.

And then think of *me!* It would get around that Huck Finn helped a nigger to get his freedom. I would hope to never see anybody from that town again. Or else I'd be ready to get down and lick his boots for shame.

That's just the way. A person does a low-down thing, then he don't want to take the results of it. Thinks as long as he can hide, it ain't no disgrace. That was my fix exactly.

The more I studied about this, the more my conscience went to grinding me. And the more wicked and low-down and ornery I got to feeling.

At last, it hit me all of a sudden. Here was the plain hand of Providence[4] slapping me in the face. Providence was letting me know my wickedness. I was being watched all the time from up there in heaven.

And all the while I was stealing a poor old woman's nigger. A woman that hadn't ever done me no harm. Now Providence was showing me that there's One that's always on the lookout. He ain't a-goin' to allow no such miserable doings to go only just so far and no further.

I most dropped in my tracks, I was so scared. Well, I tried the best I could to kind of soften it up somehow for myself. I said I was brung up wicked, and so I warn't so much to blame.

But something inside of me kept saying, "There was the Sunday school. You could have gone to it. If you'd have gone, they'd have learnt you there that people that acts as I'd been acting about that nigger goes to everlasting fire."

It made me shiver. And I about made up my mind to pray. I'd see if I couldn't try to quit being the kind of a boy I was and be better.

---

4 *Providence* is God's will or plan.

So I kneeled down. But the words wouldn't come. Why wouldn't they? It warn't no use to try and hide it from Him. Nor from *me,* neither. I knowed very well why they wouldn't come.

It was because my heart warn't right. It was because I warn't square. It was because I was playing double.

I was letting *on* to give up sin. But away inside of me, I was holding on to the biggest one of all. I was trying to make my mouth *say* I would do the right thing and the clean thing. I was trying to say I would go and write to that nigger's owner and tell where he was.

But deep down in me, I knowed it was a lie. And He knowed it. You can't pray a lie—I found that out.

So I was full of trouble, full as I could be. I didn't know what to do. At last, I had an idea. I says, I'll go and write the letter—and *then* see if I can pray.

Why, it was astonishing. I felt as light as a feather straight off, and my troubles all gone. So I got a piece of paper and a pencil. All glad and excited, I set down and wrote:

Miss Watson, your runaway nigger Jim is down here two miles below Pikesville. Mr. Phelps has got him. He will give him up for the reward if you send.

HUCK FINN

I felt good and all washed clean of sin. It was the first time I had ever felt so in my life. I knowed I could pray now. But I didn't do it straight off. I laid the paper down and set there thinking. I thought how good it was all this happened so. I thought how near I come to being lost and going to hell.

I went on thinking. And I got to thinking over our trip down the river. And I see Jim before me all the time. I see him in the day and in the nighttime, sometimes moonlight, sometimes storms. And we a-floatin' along, talkin' and singin' and laughin'.

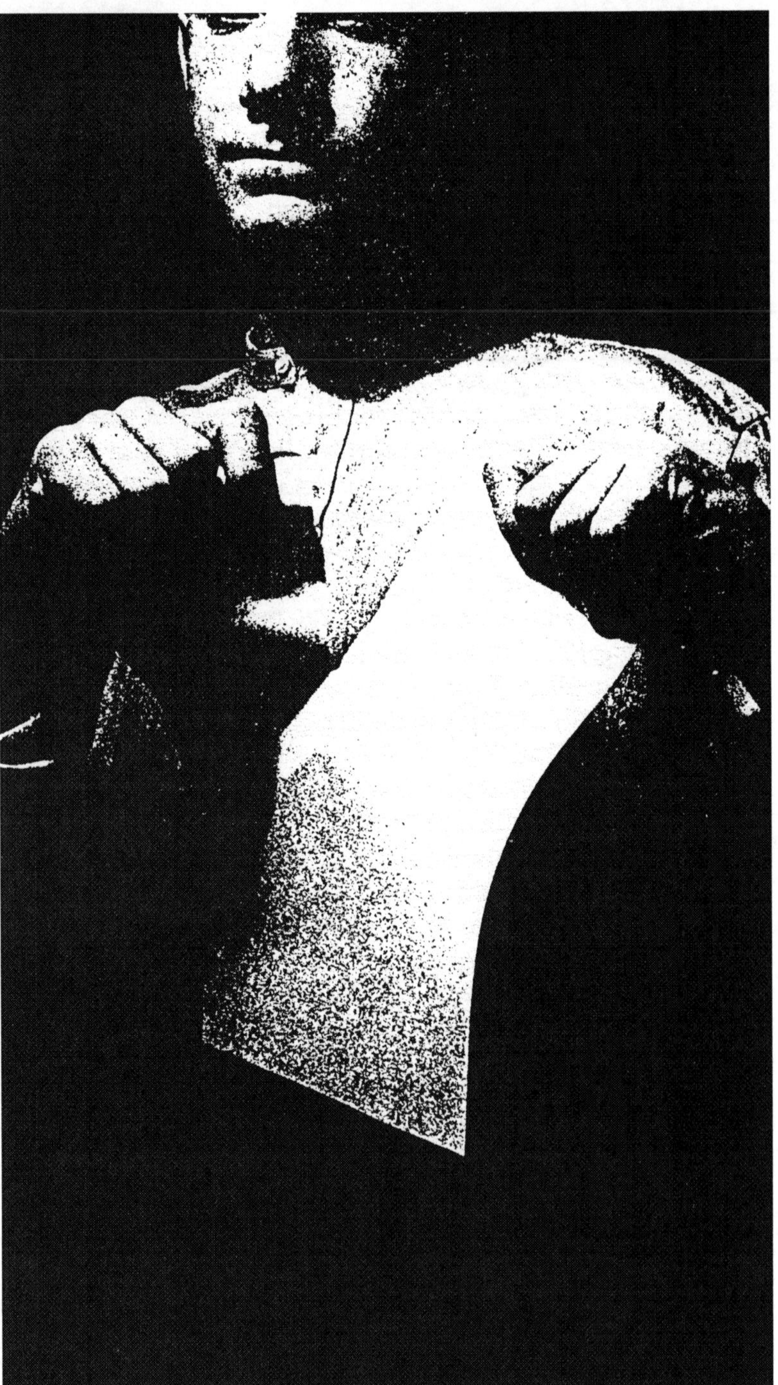

But somehow I couldn't seem to strike no places to harden me against him. It was only the other kind. I'd see him standing my watch on top of his, instead of calling me, just so I could go on sleeping.

And I saw how glad he was when I come back out of the fog. And when I come to him again in the swamp, up where the feud was. And I saw him at such-like times. He would always call me honey, and pet me. He would do everything he could think of for me. I remember how good he always was.

At last I struck the time I saved him by telling the men we had smallpox aboard. And he was so grateful. He said I was the best friend old Jim ever had in the world, and the *only* one he's got now.

Then I happened to look around, and I saw that paper. It was a close place. I took it up, and held it in my hand. I was a-tremblin'. I'd got to decide, forever, between two things. I knowed it.

I studied a minute, sort of holding my breath. Then I says to myself, all right, then, I'll *go* to hell—and tore it up.

It was awful thoughts and awful words, but they was said. And I let them stay said. I never thought no more about reforming. I shoved the whole thing out of my head.

I said I would take up wickedness again. It was in my line, being brung up to it, and the other warn't. And for a starter, I would go to work and steal Jim out of slavery again.

And if I could think up anything worse, I would do that, too. Because as long as I was in, and in for good, I might as well go the whole hog.

Then I set to thinking over how to get at it. I turned over some considerable many ways in my mind. At last, I fixed up a plan that suited me.

So then I figured the distance of a woody island that was down the river a piece. As soon as it was fairly dark, I crept out with my raft and went for it. I hid it there, and then turned in.

I slept the night through, and got up before it was light. I had my breakfast, and put on my store clothes. I tied up some others and one thing or another in a bundle. Then I took the canoe and cleared for shore.

I landed below where I judged was Phelps' place. I hid my bundle in the woods. Then I filled up the canoe with water. I loaded rocks into her and sunk her where I could find her again when I wanted her. She was about a quarter of a mile below a little steam sawmill that was on the bank.

Then I struck up the road. When I passed the mill, I saw a sign on it, "Phelps' Sawmill." Then I come to the farm houses, two or three hundred yards further along. I kept my eyes peeled. But I didn't see nobody around, though it was good daytime now.

But I didn't mind. I didn't want to see nobody just yet. I only wanted to get the lay of the land.

According to my plan, I was going to turn up there from the village, not from below. So I just took a look, and shoved along, straight for town.

Well, the very first man I saw when I got there was the duke. He was sticking up a bill for the "Royal Nonesuch." It was a three-night performance—like that other time. *They* had the cheek, them frauds! I was right on him before I could **shirk** him. He looked astonished.

He says, "Hel-*lo*! Where'd *you* come from?" Then he says, kind of glad and eager, "Where's the raft? Got her in a good place?"

I says, "Why, that's just what I was going to ask your grace."

Then he didn't look so joyful, and says, "What was your idea for asking *me?*"

"Well," I says, "I saw the king in that doggery yesterday. And I says to myself, we can't get him home for hours, till he's soberer.

"So I went a-loafin' around town to put in the time and wait. A man up and offered me ten cents. He wanted me to help him pull a skiff over the river and back to fetch a sheep. So I went along.

"We was dragging him to the boat, and the man left me ahold of the rope. He went behind him to shove him along. But the sheep was too strong for me. He jerked loose and run, and we after him.

"We didn't have no dog. So we had to chase him all over the country till we tired him out. We never got him till dark. Then we fetched him over.

"I started down for the raft. When I got there, I saw it was gone. I says to myself, they've got into trouble and had to leave. And they've took my nigger, which is the only nigger I've got in the world. And now I'm in a strange country. I ain't got no property no more, nor nothing, and no way to make my living.

"So I set down and cried. I slept in the woods all night. But what *did* become of the raft, then? And Jim—poor Jim!"

"Blamed if *I* know—that is, what's become of the raft. That old fool had made a trade and got forty dollars. When we found him in the doggery, the loafers had matched half-dollars with him. They got every cent but what he'd spent for whisky.

"When I got him home late last night, we found the raft gone. We said, 'That little rascal has stole our raft and shook us. He's run off down the river.' "

"I wouldn't shake my *nigger,* would I? The only nigger I had in the world, and the only property?"

"We never thought of that. Fact is, I reckon we'd come to consider him *our* nigger. Yes, we did consider him so. Goodness knows, we had trouble enough for him.

"So then we saw the raft was gone, and we flat broke. There warn't anything for it but to try the 'Royal Nonesuch' another shake. And I've pegged along ever since, dry as a powderhorn.[5] Where's that ten cents? Give it here."

I had considerable money, so I give him ten cents. But I begged him to spend it for something to eat, and give me some. I told him it was all the money I had. And I hadn't had nothing to eat since yesterday.

He never said nothing. The next minute, he whirls on me and says, "Do you reckon that nigger would blow on us? We'd skin him if he done that!"

---

5 A *powderhorn* was once used to carry powder for loading rifles. Powderhorns had to be kept dry or the powder would not ignite when firing a rifle.

"How can he blow? Ain't he run off?"

"No! That old fool sold him. And he never divided with me, and the money's gone."

"*Sold* him?" I says, and begun to cry. "Why, he was *my* nigger, and that was my money. Where is he? I want my nigger."

"Well, you can't *get* your nigger, that's all. So dry up your blubbering. Looky here—do you think *you'd* go and blow on us? Blamed if I think I'd trust you. Why, if you *was* to blow on us—"

He stopped. I never saw the duke look so ugly out of his eyes before. I went on a-whimperin', and says, "I don't want to blow on nobody. I ain't got no time to blow, nohow. I got to turn out and find my nigger."

He looked kind of bothered. He stood there with his bills fluttering on his arm. He was thinking, and wrinkling up his forehead.

At last he says, "I'll tell you something. We got to be here three days. Promise you won't blow, and won't let the nigger blow. I'll tell you where to find him."

So I promised, and he says, "A farmer by the name of Silas Ph—" and then he stopped. You see, he started to tell me the truth. But then he stopped that way, and begun to study and think it again. I reckoned he was changing his mind.

And so he was. He wouldn't trust me. He wanted to make sure of having me out of the way the whole three days. So pretty soon he says, "The man that bought him is named Abram Foster—Abram G. Foster. He lives forty miles back here in the country. He's on the road to Lafayette."

"All right," I says. "I can walk it in three days. And I'll start this very afternoon."

"No you won't, you'll start *now.* Don't you lose any time about it, neither, nor do any gabbing by the way. Just keep a tight tongue in your head and move right along. Then you won't get into trouble with *us,* do you hear?"

That was the order I wanted, and that was the one I played for. I wanted to be left free to work my plans.

"So clear out," he says. "You can tell Mr. Foster whatever you want to. Maybe you can get him to believe that Jim *is* your nigger. Some idiots don't require documents. At least I've heard that it's that way down South here.

"And you can tell him the handbill and the reward's **bogus.** Maybe he'll believe you. Explain to him what the idea was for getting 'em out. Go along, now. Tell him anything you want to. But mind you don't work your jaw any *between* here and there."

So I left, and struck for the back country. I didn't look around, but I kind of felt like he was watching me. But I knowed I could tire him out at that. I went straight out in the country as much as a mile before I stopped. Then I doubled back through the woods toward Phelps'.

I reckoned I better start in on my plan straight off without fooling around. I wanted to stop Jim's mouth till these fellows could get away. I didn't want no trouble with their kind. I'd seen all I wanted to of them, and wanted to get entirely shut of them.

Chapter 32

I Have a New Name

VOCABULARY PREVIEW

The following words appear in this chapter. Review the list and get to know the words before you read the chapter.

distress—disturb; trouble
droning—humming or buzzing sounds
resurrection—rising from the dead
waylay—stop; delay

When I got there, it was all still and Sunday-like, and hot and sunshiny. The hands was gone to the fields. There was them kind of faint **dronings** of bugs and flies in the air. It makes it seem so lonesome and like everybody's dead and gone.

Then a breeze fans along and quivers the leaves. It makes you feel mournful. You feel like it's spirits whispering—spirits that's been dead ever so many years. And you always think they're talking about *you.* As a general thing, it makes a body wish *he* was dead, too, and done with it all.

Phelps' was one of these little one-horse cotton plantations. They all look alike. A rail fence went 'round a two-acre yard. A stile was made out of logs sawed off and upended in steps. Kind of like barrels of different length. They were to climb over the fence with, and for the women to stand on when they are going to jump onto a horse.

There were some sickly grass patches in the big yard. But mostly it was bare and smooth. It was like an old hat with the nap[1] rubbed off. There was a big double log house for the white folks. It had cut logs, with the chinks stopped up with mud or mortar. These mud stripes had been whitewashed some time or another.

1 *Nap* is the fuzziness of suede or other cloth.

There was a round-log kitchen. It had a big, broad, open but roofed passage joining it to the house. There was a log smoke house back of the kitchen. Three little log nigger cabins were in a row on the other side of the smoke house.

One little hut was all by itself way down against the back fence. Some outbuildings were down a piece the other side. There was an ash hopper[2] and a big kettle to boil soap in by the little hut.

A bench was by the kitchen door, with a bucket of water and a gourd. A hound was asleep there in the sun. More hounds were asleep 'round about.

About three shade trees were way off in a corner. Some currant bushes and gooseberry bushes were in one place by the fence. Outside of the fence was a garden and a watermelon patch. Then the cotton fields began, and after the fields the woods.

I went around and clumb over the back stile by the ash hopper. I started for the kitchen. When I got a little ways, I heard the dim hum of a spinning wheel. It was wailing along up and sinking along down again. Then I knowed for certain I wished I was dead. For that *is* the lonesomest sound in the whole world.

I went right along, not fixing up any particular plan. I just trusted to Providence to put the right words in my mouth when the time come. I'd noticed that Providence always did put the right words in my mouth if I left it alone.

When I got halfway, first one hound and then another got up and went for me. Of course I stopped and faced them, and kept still. And such another powwow as they made!

In a quarter of a minute, I was a kind of a hub of a wheel, as you may say. The spokes was made out of dogs. A circle of fifteen of them packed together around me, a-barkin' and a-howlin'. Their necks and noses stretched up towards me.

There was more a-comin'. You could see them sailing over fences and around corners from everywheres.

A nigger woman come tearing out of the kitchen. She had a rolling pin in her hand. She sang out, "Begone! You Tige! You Spot! Begone sah!"

---

2 An *ash hopper* stores lye used for making soap.

And she fetched first one and then another of them a clip and sent them howling. Then the rest followed. The next second, half of them come back. They wagged their tails around me and made friends with me. There ain't no harm in a hound nohow.

And behind the woman comes a little nigger girl and two little nigger boys. They had nothing on but tow-linen shirts. They hung on to their mother's gown, and peeped out from behind her at me, bashful. That's the way they always do.

And here comes the white woman running from the house. She's about forty-five or fifty years old and bareheaded. She has her spinning stick in her hand.

Behind her comes little white children. They're acting the same way the little niggers was doing. She was smiling all over so she could hardly stand—and says, "*It's you,* at last! *Ain't it*"

I out with a "Yes, ma'am" before I thought.

She grabbed me and hugged me tight. Then she gripped me by both hands and shook and shook. The tears come in her eyes and run down over. She couldn't seem to hug and shake enough.

She kept saying, "You don't look as much like your mother as I reckoned you would. But law sakes, I don't care about that. I'm *so* glad to see you! Dear, dear, it does seem like I could eat you up! Children, it's your cousin Tom! Tell him howdy."

But they ducked their heads, and put their fingers in their mouths. They hid behind her. So she run on.

"Lize, hurry up and get him a hot breakfast right away. Or did you get your breakfast on the boat?"

I said I had got it on the boat. So then she started for he house, leading me by the hand. The children tagged after.

When we got there, she set me down in a chair. She set herself down on a little low stool in front of me. Then she held both of my hands.

She says, "Now I can have a *good* look at you. And laws-a-me, I've been hungry for it a many and a many a time, all these long years. And it's come at last! We been expecting you a couple of days and more. What kept you? Boat get aground?"[3]

"Yes ma'am—she—"

---

3 When a boat gets aground, it is stranded in shallow water. This can happen if a boat gets too close to shore or to a sandbar.

"Don't say yes ma'am. Say Aunt Sally. Where'd she get aground?"

I didn't rightly know what to say. I didn't know whether the boat would be coming up the river or down. But I got a good deal on instinct. And my instinct said she would be coming up—from down towards Orleans.

That didn't help me much, though. I didn't know the names of bars down that way. I saw I'd got to invent a bar. Or I'd got to forget the name of the one we got aground on—or—

Now I struck an idea, and came out with it. "It warn't the grounding. That didn't keep us back but a little. We blowed out a cylinder head."

"Good gracious! Anybody hurt?"

"No ma'am. Killed a nigger."

"Well, it's lucky, because sometimes people do get hurt. Two years ago last Christmas, your Uncle Silas was coming up from New Orleans on the old *Lally Rook.* She blowed out a cylinder head and crippled a man. I think he died afterwards.

"He was a Baptist. Your Uncle Silas knowed a family in Baton Rouge that knowed his people well. Yes, I remember now, he *did* die. Mortification[4] set in, and they, had to amputate him.

"But it didn't save him. Yes, it was mortification—that was it. He turned blue all over. And he died in the hope of a glorious **resurrection**. They say he was a sight to look at.

"Your uncle's been up to the town every day to fetch you. And he's gone again, not more than an hour ago. He'll be back any minute now. You must have met him on the road, didn't you? Oldish man, with a—"

"No, I didn't see nobody, Aunt Sally. The boat landed just at daylight. I left my baggage on the dock. Then I went looking around the town and out a piece in the country. I wanted to put in the time and not get here too soon. So I come down the back way.

"Who'd you give the baggage to?"

"Nobody."

---

4 *Mortification* here means "gangrene," which decays the flesh due to a lack of blood. The body part with gangrene has to be amputated or cut off. Usually, mortification means "embarrassment" or "shame."

"Why, child, it'll be stole!"

"Not where I hid it I reckon it won't," I says.

"How'd you get your breakfast so early on the boat?"

It was kind of thin ice, but I says, "The captain saw me standing around. He told me I better have something to eat before I went ashore. So he took me in the texas to the officers' lunch. He give me all I wanted."

I was getting so uneasy I couldn't listen good. I had my mind on the children all the time. I wanted to get them out to one side and pump them a little. Then I could find out who I was. But I couldn't get no chance, Mrs. Phelps kept it up and run on so.

Pretty soon, she made the cold chills streak all down my back, 'cause she says, "But here we're a-runnin' on this way. And you ain't told me a word about Sis, nor any of them. Now I'll just rest my voice a little, and you start up yours.

"Just tell me *everything*. Tell me all about 'em all, every one of 'em. Tell me how they are, and what they're doing, and what they told you to tell me. Tell me every last little thing you can think of."

Well, I see I was up a stump—and up it good. Providence had stood by me this far all right. But I was hard and tight aground now. I see it warn't a bit of use to try to go ahead. I'd *got* to throw up my hand.

So I says to myself, here's another place where I got to risk the truth. I opened my mouth to begin. But she grabbed me and hustled me in behind the bed.

She says, "Here he comes! Stick your head down lower. There, that'll do. You can't be seen now. Don't let on you're here. I'll play a joke on him. Children, don't you say a word."

I see I was in a fix now. But it warn't no use to worry. There warn't nothing to do but just hold still. I must try and be ready to stand from under when the lightning struck.

I had just one glimpse of the old gentleman when he come in. Then the bed hid him. Mrs. Phelps, she jumps for him, and says, "Has he come?"

"No," says her husband.

"Good-*ness* gracious!" she says. "What in the world can

have become of him?"

"I can't imagine," says the old gentleman. "And I must say, it makes me dreadful uneasy."

"Uneasy!" she says. "I'm ready to go distracted![5] He *must* have come, and you've missed him along the road. I *know* it's so—something *tells* me so."

"Why, Sally, I *couldn't* miss him along the road. *You* know that."

"But oh, dear, dear, what *will* Sis say! He must have come! You must have missed him. He—"

"Oh, don't **distress** me any more than I'm already distressed. I don't know what in the world to make of it. I'm at my wit's end. I don't mind admitting that I'm right down scared.

"But there's no hope that he's come. He *couldn't* come and me miss him. Sally, it's terrible—just terrible. Something's happened to the boat, sure!"

"Why, Silas! Look yonder! Up the road! Ain't that somebody coming?"

He sprung to the window at the head of the bed. That give Mrs. Phelps the chance she wanted.

She stooped down quick at the foot of the bed and give me a pull. Out I come. When he turned back from the window, there she stood. She was a-beamin' and a-smilin' like a house afire. I was standing pretty meek and sweaty alongside.

The old gentleman stared, and says, "Why, who's that?"

"Who do you reckon 'tis?"

"I ain't no idea. Who *is* it?"

"It's *Tom Sawyer!*"

By jings, I most slumped through the floor! But there warn't no time to swap knives. The old man grabbed me by the hand and shook, and kept on shaking. All the time how the woman did dance around and laugh and cry. Then how they both did fire off questions about Sid, and Mary, and the rest of the tribe.

But if they was joyful, it warn't nothing to what I was. It was like being born again, I was so glad to find out who I was.

Well, they froze to me for two hours. At last, my chin was so tired it couldn't hardly go any more. I had told them more about

---

5 *Distracted* here means "crazy" or "insane."

my family—I mean the Sawyer family—than ever happened to any six Sawyer families.

And I explained all about how we blowed out a cylinder head at the mouth of White River. It took us three days to fix it. Which was all right, and worked first-rate. *They* didn't know but what it would take three days to fix it. If I'd have called it a bolt head, it would have done just as well.

Now I was feeling pretty comfortable all down one side. But pretty uncomfortable all up the other. Being Tom Sawyer was easy and comfortable. It stayed easy and comfortable, till by and by, I hear a steamboat coughing along down the river.

Then I says to myself, suppose Tom Sawyer comes down on that boat? And suppose he steps in here any minute? He might sing out my name before I can throw him a wink to keep quiet.

Well, I couldn't *have* it that way. It wouldn't do at all. I must go up the road and **waylay** him. So I told the folks I reckoned I would go up to the town and fetch down my baggage.

The old gentleman was for going along with me. But I said no, I could drive the horse myself. I'd rather he wouldn't take no trouble about me.

Chapter 33

The Pitiful Ending of Royalty

VOCABULARY PREVIEW

The following words appear in this chapter. Review the list and get to know the words before you read the chapter.

audacious—bold; daring
estimation—opinion; viewpoint
impudent—brash; shameless
persuaded—convinced; urged
rapscallions—rascals; troublemakers

So I started for town in the wagon. When I was halfway, I see a wagon coming. Sure enough, it was Tom Sawyer. I stopped and waited till he come along.

I says, "Hold on!" and it stopped alongside. His mouth opened up like a trunk, and stayed so. He swallowed two or three times like a person that's got a dry throat. Then he says, "I ain't ever done you no harm. You know that. So, then, what you want to come back and haunt *me* for?"

I says, "I ain't come back. I ain't been *gone.*"

When he heard my voice, it righted him up some. But he warn't quite satisfied yet. He says, "Don't you play nothing on me, 'cause I wouldn't on you. Honest Injun, you ain't a ghost?"

"Honest Injun, I ain't," I says.

"Well—I—well, that ought to settle it, of course. But I can't somehow seem to understand it no way. Look here, warn't you ever murdered *at all?"*

"No. I warn't ever murdered at all. I played it on them. You come in here and feel of me if you don't believe me."

So he done it, and it satisfied him. He was that glad to see me again, he didn't know what to do. And he wanted to know all about it right off. It was a grand adventure, and mysterious, and so it was right in his line.

But I said, leave it alone till by and by. I told his driver to wait, and we drove off a little piece. I told him the kind of a fix I was in. What did he reckon we better do? He said, let him alone a minute, and don't disturb him.

So he thought and thought, and pretty soon, he says, "It's all right. I've got it. Take my trunk in your wagon, and let on it's yours. You turn back and fool along slow. Get to the house about the time you ought to.

"I'll go straight towards town a piece, and take a fresh start. I'll get there a quarter or a half an hour after you. You needn't let on to know me at first."

I says, "All right, but wait a minute. There's one more thing—a thing that *nobody* don't know but me. And that is, there's a nigger here that I'm a-tryin' to steal out of slavery. His name is *Jim*—old Miss Watson's Jim."

He says, "What? Why, Jim is—"

He stopped and went to studying.

I says, "*I* know what you'll say. You'll say it's dirty, low-down business. But what if it is? *I'm* low-down. And I'm a-goin' to steal him, and I want you to keep mum and not let on. Will you?"

His eyes lit up, and he says, "I'll *help* you steal him!"

Well, I let go all holds then, like I was shot. It was the most astonishing speech I ever heard. And I'm bound to say Tom Sawyer fell considerable in my **estimation**. Only I couldn't believe it. Tom Sawyer a *nigger-stealer!*

"Oh, shucks!" I says. "You're joking."

"I ain't joking, either."

"Well, then," I says, "joking or no joking, don't forget. If you hear anything said about a runaway nigger, remember that *you* don't know nothing about him. And *I* don't know nothing about him."

Then he took the trunk and put it in my wagon. He drove off his way and I drove mine. But of course I forgot all about driving slow on accounts of being glad and full of thinking. So I got home a heap too quick for that length of a trip.

The old gentleman was at the door, and he says, "Why, this is wonderful! Whoever would have thought it was in that mare to do it? I wish we'd have timed her. And she ain't sweated a hair—not a hair. It's wonderful.

"Why," says he, "I wouldn't take a hundred dollars for that horse now. I wouldn't, honest. And yet I'd have sold her for fifteen before. I thought 'twas all she was worth."

That's all he said. He was the most innocent, best old soul I ever saw. But it warn't surprising. He warn't only just a farmer, he was a preacher, too.

He had a little one-horse log church down back of the plantation. He built it himself at his own expense. It was for a church and a schoolhouse. He never charged nothing for his preaching, and it was worth it, too. There was plenty other farmer-preachers like that, down South. They done the same way.

In about half an hour, Tom's wagon drove up to the front step. Aunt Sally, she saw it through the window. It was only about fifty yards. She says, "Why, there's somebody come! I wonder who 'tis? Why, I do believe it's a stranger."

Then she said to one of the children, "Jimmy, run and tell Lize to put on another plate for dinner."

Everybody made a rush for the front door. Because, of course, a stranger don't come *every* year. And so he stirs up more interest than yellow fever,[1] when he does come.

Tom was over the stile and starting for the house. The wagon was spinning up the road for the village. We was all bunched in the front door. Tom had his store clothes on, and an audience. That was always nuts for Tom Sawyer.

It warn't no trouble to him to throw in an amount of suitable style. Not in them circumstances. He warn't a boy to go meekly along up that yard like a sheep. No, he come calm and important, like the ram.

When he got a-front of us, he lifts his hat ever so gracious and dainty. It was like it was the lid of a box that had butterflies asleep in it. And he didn't want to disturb them. He says, "Mr. Archibald Nichols, I suppose?"

---

1 *Yellow fever* is a tropical disease spread by mosquitoes.

"No, my boy," says the old gentleman. "I'm sorry to say that your driver has deceived you. Nichols' place is down a matter of three miles more. Come in, come in."

Tom, he took a look back over his shoulder, and says, "Too late—he's out of sight."

"Yes, he's gone, my son, and you must come in and eat your dinner with us. Then we'll hitch up and take you down to Nichols'."

"Oh, I *can't* make you so much trouble. I couldn't think of it. I'll walk—I don't mind the distance."

"But we won't let you walk. It wouldn't be Southern hospitality to do it. Come right in."

"Oh, *do,* " says Aunt Sally. "It ain't a bit of trouble to us, not a bit in the world. You *must* stay. It's a long, dusty three miles. We *can't* let you walk.

"And, besides, I've already told 'em to put on another plate when I saw you coming. So you mustn't disappoint us. Come right in and make yourself at home."

So Tom thanked them very hearty and handsome. He let himself be **persuaded,** and come in. When he was in, he said he was a stranger from Hicksville, Ohio. He said his name was William Thompson—and he made another bow.

Well, he run on, and on, and on. He made up stuff about Hicksville and everybody in it he could invent. I was getting a little nervous. I wondered how this was going to help me out of my scrape.

He was still talking along. Then at last, he reached over and kissed Aunt Sally right on the mouth. Then he settled back again in his chair comfortable. He was going to keep on talking. But Aunt Sally jumped up and wiped it off with the back of her hand, and says, "You **audacious** puppy!"

He looked kind of hurt, and says, "I'm surprised at you, ma'am."

"You're surp—Why, what do you reckon *I* am? I've a good notion to take and—Say, what do you mean by kissing me?"

He looked kind of humble, and says, "I didn't mean nothing, ma'am. I didn't mean no harm. I—I—thought you'd like it."

"Why, you born fool!" She took up the spinning stick. It seemed like it was all she could do to keep from giving him a crack with it. "What made you think I'd like it?"

"Well, I don't know. Only, they—they—told me you would."

"They told you I would. Whoever told you's *another* lunatic. I never heard the beat of it. Who's *they?"*

"Why, everybody. They all said so, ma'am."

It was all she could do to hold in. Her eyes snapped, and her fingers worked like she wanted to scratch him. She says, "Who's 'everybody'? Out with their names, or there'll be an idiot short."

He got up and looked distressed, and fumbled for his hat, and says, "I'm sorry, and I warn't expecting it. They told me to. They all told me to. They all said, kiss her, and said she'd like it. They all said it—every one of them. But I'm sorry, ma'am, and I won't do it no more. I won't, honest."

"You won't, won't you? Well, I should *reckon* you won't!"

"No ma'am, I'm honest about it. I won't ever do it again—till you ask me."

"Till I *ask* you! Well, I never see the beat of it in my born days! I bet you'll be the Methusalem-numbskull[2] of creation before ever *I* ask you—or the likes of you."

"Well," he says, "it does surprise me so. I can't make it out somehow. They said you would, and I thought you would. But—"

He stopped and looked around slow. It was like he wished he could run across a friendly eye somewheres. He fetched the old gentleman's, and says, "Didn't *you* think she'd like me to kiss her, sir?"

"Why, no. I—I—well, no, I believe I didn't."

Then Tom looks on around the same way to me, and says, "Tom, didn't *you* think Aunt Sally'd open out her arms and say, 'Sid Sawyer—' "

"My land!" she says, breaking in and jumping for him.

2 Aunt Sally means Methuselah. He was a character in the Bible who lived to be 969 years old.

"You **impudent** young rascal, to fool a body so—"

She was going to hug him, but he fended her off, and says, "No, not till you've asked me first."

So she didn't lose no time, but asked him. She hugged him and kissed him over and over again. Then she turned him over to the old man, and he took what was left.

And after they got a little quiet again, she says, "Why, dear me, I never saw such a surprise. We warn't looking for *you* at all, but only Tom. Sis never wrote me about anybody coming but him."

"It's because it warn't *intended* for any of us to come but Tom," he says. "But I begged and begged. At the last minute, she let me come, too.

"So, coming down the river, me and Tom had an idea. We thought it would be a first-rate surprise for him to come here to the house first. Then I could by and by tag along and drop in. I'd let on to be a stranger.

"But it was a mistake, Aunt Sally. This ain't no healthy place for a stranger to come."

"No—not for impudent whelps,[3] Sid. You ought to had your jaws boxed. I ain't been so put out since I don't know when.

"But I don't care, I don't mind the terms. I'd be willing to stand a thousand such jokes to have you here. Well, to think of that performance! I don't deny it. I was most putrefied[4] with astonishment when you give me that smack."

We had dinner out in that broad open passage between the house and the kitchen. There was things enough on that table for seven families. It was all hot, too. There was none of your flabby, tough meat that's laid in a cupboard in a damp cellar all night. You know, the stuff that tastes like a hunk of old cold cannibal in the morning.

Uncle Silas asked a pretty long blessing over it. But it was worth it. It didn't cool it a bit, neither. Though I've seen them kind of interruptions do that lots of times.

---

3 A *whelp* is a puppy.

4 *Putrefied* actually means "rotted" or "decayed." Aunt Sally really means "petrified" or "completely startled."

There was a considerable good deal of talk all the afternoon. Me and Tom was on the lookout all the time. But it warn't no use. They didn't happen to say nothing about any runaway nigger. We was afraid to try to work up to it.

But at supper, at night, one of the little boys says, "Pa, may Tom and Sid and me go to the show?"

"No," says the old man. "I reckon there ain't going to be any. You couldn't go even if there was. The runaway nigger told Burton and me all about that disgraceful show.

"Burton said he would tell the people. So I reckon they've drove the audacious loafers out of town before this time."

So there it was! But *I* couldn't help it.

Tom and me was to sleep in the same room and bed. So, being tired, we bid good night and went up to bed right after supper.

Then we clumb out of the window and down the lightning rod. We shoved for the town. I didn't believe anybody was going to give the king and the duke a hint. So if I didn't hurry up and give them one, they'd get into trouble, sure.

On the road, Tom told me all about how it was reckoned I was murdered. He told how Pap disappeared pretty soon and didn't come back no more. And there was a stir when Jim run away.

And I told Tom all about our "Royal Nonesuch" **rapscallions**. And I told as much of the raft voyage as I had time to.

Then we struck into the town and up through the middle of it. It was as much as half after eight then. Here comes a raging rush of people with torches. They made an awful whooping and yelling. They were banging tin pans and blowing horns.

We jumped to one side to let them go by. As they went by, I saw they had the king and the duke straddled on a rail. That is, I knowed it *was* the king and the duke. But they was all over tar and feathers.

They didn't look like nothing in the world that was human. They just looked like a couple of monstrous big soldier-plumes.

Well, it made me sick to see it. I was sorry for them poor pitiful rascals. It seemed like I couldn't ever feel any hardness against them any more in the world. It was a dreadful thing to see. Human beings *can* be awful cruel to one another.

We saw we was too late—couldn't do no good. We asked some stragglers about it. They said everybody went to the show looking very innocent. They laid low and kept dark.

They waited till the poor king was in the middle of his prancings on the stage. Somebody give a signal, and the house rose up and went for them.

So we poked along back home. I warn't feeling so brash as I was before. I felt kind of ornery, and humble, and to blame, somehow. Though I hadn't done nothing.

But that's always the way. It don't make no difference whether you do right or wrong. A person's conscience ain't got no sense. It just goes for him *anyway.*

If I had a yellow dog that didn't know more than a person's conscience does, I would poison him. It takes up more room than all the rest of a person's insides. And yet it ain't no good, nohow. Tom Sawyer, he says the same.

Chapter 34

We Cheer Up Jim

VOCABULARY PREVIEW

The word below appears in this chapter. Review the definition and get to know the meaning before you read the chapter.

acquainted—aware; familiar

We stopped talking, and got to thinking. By and by, Tom says, "Looky here, Huck. What fools we are not to think of it before! I bet I know where Jim is."

"No! Where?"

"In that hut down by the ash hopper. Why, looky here. When we was at dinner, didn't you see a nigger man go in there with some vittles?"

"Yes."

"What did you think the vittles was for?"

"For a dog."

"So did I. Well, it wasn't for a dog."

"Why?"

"Because part of it was watermelon."

"So it was—I noticed it. Well, it does beat all. I never thought about a dog not eating watermelon. It shows how a body can see and don't see at the same time."

"Well, the nigger unlocked the padlock when he went in. And he locked it again when he came out. He gave uncle a key about the time we got up from the table. It was the same key, I bet.

"Watermelon shows man, lock shows prisoner. It ain't likely there's two prisoners on such a little plantation. Not here where the people's all so kind and good. Jim's the prisoner.

"All right. I'm glad we found it out detective fashion. I wouldn't give shucks for any other way. Now you work your mind. Study out a plan to steal Jim. I will study out one, too. We'll take the one we like the best."

What a head for just a boy to have! If only I had Tom Sawyer's head. I wouldn't trade it off to be a duke, nor mate of a steamboat, nor clown in a circus. I wouldn't trade it for nothing I can think of.

I went to thinking out a plan. But it was only just to be doing something. I knowed very well where the right plan was going to come from.

Pretty soon, Tom says, "Ready?"

"Yes," I says.

"All right—bring it out."

"My plan is this," I says. "We can easily find out if it's Jim in there. Then get up my canoe tomorrow night, and fetch my raft over from the island. We'll wait for the first dark night that comes. Then we'll steal the key out of the old man's britches after he goes to bed.

"We'll shove off down the river on the raft with Jim. We'll hide daytimes and run nights, the way me and Jim used to do before. Wouldn't that plan work?"

"*Work?* Why certainly it would work, like rats a-fightin'. But it's too blamed simple. There ain't nothing *to* it. What's the good of a plan that ain't no more trouble than that? It's as mild as goose milk. Why, Huck, it wouldn't make no more talk than breaking into a soap factory."

I never said nothing. I warn't expecting nothing different. I knowed mighty well that he would get *his* plan ready. And it wouldn't have none of them objections to it.

And it didn't. He told me what it was. I saw in a minute it was worth fifteen of mine for style. It would make Jim just as free a man as mine would. And maybe get us all killed besides. So I was satisfied. I said we would waltz in on it.

I needn't tell what it was here. I knowed it wouldn't stay the way it was. I knowed he would be changing it around every which way as he went along. He'd heave in new bulliness wherever he got a chance. And that is what he done.

Well, one thing was dead sure. Tom Sawyer was in earnest. He was actually going to help steal that nigger out of slavery. That was the thing that was too much for me.

Here was a boy that was respectable and well brung up. He

had a character to lose, and his folks at home that had characters. He was bright and not leather-headed. He was knowing and not ignorant, and not mean, but kind.

And yet here he was. He didn't have no more pride, or tightness, or feeling, than to stoop to this business. He would make himself a shame, and his family name a shame, before everybody. I *couldn't* understand it no way at all.

It was outrageous. I knowed I ought to just up and tell him so, and so be his true friend. I could let him quit the thing right where he was and save himself. And I *did* start to tell him. But he shut me up, and says, "Don't you reckon I know what I'm about? Don't I generally know what I'm about?"

"Yes."

"Didn't I *say* I was going to help steal the nigger?"

"Yes."

"*Well,* then."

That's all he said, and that's all I said. It warn't no use to say any more. When he said he'd do a thing, he always done it.

But I couldn't make out why he was willing to go into this thing. So I just let it go. I never bothered no more about it. If he was bound to have it so, *I* couldn't help it.

When we got home, the house was all dark and still. So we went down to the hut by the ash hopper to examine it. We went through the yard so as to see what the hounds would do. They knowed us. They didn't make much noise. No more than country dogs is always doing when anything comes by in the night.

When we got to the cabin, we took a look at the front and the two sides. The north side was the side I wasn't **acquainted** with. There we found a square window hole. It was up tolerable high, with just one thick board nailed across it.

I says, "Here's the ticket. This hole's big enough for Jim to get through if we wrench off the board."

Tom says, "It's as simple as tit-tat-toe,[1] three in a row. And as easy as playing hooky. I should *hope* we can find a way that's a little more complicated than *that,* Huck Finn."

"Well, then," says I, "how'll it do to saw him out? The way

1 *Tit-tat-toe* is the same game as tic-tac-toe.

I done before I was murdered that time?"

"That's more *like* it," he says. "It's real mysterious, and troublesome, and good," he says. "But I bet we can find a way that's twice as long. There ain't no hurry. Let's keep on looking around."

Between the hut and the fence, on the back side, was a lean-to.[2] It joined the hut at the eaves, and was made out of plank. It was as long as the hut, but narrow. It was only about six foot wide. The door to it was at the south end, and was padlocked.

Tom went to the soap kettle and searched around. He fetched back the iron thing they lift the lid with. So he took it and pried out one of the staples.

The chain fell down, and we opened the door and went in. We shut it, and struck a match. We saw the shed was only built against the cabin and hadn't no connection with it.

There warn't no floor to the shed. Nor was there nothing much in it. Just some old rusty played-out hoes and spades and picks and a crippled plow. The match went out, and so did we. We shoved in the staple again, and the door was locked as good as ever.

Tom was joyful. He says, "Now we're all right. We'll *dig* him out. It'll take about a week!"

Then we started for the house. I went in the back door. You only have to pull a buckskin latchstring. They don't fasten doors. But that warn't romantical enough for Tom Sawyer. There warn't no way for him but to climb up the lightning rod.

But he only got up halfway about three times. And he missed fire and fell every time. The last time, he most busted his brains out. He thought he'd got to give it up. But after he was rested, he figured he would give her one more turn for luck. This time he made the trip.

In the morning, we was up at break of day. We went down to the nigger cabins to pet the dogs. And we wanted to make friends with the nigger that fed Jim—if it *was* Jim that was being fed.

The niggers was just getting through breakfast and starting for the fields. Jim's nigger was piling up a tin pan with bread and meat and things. Whilst the others was leaving, the key come

---

2 A *lean-to* is a small shelter with a roof that slopes to the ground.

from the house.

This nigger had a good-natured, chuckleheaded face. His hair was all tied up in little bunches with thread. That was to keep witches off.

He said the witches was pestering him awful these nights. They was making him see all kinds of strange things. He was hearing all kinds of strange words and noises. He didn't believe he was ever witched so long before in his life.

He got worked up, and got to running on about his troubles. He forgot all about what he'd been a-goin' to do. So Tom says, "What's the vittles for? Going to feed the dogs?"

The nigger kind of smiled around gradually over his face. It's like when you heave a brickbat[3] in a mud puddle. Then he says, "Yes, Master Sid, *a* dog. Curious dog, too. Does you want to go en' look at him?"

"Yes."

I nudged Tom, and whispers, "You going, right here in the daybreak? *That* warn't the plan."

"No, it warn't," Tom says. "But it's the plan now."

So, drat him, we went along. But I didn't like it much. When we got in it was dark. We couldn't hardly see anything. But Jim was there, sure enough, and could see us. And he sings out, "Why, *Huck*! En' good *land!* Ain't dat Mister Tom?"

I just knowed how it would be. I just expected it. I didn't know nothing to do. If I had, I couldn't have done it. That nigger busted in and says, "Why, de gracious sakes! Do he know you gentlemen?"

We could see pretty well now. Tom, he looked at the nigger, steady and kind of wondering. He says, "Does *who* know us?"

"Why, dis here runaway nigger."

"I don't reckon he does. What put that into your head?"

"What *put* it there? Didn't he just dis minute sing out like he knowed you?"

Tom says, in a puzzled-up kind of way, "Well, that's mighty curious. *Who* sung out? *When* did he sing out? *What* did he sing out?"

And Tom turns to me, perfectly calm, and says, "Did *you*

---

3 A *brickbat* is a piece of brick that is used as a weapon when thrown.

hear anybody sing out?"

Of course there warn't nothing to be said but the one thing. So I says, "No. *I* ain't heard nobody say nothing."

Then he turns to Jim. He looks him over like he never saw him before, and says, "Did you sing out?"

"No, sah," says Jim. "I ain't said nothing, sah."

"Not a word?"

"No, sah. I ain't said a word."

"Did you ever see us before?"

"No, sah. Not as *I* knows on."

So Tom turns to the nigger who was looking wild and distressed. Tom says, kind of severe, "What do you reckon's the matter with you, anyway? What made you think somebody sung out?"

"Oh, it's de dad-blamed witches, sah. I wished I was dead, I do. Dey's always at it, sah. En' dey do mos' kill me, dey scares me so. Please don't tell nobody about it, sah. Or ole Master Silas, he'll scold me. 'Cause he say dey *ain't* no witches.

"I just wish to goodness he was here now. *Den* what would he say! I just bet he couldn't find no way to git around it *dis* time.

"But it's always just so. People dat's *set,* stays set. Dey won't look into nothin' en' find it out for deyselves. Den *you* find it out en' tell 'em 'bout it. But dey don't believe you."

Tom give him a dime. He said we wouldn't tell nobody. He told him to buy some more thread to tie up his hair with.

Then he looks at Jim, and says, "I wonder if Uncle Silas is going to hang this nigger. If I was to catch a nigger that was ungrateful enough to run away, *I* wouldn't give him up. I'd hang him."

The nigger stepped to the door to look at the dime. He bit it to see if it was good. Then Tom whispered to Jim and says, "Don't ever let on to know us. And if you hear any digging going on nights, it's us. We're going to set you free."

Jim only had time to grab us by the hand and squeeze it. Then the nigger come back. We said we'd come again some time if the nigger wanted us to. He said he would, especially if it was dark. The witches went for him mostly in the dark. It was good to have folks around then.

Chapter 35

Dark, Deep-Laid Plans

VOCABULARY PREVIEW

The following words appear in this chapter. Review the list and get to know the words before you read the chapter.

conveniences—helpful tools or equipment
distinctions—slight differences; minor points
regulations—rules

It would be most an hour yet till breakfast. So we left and struck down into the woods.

Tom said we got to have *some* light to see how to dig by. A lantern makes too much, and might get us into trouble. What we must have was a lot of them rotten chunks that's called fox fire.[1] It just makes a soft kind of a glow when you lay them in a dark place. We fetched an armful and hid it in the weeds. Then we set down to rest.

Tom says, kind of dissatisfied, "Blame it, this whole thing is just as easy and awkward as it can be. It makes it so rotten difficult to get up a difficult plan.

"There ain't no watchman to be drugged. Now there *ought* to be a watchman. There ain't even a dog to give a sleeping mixture to.

"And there's Jim chained by one leg, with a ten-foot chain, to the leg of his bed. Why, all you got to do is to lift up the bedstead. Then you slip off the chain.

"And Uncle Silas, he trusts everybody. He sends the key to the pumpkin-headed nigger. He don't even send nobody to watch the nigger. Jim could have got out of that window hole before this. Only there wouldn't be no use trying to travel with a ten-foot chain on his leg.

"Why, drat it, Huck. It's the stupidest arrangement I ever

1 *Fox fire* is glowing fungus on rotting wood.

saw. You got to invent *all* the difficulties. Well, we can't help it. We got to do the best we can with the materials we've got.

"Anyhow, there's one thing. There's more honor in getting him out through a lot of difficulties and dangers. But there warn't one of them furnished to us by the people whose duty it was to furnish them. We had to contrive them all out of our own head.

"Now look at just that one thing of the lantern. Let's come down to cold facts. We simply got to *let on* that a lantern's risky. Why, we could work with a torchlight procession if we wanted to, *I* believe.

"Now, whilst I think of it. We got to hunt up something to make a saw out of the first chance we get."

"What do we want of a saw?"

"What do we *want* of a saw? Ain't we got to saw the leg of Jim's bed off? So as to get the chain loose?"

"Why, you just said a body could lift up the bedstead and slip the chain off."

"Well, if that ain't just like you, Huck Finn. You *can* get up the infant-schooliest ways of going at a thing. Why, ain't you ever read any books at all? Baron Trenck, nor Casanova, nor Benvenuto Chelleeny, nor Henri IV?[2] Nor none of them heroes? Who ever heard of getting a prisoner loose in such an old-maidy way as that?

"No. The way all the best authorities does is to saw the bed leg in two. You leave it just *so,* and swallow the sawdust, so it can't be found. Then you put some dirt and grease around the sawed place. That way the very keenest seneschal[3] can't see no sign of its being sawed. He thinks the bed leg is perfectly sound.

"Then, the night you're ready, fetch the leg a kick, and down she goes. Slip off your chain, and there you are. Nothing to do but throw your rope ladder over the battlements. Then you slide down it and break your leg in the moat. Because a rope ladder is nineteen foot too short, you know.

---

2 Baron Friedrich von der Trenck (1726–1794) was an Austrian soldier. Giovanni Casanova (1725–1798) was an Italian lover and adventurer. Benvenuto Cellini (1500–1571) was a Florentine sculptor. Henry IV (1553–1610) was King of France. All were know for daring escape plans. (Tom mispronounces some names.)

3 A *seneschal* was a powerful official of the Middle Ages, the period from A.D. 500–1500. Here, Tom uses *seneschal* to mean "guard."

"And there's your horses and your trusty vassals.[4] They scoop you up and fling you across a saddle. Then away you go to your native Languedoc, or Navarre,[5] or wherever it is.

"It's gaudy, Huck. I wish there was a moat to this cabin. If we get time, the night of the escape, we'll dig one."

I says, "What do we want of a moat? We're going to snake him out from under the cabin."

But he never heard me. He had forgot me and everything else. He had his chin in his hand, thinking. Pretty soon, he sighs and shakes his head. Then he sighs again, and says, "No, it wouldn't do. There ain't necessity enough for it."

"For what?" I says.

"Why, to saw Jim's leg off," he says.

"Good land!" I says. "Why, there ain't *no* need for it. What would you want to saw his leg off for, anyway?"

"Well, some of the best authorities has done it. They couldn't get the chain off. So they just cut their hand off and got away. And a leg would be better still.

"But we got to let that go. There ain't need enough in this case. Besides, Jim's a nigger. He wouldn't understand the reasons for it. He wouldn't know how it's the custom in Europe. So we'll let it go.

"But there's one thing—he can have a rope ladder. We can tear up our sheets and make him a rope ladder easy enough. And we can send it to him in a pie. It's mostly done that way. And I've eaten worse pies."

"Why, Tom Sawyer, how you talk," I says. "Jim ain't got no use for a rope ladder."

"He *has* got use for it. How *you* talk, you better say. You don't know nothing about it. He's *got* to have a rope ladder. They all do."

"What in the nation can he *do* with it?"

"*Do* with it? He can hide it in his bed, can't he? That's what they all do. And he's got to do it, too.

"Huck, you don't ever seem to want to do anything that's regular. You want to be starting something fresh all the time.

---

4 *Vassals* were servants or slaves during the Middle Ages.

5 *Languedoc* was a district of southern France, and Navarre was in northern Spain.

Suppose he *don't* do nothing with it? Ain't it there in his bed, for a clue, after he'd gone?

"And don't you reckon they'll want clues? Of course they will. And you wouldn't leave them any? That would be a *pretty* howdy-do, *wouldn't* it! I never heard of such a thing."

"Well," I says, "if it's in the **regulations**, and he's got to have it, all right. Let him have it. I don't wish to go back on no regulations.

"But there's one thing, Tom Sawyer. What if we do go tearing up our sheets to make Jim a rope ladder? We're going to get into trouble with Aunt Sally, just as sure as you're born.

"Now, the way I look at it," says I, "a hickory-bark ladder don't cost nothing. And it don't waste nothing. It is just as good to load up a pie with, and hide in a straw tick, as any rag ladder you can start.

"And as for Jim, he ain't had no experience. So *he* don't care what kind of a—"

"Oh, shucks, Huck Finn. If I was as ignorant as you, I'd keep still. That's what *I'd* do. Who ever heard of a state prisoner escaping by a hickory-bark ladder? Why, it's just ridiculous."

"Well, all right, Tom, fix it your own way. But if you'll take my advice, you'd let me borrow a sheet off the clothes line."

He said that would do. And that gave him another idea, and he says, "Borrow a shirt, too."

"What do we want of a shirt, Tom?"

"Want it for Jim to keep a journal on."

"Journal your granny. *Jim* can't write."

"Suppose he *can't* write. He can make marks on the shirt, can't he? We'll make him a pen out of an old pewter spoon, or a piece of an old iron barrel hoop."

"Why, Tom, we can pull a feather out of a goose and make him a better one. And quicker, too."

"*Prisoners* don't have geese running around the dungeon-keep to pull pens out of, you muggins. They *always* make their pens out of the hardest, toughest, troublesomest piece of old brass candlestick. Or they use something like that that they can get their hands on.

"It takes them weeks and weeks and months and months

to file it out, too. They've got to do it by rubbing it on the wall. *They* wouldn't use a goose quill if they had it. It ain't regular."

"Well, then, what'll we make him the ink out of?"

"Many makes it out of iron rust and tears. But only the common sort and women do that. The best authorities uses their own blood. Jim can do that.

"When he wants, he can send any little common ordinary mysterious message to let the world know where he's captive. He can write that on the bottom of a tin plate with a fork. Then he can throw it out of the window. The Iron Mask[6] always done that. And it's a blamed good way, too."

"Jim ain't got no tin plate. They feed him in a pan."

"That ain't nothing. We can get him some."

"Ain't nobody can *read* his plates."

"That ain't got anything to *do* with it, Huck Finn. All *he's* got to do is to write on the plate and throw it out. You don't *have* to be able to read it. Why, half the time you can't read anything a prisoner writes. Not on a tin plate or anywhere else."

"Well, then what's the sense in wasting the plates?"

"Why, blame it all, it ain't the *prisoner's* plates."

"But it's *somebody's* plates, ain't it?"

"Well, suppose it is? What does the *prisoner* care whose—"

He broke off there, because we heard the breakfast horn blowing. So we cleared out for the house.

Along during the morning, I borrowed a sheet and a white shirt off of the clothes line. I found an old sack and put them in it. And we went down and got the fox fire, and put that in too.

I called it borrowing, because that was what Pap always called it. But Tom said it warn't borrowing, it was stealing. He said we was representing prisoners. And prisoners don't care how they get a thing. Just so they get it. Nobody don't blame them for it, either.

It ain't no crime in a prisoner to steal the thing he needs to get away with, Tom said. It's his right. And so, as long as we was representing a prisoner, we had a perfect right to steal anything on this place. We just had to have the least use for it to

---

6 The Man in the Iron Mask was the hero of Alexandre Dumas' *The Viscount of Bragelonne* (1848-50).

get ourselves out of prison with.

He said if we warn't prisoners, it would be a very different thing. Nobody but a mean, ornery person would steal when he warn't a prisoner. So we figured we would steal everything there was that come handy.

And yet he made a mighty fuss one day after that. I stole a watermelon out of the nigger patch and eat it. He made me go and give the niggers a dime without telling them what it was for.

Tom said that what he meant was, we could steal anything we *needed.* Well, I said, I needed the watermelon. But he said I didn't need it to get out of prison with. There's where the difference was. He said it would have been all right if I'd have wanted it to hide a knife in. I could smuggle it to Jim to kill the seneschal with.

So I let it go at that. But I couldn't see no advantage in my representing a prisoner. Not if I had to set down and chaw over a lot of gold-leaf **distinctions** like that every time I see a chance to hog a watermelon.

Well, as I was saying, we waited that morning till everybody was settled down to business. Nobody was in sight around the yard. Then Tom carried the sack into the lean-to. I stood off a piece to keep watch.

By and by, he come out. We went and set down on the woodpile to talk. He says, "Everything's all right now except tools. That's easy fixed."

"Tools?" I says.

"Yes."

"Tools for what?"

"Why, to dig with. We ain't a-goin' to *gnaw* him out, are we?"

I says, "Ain't them old crippled picks and things in there good enough to dig a nigger out with?"

He turns on me, looking pitying enough to make a body cry. He says, "Huck Finn, did you *ever* hear of a prisoner having picks and shovels? Did he ever have all the modern **conveniences** in his wardrobe to dig himself out with?

"Have you got any senses in you at all? Now I want to ask you, what kind of a chance would *that* give him to be a hero?

Why, they might as well lend him the key and be done with it.

"Picks and shovels—why, they wouldn't furnish 'em to a king."

"Well, then," I says, "we don't want the picks and shovels. So what do we want?"

"A couple of kitchen knives."

"To dig the foundations out from under that cabin with?"

"Yes."

"Confound it, it's foolish, Tom."

"It don't make no difference how foolish it is. It's the *right* way. And it's the regular way. There ain't no *other* way, that ever *I* heard of. And I've read all the books that gives any information about these things.

"They always dig out with a kitchen knife. And not through dirt, mind you. Generally it's through solid rock. And it takes them weeks and weeks and weeks, and for ever and ever.

"Why, look at one of them prisoners. He was in the bottom dungeon of Castle Deef, in the harbor of Marseilles.[7]

He dug himself out that way. How long was he at it, you reckon?"

"I don't know."

"Well, guess."

"I don't know. A month and a half."

"*Thirty-seven years*—and he come out in China. That's the kind. I wish the bottom of *this* fortress was solid rock."

"*Jim* don't know nobody in China."

"What's *that* got to do with it? Neither did that other fellow. But you're always a-wanderin' off on a side issue. Why can't you stick to the main point?"

"All right, *I* don't care where he comes out. Just so he *comes* out. And Jim don't either, I reckon. But there's one thing, anyway. Jim's too old to be dug out with a kitchen knife. He won't last."

"Yes, he will *last,* too. You don't reckon it's going to take thirty-seven years to dig him out, do you? Not through a *dirt* foundation?"

7 In Alexandre Dumas' *The Count of Monte Cristo*, the hero escapes from the Chateau d'If on an island in the Marseilles harbor.

"How long will it take, Tom?"

"Well, we can't risk being as long as we ought to. It may not take very long for Uncle Silas to hear from down there by New Orleans. He'll hear Jim ain't from there. Then his next move will be to advertise Jim, or something like that.

"So we can't risk being as long digging him out as we ought to. By rights, I reckon we ought to be a couple of years. But we can't.

"Things being so uncertain, what I recommend is this. That we really dig right in, as quick as we can. After that, we can *let on,* to ourselves, that we was at it thirty-seven years. Then we can snatch him out and rush him away the first time there's an alarm. Yes, I reckon that'll be the best way."

"Now, there's *sense* in that," I says. "Letting on don't cost nothing. Letting on ain't no trouble. If it's any object, I don't mind letting on we was at it a hundred and fifty years.

"It wouldn't strain me none, after I got my hand in. So I'll mosey along now, and steal a couple of kitchen knives."

"Steal three," he says. "We want one to make a saw out of."

"Tom, I hope it ain't unregular and wicked to suggest it," I says. "But there's an old rusty saw blade around yonder. It's sticking under the weatherboarding behind the smokehouse."

Tom looked kind of weary and discouraged, and says, "It ain't no use to try to learn you nothing, Huck. Run along and steal the knives—three of them." So I done it.

Chapter 36

Trying to Help Jim

VOCABULARY PREVIEW

The following words appear in this chapter. Review the list and get to know the words before you read the chapter.

hearty—strong; brave
keeled—passed out; fainted
principle—high standards; knowledge of right and wrong
sociable—friendly

We waited till we reckoned everybody was asleep that night. Then we went down the lightning rod, and shut ourselves up in the lean-to. We got out our pile of fox fire, and went to work.

We cleared everything out of the way, about four or five foot along the middle of the bottom log. Tom said we was right behind Jim's bed now. We'd dig in under it.

He said when we got through there, nobody in the cabin would ever know there was a hole there. Jim's bedspread hung down most to the ground. You'd have to raise it up and look under to see the hole.

So we dug and dug with the kitchen knives till most midnight. Then we was dog-tired, and our hands was blistered. And yet you couldn't see we'd done anything, hardly.

At last I says, "This ain't no thirty-seven-year job. This is a thirty-eight-year job, Tom Sawyer."

He never said nothing. But he sighed, and pretty soon he stopped digging. For a good little while, I knowed that he was thinking. Then he says, "It ain't no use, Huck. It ain't a-goin' to work. If we was prisoners it would.

"Then we'd have as many years as we wanted, and no hurry. And we wouldn't get but a few minutes to dig, every day, while they was changing watches. So our hands wouldn't get blistered.

"We could keep it up right along, year in and year out. We

could do it right, and the way it ought to be done. But *we* can't fool along. We got to rush. We ain't got no time to spare.

"We can't put in another night this way. If we did, we'd have to knock off for a week to let our hands get well. We couldn't touch a kitchen knife with them sooner."

"Well, then, what we going to do, Tom?"

"I'll tell you. It ain't right, and it ain't moral, and I wouldn't like it to get out. But there ain't only just the one way. We got to dig him out with the picks. We'll *let on* it's kitchen knives."

"Now you're *talking!"* I says. "Your head gets leveler and leveler all the time, Tom Sawyer," I says. "Picks is the thing, moral or not moral.

"As for me, I don't care shucks for the morality of it, nohow. It's like when I start in to steal a nigger, or a watermelon, or a Sunday school book. I ain't no ways particular how it's done so it's done.

"What I want is my nigger. What I want is my watermelon. What I want is my Sunday school book. So what if a pick's the handiest thing? Then that's the thing I'm a-goin' to dig that nigger or that watermelon or that Sunday school book out with. I don't give a dead rat what the authorities thinks about it, neither."

"Well," Tom says, "there's an excuse for picks and letting on in a case like this. If it warn't so, I wouldn't approve of it. Nor I wouldn't stand by and see the rules broke. Right is right, and wrong is wrong. A body ain't got no business doing wrong when he ain't ignorant and knows better.

"It might answer for *you* to dig Jim out with a pick, *without* letting on. You don't know no better. But it wouldn't for me, because I do know better. Give me a kitchen knife."

He had his own by him, but I handed him mine. He flung it down, and says, "Give me a *kitchen knife.*"

I didn't know just what to do—but then I thought. I scratched around amongst the old tools. I got a pickax and give it to him. He took it and went to work, and never said a word.

He was always just that particular. Full of **principle**.

So then I got a shovel. Then we picked and shoveled in turn, and made the fur fly. We stuck to it about a half an hour. That was as long as we could stand up. But we had a good deal of a hole to show for it.

When I got upstairs, I looked out at the window. I saw Tom doing his level best with the lightning rod. But he couldn't come up it, his hands was so sore. At last he says, "It ain't no use, it can't be done. What you reckon I better do? Can't you think of no way?"

"Yes," I says, "but I reckon it ain't regular. Come up the stairs, and let on it's a lightning rod."

So he done it.

Next day, Tom stole a pewter spoon and a brass candlestick in the house. These were for to make some pens for Jim out of. And he took six tallow candles.

I hung around the nigger cabins and laid for a chance. At last I stole three tin plates. Tom says it wasn't enough. But I said nobody wouldn't ever see the plates that Jim throwed out. They'd fall in the dog fennel[1] and jimsonweeds under the window hole. Then we could tote them back and he could use them over again. So Tom was satisfied.

Then he says, "Now, the thing to study out is, how to get the things to Jim."

"Take them in through the hole," I says, "when we get it done."

He only just looked scornful. He said something about nobody ever heard of such an idiotic idea. Then he went to studying. By and by, he said he had figured out two or three ways. But there warn't no need to decide on any of them yet. Said we'd got to reach Jim first.

That night, we went down the lightning rod a little after ten. We took one of the candles along. We listened under the window hole, and heard Jim snoring. So we pitched it in, and it didn't wake him. Then we whirled in with the pick and shovel. In about two hours and a half, the job was done.

We crept in under Jim's bed and into the cabin. We pawed around and found the candle and lit it. We stood over Jim awhile, and found him looking **hearty** and healthy. Then we woke him up gentle and little by little.

---

1 *Dog fennel* is a kind of herb.

He was so glad to see us, he most cried. He called us honey, and all the pet names he could think of. He was for having us hunt up a cold chisel to cut the chain off of his leg with right away. Then we could clear out without losing any time.

But Tom showed him how unregular it would be. He set down and told him all about our plans. He told how we could alter them in a minute any time there was an alarm. He said not to be the least afraid. We would see he got away, *sure.*

So Jim, he said it was all right. We set there and talked over old times awhile. Then Tom asked a lot of questions. Jim told him Uncle Silas come in every day or two to pray with him, and Aunt Sally come in to see if he was comfortable and had plenty to eat. Both of them was kind as they could be.

Tom says, "Now I know how to fix it. We'll send you some things by them."

I said, "Don't do nothing of the kind. It's one of the most jackass ideas I ever struck."

But he never paid no attention to me. He went right on. It was his way when he'd got his plans set. So he told Jim how we'd have to smuggle in the rope ladder pie and other large things by Nat, the nigger that fed him. Jim must be on the lookout, and not be surprised. He must not let Nat see him open them.

We would also put small things in Uncle's coat pockets. Jim must steal them out. We would tie things to Aunt's apron strings or put them in her apron pocket, if we got a chance. Tom told him what they would be and what they was for.

And he told him how to keep a journal on the shirt with his blood, and all that. He told him everything.

Jim, he couldn't see no sense in the most of it. But he figured we was white folks and knowed better than him. So he was satisfied. He said he would do it all just as Tom said.

Jim had plenty corncob pipes and tobacco. So we had a right down good **sociable** time. Then we crawled out through the hole, and so home to bed. Our hands looked like they'd been chawed.

Tom was in high spirits. He said it was the best fun he ever had in his life, and the most intellectual. He said he wished he could see his way to it. Then we would keep it up all the rest of our lives. We would leave Jim to our children to get out. He believed Jim would come to like it better and better the more he got used to it.

He said that in that way, it could be strung out as much as eighty years. Then it would be the best time on record. And he said it would make us all celebrated that had a hand in it.

In the morning, we went out to the woodpile. We chopped up the brass candlestick into handy sizes. Tom put them and the pewter spoon in his pocket.

Then we went to the nigger cabins. I drew Nat's attention away. Then Tom shoved a piece of candlestick into the middle of the corn pone that was in Jim's pan.

We went along with Nat to see how it would work. It just worked noble. When Jim bit into it, it most mashed all his teeth out. There warn't ever anything could have worked better. Tom said so himself.

Jim, he never let on but what it was only just a piece of rock. Or maybe something like that that's always getting into bread, you know. But after that, he never bit right into nothing. He jabbed his fork into it three or four places first. While we was a-standin' there in the dimmish light, here comes a couple of the hounds, bulging in from under Jim's bed. They kept on piling in till there was eleven of them. There warn't hardly room in there to get your breath.

By jings, we forgot to fasten that lean-to door! The nigger Nat, he only just hollered "Witches" once. And he keeled over onto the floor amongst the dogs. He begun to groan like he was dying.

Tom jerked the door open and flung out a slab of Jim's meat. The dogs went for it. In two seconds, he was out himself and back again and shut the door. I knowed he'd fixed the other door, too.

Then he went to work on the nigger. He coaxed him and petted him. He asked him if he'd been imagining he saw something again. Nat raised up, and blinked his eyes around.

Nat says, "Master Sid, you'll say I's a fool. But I see most a million dogs, or devils, or something. I wish I may die right here in my tracks if I don't believe I did. I did, most surely. Master

Sid, felt 'em. *I felt* 'em, sah. Dey was all over me.

"Dad-fetched, I just wish I could git my hands on one of dem witches just once. Only just once. It's all *I'd* ask. But mostly I wish dey'd let me alone, I does."

Tom says, "Well, I tell you what *I* think. What makes them come here just at this runaway nigger's breakfast time? It's because they're hungry, that's the reason. You make them a witch pie. That's the thing for *you* to do."

"But my land, Master Sid. How's I goin' to make 'em a witch pie? I don't know how to make it. I ain't ever heard of such a thing before."

"Well, then, I'll have to make it myself."

"Will you do it, honey? Will you? I'll worship de ground under your foot, I will!"

"All right, I'll do it, seeing it's you. You've been mighty good to us and showed us the runaway nigger. But you got to be mighty careful. When we come around, you turn your back. Then whatever we've put in the pan, don't let on you see it at all.

"And don't you look when Jim unloads the pan. Something might happen, I don't know what. And above all, don't you *handle* the witch things."

"Handle 'em, Master Sid? What is you a-talkin' 'bout? I wouldn't lay de weight of my finger on 'em. Not for ten hundred thousand billion dollars, I wouldn't."

Chapter 37 (Summary)

Jim Gets His Witch Pie

Even before they sat down to breakfast, Huck and Tom were scheming. They stuck a nail into the band of Uncle Silas' hat and a spoon in his coat pocket for Jim to swipe later.

At the breakfast table, Aunt Sally was in a foul mood because so many household things were missing. She remarked that the rats could be blamed for taking the candles. But she wondered about Uncle Silas' lost shirt and the spoon and all the other things. Huck felt mighty uncomfortable listening to her. But he kept quiet about what he knew.

Later Tom and Huck built a fire in the woods and baked a "witch pie" for the rope ladder. They put the pie and some tin plates on Jim's tray, and Nat carried it in to him. As directed by Tom, Jim hid the ladder, used the nail to put some nonsense marks on a plate, and threw the plate out the window.

Chapter 38 (Summary)

"Here a Captive Heart Busted"

Tom's elaborate scheme for Jim's "proper" escape grew even more complex. According to Tom, captives *always* scribbled messages on prison walls, so Jim must too. Jim wasn't thrilled with the idea. For one thing, he didn't even know how to write. But he went along with it to please Tom.

Tom set about making up a fitting message and coat of arms for Jim to scratch onto the wall. He came up with several ridiculous sayings, among them "Here a captive heart busted." Then Tom figured that log walls weren't good enough. Jim must carve all this into stone. So Tom and Huck, along with Jim (who could easily leave his prison at any time), lugged a large grindstone from the mill to the cabin.

But Tom wasn't finished with Jim yet. If Jim was to be a "noble" prisoner, he must have spiders and rats and snakes to keep him company. And he must tame them all and entertain them with music from a Jew's harp.

No amount of pleading from Jim could convince Tom to abandon this frightful plan. At last, Tom lost patience with him. He scolded Jim for not appreciating the chance to become a famous prisoner. Jim apologized, and Huck and Tom headed for bed.

Chapter 39 (Summary)

Tom Writes Nonnamous Letters

In the morning Huck and Tom captured some rats and garter snakes for Jim. But the creatures managed to get loose inside the house, causing Aunt Sally to be jumpy for days.

Tom and Huck trapped more rats and snakes. They delivered the creatures to Jim's cabin, along with a variety of spiders, bugs, and frogs. After a time, Jim could hardly stand it in the cabin. It was especially awful at night. Then the animals and insects took turns tormenting him while he tried to sleep.

Tom, on the other hand, felt everything was moving along well. But he sped up his plan when he heard Uncle Silas was going to advertise Jim in the St. Louis and New Orleans newspapers. Tom decided it was time for the anonymous letters.

The first letter that Huck secretly delivered to the family merely warned of upcoming trouble. The second letter was more to the point. The "author" was a member of a gang that planned to steal Jim. The writer claimed that the theft was to be pulled off that night.

These letters weren't all that frightened Uncle Silas' family. The pictures of a skull and crossbones and a coffin that Tom and Huck left around gave the family a huge case of the jitters.

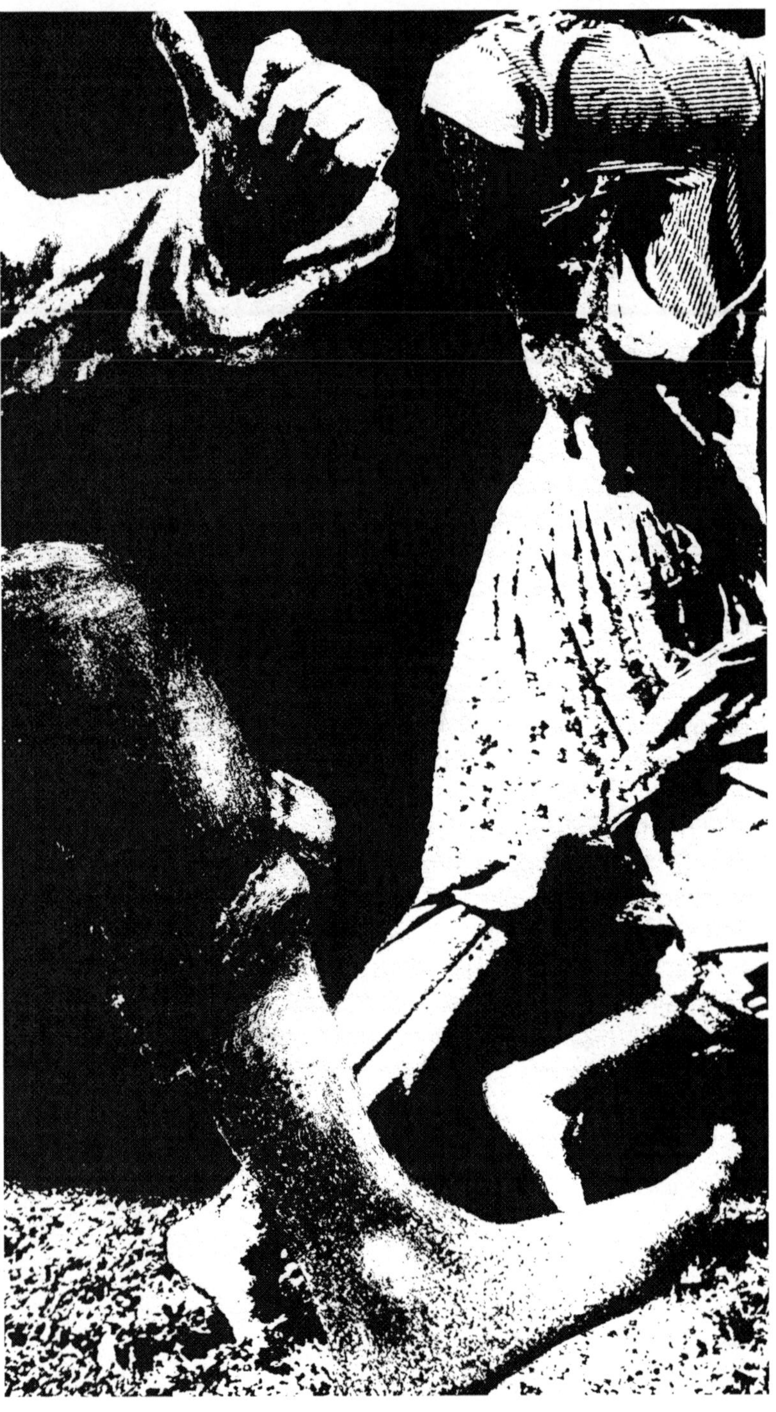

Chapter 40

A Mixed-up and Splendid Rescue

VOCABULARY PREVIEW

The following words appear in this chapter. Review the list and get to know the words before you read the chapter.

anxious—worried; troubled
consulting—considering; talking over
desperadoes—criminals; gangsters
elegant—grand; superior
evasion—escape; flight
stealthily—quietly; secretly

We was feeling pretty good after breakfast. We took my canoe and went over the river a-fishin', with a lunch. We had a good time, and took a look at the raft and found her all right.

We got home late to supper. We found them in such a sweat and worry, they didn't know which end they was standing on. They made us go right off to bed the minute we was done supper.

They wouldn't tell us what the trouble was. They never let on a word about the new letter. But they didn't need to. We knowed as much about it as anybody did.

As soon as we was half upstairs and Aunt Sally's back was turned, we slid for the cellar cupboard. We loaded up a good lunch and took it up to our room and went to bed.

We got up about half past eleven. Tom put on Aunt Sally's dress that he stole and was going to start with the lunch, but says, "Where's the butter?"

"I laid out a hunk of it," I says, "on a piece of corn pone."

"Well, you *left* it laid out, then. It ain't here."

"We can get along without it," I says.

"We can get along *with* it, too," he says. "Just you slide down cellar and fetch it. And then mosey right down the lightning rod and come along.

"I'll go and stuff the straw into Jim's clothes to represent his mother in disguise. I'll be ready to *ba* like a sheep and shove soon as you get there."[1]

So out he went, and down cellar went I. The hunk of butter, big as a person's fist, was where I had left it. So I took up the slab of corn pone with it on. I blowed out my light, and started upstairs very sneaky.

I got up to the main floor all right, but here comes Aunt Sally with a candle. I clapped the truck in my hat, and clapped my hat on my head.

The next second she see me, and she says, "You been down cellar?"

"Yes ma'am."

"What you been doing down there?"

"Nothin'."

"Nothin'!"

"No ma'am."

"Well, then, what possessed you to go down there this time of night?"

"I don't know, ma'am."

"You don't *know?* Don't answer me that way. Tom, I want to know what you been *doing* down there."

"I ain't been doing a single thing, Aunt Sally. I hope to gracious if I have."

I reckoned she'd let me go now, and as a general thing she would. But I suppose there was too many strange things going on. She was just in a sweat about every little thing that warn't yardstick straight.

So she says, very decided, "You just march into that setting room and stay there till I come. You been up to something you had no business to. I bet I'll find out what it is before *I'm* done with you."

So she went away as I opened the door and walked into the setting room. My, but there was a crowd there! Fifteen farmers,

---

1 In chapter 39, Tom added Jim's mother to the escape plan. Tom claimed that it was routine for the prisoner's mother to change clothes with the prisoner and stay in the prisoner's place. And in one of the anonymous letters, Tom informed the Phelpses that the sheep's "ba" was the signal that the gang members were in the cabin stealing Jim.

and every one of them had a gun. I was most powerful sick, and slunk to a chair and set down.

They was setting around, some of them talking a little, in a low voice. All of them were fidgety and uneasy. They tried to look like they warn't, but I knowed they was. They was always taking off their hats, and putting them on. And they was scratching their heads, and changing their seats, and fumbling with their buttons.

I warn't easy myself. But I didn't take my hat off, all the same. I did wish Aunt Sally would come and get done with me. She could lick me if she wanted to. Then I could get away and tell Tom how we'd overdone this thing.

We'd gotten ourselves into a thundering hornet's nest. So we should stop fooling around straight off. We should clear out with Jim before these rips got out of patience and come for us.

At last she come and begun to ask me questions. But I *couldn't* answer them straight. I didn't know which end of me was up.

These men was in a real fidget now. Some of them was wanting to start right *now* and lay for them **desperadoes**. They said it warn't but a few minutes to midnight. Others was trying to get them to hold on and wait for the sheep signal.

And here was Aunty pegging away at the questions. I was a-shakin' all over and ready to sink down in my tracks. I was that scared. The place was getting hotter and hotter. The butter begun to melt and run down my neck and behind my ears.

Pretty soon, one of them says, *"I'm* for going and getting in the *cabin first* and right *now.* We'll catch them when they come."

I most dropped. A streak of butter come a-tricklin' down my forehead. Aunt Sally, she sees it, and turns white as a sheet. She says, "For the land's sake, what is the matter with the child? He's got the brain fever as sure as you're born. And they're oozing out!"

And everybody runs to see, and she snatches off my hat. Out comes the bread and what was left of the butter.

She grabbed me, and hugged me, and says, "Oh, what a turn you did give me! And how glad and grateful I am it ain't no worse. For luck's against us, and it never rains but it pours.

"When I see that truck, I thought we'd lost you. For I knowed by the color and all it was just like your brains would be if—

"Dear, dear," says she. "Why didn't you *tell* me that was what you'd been down there for. *I* wouldn't have cared. Now clear out to bed, and don't let me see no more of you till morning!"

I was upstairs in a second, and down the lightning rod in another one. I took off through the dark for the lean-to.

I couldn't hardly get no words out, I was so **anxious**. But I told Tom as quick as I could we must jump for it now. We didn't have a minute to lose. The house was full of men, yonder, with guns!

His eyes just blazed, and he says, "No! Is that so? *Ain't* it bully! Why, Huck, if it was to do over again, I bet I could fetch two hundred! If we could put it off till—"

"Hurry! *Hurry!*" I says. "Where's Jim?"

"Right at your elbow. If you reach out your arm, you can touch him. He's dressed, and everything's ready. Now we'll slide out and give the sheep signal."

But then we heard the tramp of men coming to the door. We heard them begin to fumble with the padlock.

A man said, "I *told* you we'd be too soon. They haven't come. The door is locked. Here, I'll lock some of you in the cabin. You lay for 'em in the dark, and kill 'em when they come. The rest scatter around a piece. Listen if you can hear 'em coming."

So in they come, but couldn't see us in the dark. They most trod on us whilst we was hustling to get under the bed. But we got under all right, and out through the hole, swift and soft. Jim went first, me next, and Tom last. This was according to Tom's orders.

Now we was in the lean-to, and heard trampings close by outside. So we crept to the door. Tom stopped us there and put his eye to the crack. But he couldn't make out nothing, it was so dark.

He whispered and said he would listen for the steps to get further. When he nudged us, Jim must glide out first, and him last. So he set his ear to the crack and listened, and listened, and listened.

The steps was a-scrapin' around out there all the time. At last he nudged us. We slid out and stooped down, not breathing, and not making the least noise. We slipped **stealthily** towards the fence in Injun file.

We got to it all right, and me and Jim over it. But Tom's britches catched fast on a splinter on the top rail. Then he hear the steps coming, so he had to pull loose. That snapped the splinter and made a noise. As he dropped in our tracks and started, somebody sings out, "Who's that? Answer, or I'll shoot!"

But we didn't answer. We just took off quick as we could. Then there was a rush, and a *bang, bang, bang!* The bullets fairly whizzed around us. We heard them sing out, "Here they are! They've broke for the river! After 'em, boys, and turn loose the dogs!"

So here they come, full speed. We could hear them because they wore boots and yelled. But we didn't wear no boots and didn't yell.

We was in the path to the mill. When they got pretty close onto us, we dodged into the bush and let them go by. Then we dropped in behind them.

They'd had all the dogs shut up, so they wouldn't scare off the robbers. But by this time, somebody had let them loose. Here they come, making powwow enough for a million.

But they was our dogs. So we stopped in our tracks till they catched up. Then they see it warn't nobody but us, and no excitement to offer them. So they only just said howdy, and tore right ahead towards the shouting and clattering.

Then we got energy again. We whizzed along after them till we was nearly to the mill. Then we struck up through the bush to where my canoe was tied. We hopped in and pulled for dear life towards the middle of the river. We didn't make no more noise than we was obliged to.

Then we struck out, easy and comfortable, for the island where my raft was. We could hear them yelling and barking at each other all up and down the bank. Then we was so far away, the sounds got dim and died out.

When we stepped onto the raft, I says, "*Now,* old Jim, you're a free man *again.* And I bet you won't ever be a slave no more."

"En' a mighty good job it was, too, Huck. It was planned beautiful, en' it was *done* beautiful. En' there ain't *nobody* can git up a plan dat's more mixed up en' splendid den what dat one was."

We was all glad as we could be. But Tom was the gladdest of all because he had a bullet in the calf of his leg.

When me and Jim heard that, we didn't feel as brash as what we did before. It was hurting him considerable and bleeding. So we laid him in the wigwam. We tore up one of the duke's shirts for to bandage him.

But he says, "Give me the rags. I can do it myself. Don't stop now. Don't fool around here, and the **evasion** moving along so handsome. Man the sweeps, and set her loose!

"Boys," Tom says, "we done it **elegant**! 'Deed we did. I wish *we'd* have had a part of Louis XVI's escape. There wouldn't have been no 'Son of Saint Louis, ascend to heaven!'[2] wrote down in *his* biography.

"No sir, we'd have whooped him over the *border.* That's what we'd have done with *him.* We'd have done it just as slick as nothing at all, too. Man the sweeps—man the sweeps!"

But me and Jim was **consulting**—and thinking. And after we'd thought a minute, I says, "Say it, Jim."

So he says, "Well, den, dis is de way it look to me, Huck. If it was *him* dat was bein' set free, en' one of de boys was to get shot, would he say, 'Go on en' save '*em.* Never mind 'bout a doctor for to save dis one'?

"Is dat like Master Tom Sawyer? Would he say dat? You *bet* he wouldn't! *Well,* den, is *Jim* goin' to say it? No, sah. I don't budge a step out of dis place without a *doctor.* Not if it's forty years!"

I knowed he was white inside, and I reckoned he'd say what he did say. So it was all right now. I told Tom I was a-goin' for a doctor.

He raised considerable fuss about it. But me and Jim stuck to it and wouldn't budge. He was for crawling out and setting the raft loose himself. But we wouldn't let him. Then he give us a piece of his mind, but it didn't do no good.

2 Louis XVI was said to have made this statement before he was put to death in 1793.

So when he sees me getting the canoe ready, he says, "Well, then, if you're bound to go, I'll tell you what to do when you get to the village. Shut the door and blindfold the doctor tight and fast. Make him swear to be as silent as the grave.

"Then put a purse full of gold in his hand. Take and lead him all around the back alleys and everywheres in the dark. Then fetch him here in the canoe, in a roundabout way amongst the islands.

"Search him and take his chalk away from him. Don't give it back to him till you get him back to the village. Or else he will chalk this raft so he can find it again. It's the way they all do."

So I said I would, and left. Jim was to hide in the woods when he saw the doctor coming till he was gone again.

Chapter 41

"Must 'A' Been Spirits"

VOCABULARY PREVIEW

The following words appear in this chapter. Review the list and get to know the words before you read the chapter.

faculties—abilities
fluster—confusion
singular—unusual; unique
tedious—detailed

The doctor was an old man—a very nice, kind-looking old man—when I got him up. I told him me and my brother was over on Spanish Island hunting yesterday afternoon. We camped on a piece of a raft we found.

About midnight, my brother must have kicked his gun in his dreams. It went off and shot him in the leg. I said we wanted him to go over there and fix it. But we didn't want him to say nothing about it, nor let anybody know. We wanted to come home this evening and surprise the folks.

"Who is your folks?" he says.

"The Phelpses, down yonder."

"Oh," he says. And after a minute, he says, "How'd you say he got shot?"

"He had a dream," I says, "and it shot him."

"**Singular** dream," he says.

So he lit up his lantern, and got his saddlebags, and we started. But when he saw the canoe, he didn't like the look of her. He said she was big enough for one, but didn't look pretty safe for two.

I says, "Oh, you needn't be afeard, sir. She carried the three of us easy enough."

"What three?"

"Why, me and Sid, and—and—and *the guns*. That's what I mean."

"Oh," he says.

But he put his foot on the gunnel[1] and rocked her. He shook his head, and said he reckoned he'd look around for a bigger one.

But they was all locked and chained. So he took my canoe, and said for me to wait till he come back. Or he said I could hunt around further. Or maybe I better go down home and get them ready for the surprise if I wanted to.

But I said I didn't. So I told him just how to find the raft. Then he started.

I struck an idea pretty soon. I says to myself, supposin' he can't fix that leg just in three shakes of a sheep's tail, as the saying is? Supposin' it takes him three or four days? What are we going to do? Lay around there till he lets the cat out of the bag?

No, sir. I know what *I'll* do. I'll wait until he comes back. If he says he's got to go back again, I'll get down there, too, if I swim.

And we'll take and tie him, and keep him, and shove out down the river. When Tom's done with him, we'll give him what it's worth, or all we got. Then we'll let him get ashore.

So then I crept into a lumber pile to get some sleep. Next time I waked up, the sun was way up over my head! I shot out and went for the doctor's house. But they told me he'd gone away in the night some time or other. They said he warn't back yet.

Well, thinks I, that looks powerful bad for Tom. I'll dig out for the island right off. So away I shoved. I turned the corner, and nearly rammed my head into Uncle Silas' stomach!

He says, "Why, *Tom!* Where you been all this time, you rascal?"

"I ain't been nowheres," I says. "Only just hunting for the runaway nigger—me and Sid."

"Why, where ever did you go?" he says. "Your aunt's been mighty uneasy."

"She needn't," I says, "because we was all right. We

---

1 A *gunnel* is more commonly known as a gunwale. In this case, it is the upper edge or rail of a small boat.

followed the men and the dogs. But they outrun us, and we lost them. But we thought we heard them on the water. So we got a canoe and took out after them and crossed over. But we couldn't find nothing of them.

"So we cruised along upshore till we got kind of tired and beat out. We tied up the canoe and went to sleep. And we never waked up till about an hour ago.

"Then we paddled over here to hear the news. Sid's at the post office to see what he can hear. I'm a-branchin' out to get something to eat for us. Then we're going home."

So then we went to the post office to get "Sid." But just as I suspected, he warn't there. So the old man, he got a letter out of the office. We waited awhile longer, but Sid didn't come.

So the old man said, come along. Let Sid foot it home, or canoe it, when he got done fooling around. But we would ride. I couldn't get him to let me stay and wait for Sid. He said there warn't no use in it. He said I must come along and let Aunt Sally see we was all right.

When we got home, Aunt Sally was that glad to see me. She laughed and cried both, and hugged me. And she give me one of them lickings of hers that don't amount to shucks. She said she'd serve Sid the same when he come.

And the place was plumb full of farmers and farmers' wives, to dinner. Such another chattering a body never heard. Old Mrs. Hotchkiss was the worst. Her tongue was a-goin' all the time.

She says, "Well, Sister Phelps, I've ransacked that there cabin over. And I believe the nigger was crazy. I says to Sister Damrell—didn't I, Sister Damrell?—He's crazy.

"Them's the very words I said. You all heard me. He's crazy. Everything shows it. Look at that there grindstone.

"Want to tell *me* that that creature's in his right mind? After scribbling all them crazy things onto a grindstone?

"Here such and such a person busted his heart. And here so and so pegged along for thirty-seven years, and all that. Natural son of Louis somebody, and such everlastin' rubbish.

"He's plumb crazy. It's what I says in the first place. It's what I says in the middle. And it's what I says last and all the time. The nigger's crazy. He's crazy as Nebokoodneezer."[2]

"And look at that there ladder made out of rags, Sister Hotchkiss," says old Mrs. Damrell. "What in the name of goodness *could* he ever want of—"

"The very words I was a-sayin' no longer ago than this minute to Sister Utterback. And she'll tell you so herself. Look at that there rag ladder. *Look* at it. What *could* he have wanted of it, Sister Hotchkiss?"

"But how in the nation'd they ever *git* that grindstone *in* there, *anyway?* And who dug that there *hole?* And who—"

"My very *words,* Brother Penrod! I was a-sayin'—pass that there saucer of molasses, won't you?—I was saying to Sister Dunlap, just this minute, how *did* they git that grindstone in there? Without *help,* mind you. Without *help!*

"There's where 'tis. Don't tell *me,* says I. There *was* help, says I. And there was *aplenty* help, too, says I. There been a *dozen* a-helpin' that nigger. And I bet I'd skin every last nigger on this place but I'd find out who done it, says I. And moreover, says I—"

"A *dozen* says you! *Forty* couldn't have done everything that's been done. Look at them kitchen knife saws and things. Look how **tedious** they've been made. Look at that bed leg sawed off with 'em—a week's work for six men. Look at that nigger made out of straw on the bed. And look at—"

"You may *well* say it, Brother Hightower! It's just as I was a-sayin' to Brother Phelps, his own self. Says he, 'What do *you* think of it, Sister Hotchkiss?' Think of what, Brother Phelps? says I. 'Think of that bed leg sawed off that way?' says he.

"*Think* of it? says I. I lay it never sawed *itself* off, says I. Somebody *sawed* it, says I. That's my opinion, take it or leave it. It may not be of no account, says I. But such as 'tis, it's my opinion, says I. And if anybody can start a better one, let him *do* it, I says to Sister Dunlap—"

"Why, dog my cats. There must have been a houseful of niggers in there every night. Every night for four weeks to have done all that work, Sister Phelps.

---

2 By *Nebokoodneezer,* Mrs. Hotchkiss really means "Nebuchadnezzar," a king of ancient Babylon. The Bible says that he went made and then ate grass like an ox.

"Look at that shirt. Every last inch of it was covered over with secret African writing done with blood! Must have been a raft of 'em at it right along, all the time, almost. Why, I'd give two dollars to have it read to me. And as for the niggers that wrote it, I reckon I'd take and lash 'em till—"

"People to *help* him, Brother Marples! Well, I reckon you'd *think* so if you'd have been in this house for a while back. Why, they've stole everything they could lay their hands on. And we was a-watchin' all the time, mind you.

"They stole that shirt right off of the line! And what about that sheet they made the rag ladder out of? There ain't no telling how many times they *didn't* steal that.[3]

"And flour, and candles, and candlesticks, and spoons, and the old warming pan. There was most a thousand things that I don't remember now. And my new calico dress.

"And me and Silas and my Sid and Tom was on the constant watch day *and* night. Just as I was a-tellin' you. Not a one of us could catch hide nor hair nor sight nor sound of them.

"And here at the last minute, lo and behold you. They slides right in under our noses and fools us. And not only fools *us* but the Injun Territory robbers, too. They actually gets *away* with that nigger safe and sound. And that with sixteen men and twenty-two dogs right on their very heels at that very time!

"I tell you, it just beats anything I ever *heard* of. Why, *spirits* couldn't have done better and been no smarter. And I reckon they must have *been* spirits. Because *you* know our dogs. There ain't no better. Well, them dogs never even got on the *track* of 'em once! You explain *that* to me if you can! *Any* of you!"

"Well, it does beat—"

"Laws alive, I never—"

"So help me, I wouldn't have been—"

"*House* thieves as well as—"

"Goodness gracious sakes, I'd have been afeard to *live* in such a—"

" 'Fraid to *live!* Why, I was that scared, I didn't dare hardly

3 In chapter 37, Tom and Huck stole and replaced one of Aunt Sally's sheets over and over. This confused her to the point that she didn't know how many sheets she had, and she never knew if she was missing a sheet or not.

go to bed, or get up, or lay down, or *set* down, Sister Ridgeway. Why, they'd steal the very—why, goodness sakes, you can guess what kind of a **fluster** *I* was in by the time midnight come last night.

"I hope to gracious if I warn't afraid they'd steal some of the family! I was just at that point. I didn't have no reasoning **faculties** no more.

"It looks foolish enough *now,* in the daytime. But I says to myself, there's my two poor boys asleep, away upstairs in that lonesome room. And I declare to goodness I was that uneasy, that I crept up there and locked 'em in! I *did.*

"And anybody would. Because, you know, when you get scared that way, it keeps running on. And it gets worse and worse all the time. Your wits get confused. You get to doing all sorts of wild things.

"By and by, you think to yourself, supposin' I was a boy, and was away up there, and the door ain't locked, and you—"

She stopped, looking kind of wondering. Then she turned her head around slow. And when her eye lit on me—I got up and took a walk.

Says I to myself, I can't explain how we come to not be in that room this morning. So I'd better go out to one side and study over it a little. But I didn't dare go far, or she'd have sent for me.

It came to be late in the day and the people all went home. Then I come in and told her the noise and shooting waked up me and "Sid." The door was locked, and we wanted to see the fun. So we went down the lightning rod, and both of us got hurt a little. We didn't never want to try *that* no more.

And then I went on and told her all what I told Uncle Silas before. Then she said she'd forgive us. And maybe it was all right enough, anyway. It was about what a body might expect of boys. All boys was a pretty harum-scarum[4] lot as far as she could see.

She was glad no harm hadn't come of it. And she judged she better put in her time being grateful that we was alive and

4 *Harum-scarum* means "reckless" or "irresponsible."

well and she had us still. She wouldn't fret over what was past and done.

So then she kissed me, and patted me on the head. Then she dropped into a kind of thoughtful mood. And pretty soon she jumps up, and says, "Why, laws-a-mercy, it's most night, and Sid not come yet! What *has* become of that boy?"

I saw my chance, so I skips up and says, "I'll run right up to town and get him," I says.

"No, you won't," she says. "You'll stay right where you are. *One's* enough to be lost at a time. If he ain't here to supper, your uncle'll go."

Well, he warn't there to supper. So right after supper, Uncle Silas went. He come back about ten, a little bit uneasy. He hadn't run across Tom's track. Aunt Sally was a good *deal* uneasy. But Uncle Silas, he said there warn't no occasion to be.

"Boys will be boys," he said. "You'll see this one turn up in the morning all sound and right."

So she had to be satisfied. But she said she'd set up for him awhile anyway. She would keep a light burning so he could see it.

And then I went up to bed. She come up with me and brought her candle. She tucked me in and mothered me so good, I felt mean. I felt like I couldn't look her in the face.

She set down on the bed and talked with me a long time.

She said what a splendid boy Sid was. She didn't seem to want to ever stop talking about him. She kept asking me every now and then if I reckoned he could have got lost, or hurt, or maybe drownded.

She kept asking if I thought he might be laying at this minute somewheres suffering or dead, and she not by to help him. So the tears would drip down silent. And I would tell her that Sid was all right, and would be home in the morning, sure.

She would squeeze my hand, or maybe kiss me. She'd tell me to say it again, and keep on saying it. It done her good, and she was in so much trouble. And when she was going away, she looked down in my eyes so steady and gentle.

She says, "The door ain't going to be locked, Tom. And

there's the window and the rod. But you'll be good, *won't* you? And you won't go? For *my* sake."

Laws knows, I *wanted* to go bad enough to see about Tom. I was all intending to go. But after that, I wouldn't have went, not for kingdoms.

But she was on my mind and Tom was on my mind. So I slept very restless. And twice I went down the rod away in the night, and slipped around front. I saw her setting there by her candle in the window. Her eyes was towards the road and the tears in them.

I wished I could do something for her, but I couldn't. I could only swear that I wouldn't never do nothing to grieve her any more. And the third time I waked up at dawn, and slid down. She was there yet, and her candle was most out. Her old gray head was resting on her hands, and she was asleep.

Chapter 42

Why They Didn't Hang Jim

VOCABULARY PREVIEW

The following words appear in this chapter. Review the list and get to know the words before you read the chapter.

flighty—restless; nervous
scamp—rascal; troublemaker
sultry—very warm and uncomfortable
symptoms—signs; indications
tapering—decreasing; fading
yarn—story; tale

The old man was uptown again before breakfast. But he couldn't get no track of Tom. Both of them set at the table thinking, and not saying nothing. They was looking mournful, and their coffee getting cold. They warn't eating anything.

And by and by, the old man says, "Did I give you the letter?"

"What letter?"

"The one I got yesterday out of the post office."

"No, you didn't give me no letter."

"Well, I must have forgot it."

So he rummaged his pockets, then went off somewheres where he had laid it down. He fetched it and give it to her.

She says, "Why, it's from St. Petersburg. It's from Sis."

I figured another walk would do me good, but I couldn't stir. But before she could break it open, she dropped it and run. She saw something. And so did I. It was Tom Sawyer on a mattress. And that old doctor, too. And Jim, in *her* calico dress. He had his hands tied behind him. A lot of people were with them.

I hid the letter behind the first thing that come handy, and rushed. She flung herself at Tom, crying, and says, "Oh, he's dead, he's dead. I know he's dead!"

And Tom, he turned his head a little. He muttered something or other, which showed he warn't in his right mind. Then she flung up her hands, and says, "He's alive, thank God! And that's enough!"

And she snatched a kiss of him, and flew for the house to get the bed ready. She scattered orders right and left at the niggers and everybody else. She talked as fast as her tongue could go, every jump of the way.

I followed the men to see what they was going to do with Jim. The old doctor and Uncle Silas followed after Tom into the house.

The men was very huffy. Some of them wanted to hang Jim for an example to all the other niggers around there.

Then they wouldn't be trying to run away like Jim done. And they wouldn't be making such a raft[1] of trouble. Or keeping a whole family scared most to death for days and nights.

But the others said, don't do it. It wouldn't answer at all. They said, "He ain't our nigger. His owner will turn up and make us pay for him, sure."

So that cooled them down a little. Some people is always the most anxious for to hang a nigger that ain't done just right. But they're always the very ones that ain't the most anxious to pay for him. Not even after they've got their satisfaction out of him.

They cussed Jim considerable, though. They give him a cuff or two side of the head once in a while. But Jim never said nothing. He never let on to know me.

They took him to the same cabin, and put his own clothes on him, and chained him again. And not to no bed leg this time, but to a big staple drove into the bottom log.

They chained his hands, too, and both legs. They said he warn't to have nothing but bread and water to eat after this. Not till his owner come, or he was sold at auction because his owner didn't come in a certain length of time.

They filled up our hole. They said a couple of farmers with guns must stand watch around about the cabin every night. A bulldog would be tied to the door in the daytime.

---

1 *Raft* here means "large amount."

About this time, they was through with the job. They was **tapering** off with kind of general good-bye cussing. Then the old doctor comes and takes a look and says, "Don't be no rougher on him than you're obliged to. He ain't a bad nigger.

"When I got to where I found the boy, I saw I couldn't cut the bullet out without some help. But he warn't in no condition for me to leave to go and get help. And he got a little worse and a little worse.

"After a long time, he went out of his head. He wouldn't let me come near him any more. He said if I chalked his raft, he'd kill me. He said no end of wild foolishness like that.

"I saw I couldn't do anything at all with him. So I says, 'I got to have *help* somehow.'

"And the minute I says it, out crawls this nigger from somewheres. He says he'll help. And he done it, too, and done it very well.

"Of course I judged he must be a runaway nigger, and there I *was!* And there I had to stick right straight along all the rest of the day and night. It was a fix, I tell you!

"I had a couple of patients with the chills. Of course I'd have liked to run up to town and see them. But I didn't dare, because the nigger might get away. Then I'd be to blame.

"And yet never a skiff come close enough for me to hail. So there I had to stick where I was until daylight this morning.

"I never saw a nigger that was a better nurse or faithfuler. Yet he was risking his freedom to do it. He was all tired out, too. I see plain enough he'd been worked quite hard lately. I liked the nigger for that. I tell you, gentlemen, a nigger like that is worth a thousand dollars—and kind treatment, too.

"I had everything I needed. And the boy was doing as well there as he would have done at home. Better, maybe, because it was so quiet. But there I *was,* with both of 'em on my hands. And there I had to stick till about dawn this morning.

"Then some men in a skiff come by. As good luck would have it, the nigger was setting by the pallet. His head was propped on his knees sound asleep.

"So I motioned them in quiet. They slipped up on him and grabbed him and tied him before he knowed what he was about.

We never had no trouble.

"The boy was in a kind of a **flighty** sleep, too. We muffled the oars and hitched the raft on. We towed her over very nice and quiet. The nigger never made the least disturbance nor said a word from the start.

"He ain't no bad nigger, gentlemen. That's what I think about him."

Somebody says, "Well, it sounds very good, doctor, I'm obliged to say."

Then the others softened up a little, too. I was mighty thankful to that old doctor for doing Jim that good turn. I was glad it was according to my judgment of him, too. For I thought he had a good heart in him and was a good man the first time I saw him.

Then they all agreed that Jim had acted very well. He was deserving to have some notice took of it and reward. So every one of them promised, right out and hearty, that they wouldn't cuss him no more.

Then they come out and locked him up. I hoped they was going to say he could have one or two of the chains took off. They was rotten heavy. Or maybe he could have meat and greens with his bread and water. But they didn't think of it.

I reckoned it warn't best for me to mix in. But I judged I'd get the doctor's **yarn** to Aunt Sally somehow or other. I'd do it as soon as I'd got through the trouble that was laying just ahead of me. Explanations, I mean. I had told all about how Sid and me put in that dratted night. How we paddled around hunting the runaway nigger. But how did I forget to mention about Sid being shot?

But I had plenty of time. Aunt Sally, she stuck to the sickroom all day and all night. And every time I saw Uncle Silas mooning around, I dodged him.

Next morning, I heard Tom was a good deal better. They said Aunt Sally was gone to get a nap. So I slips to the sickroom. If I found Tom awake, I reckoned we could put up a yarn for the family that would wash.

But he was sleeping, and sleeping very peaceful, too. And he was pale, not fire-faced the way he was when he come. So I set down and laid for him to wake.

In about half an hour, Aunt Sally comes gliding in. There I was, up a stump again! She motioned me to be still, and set down by me. She begun to whisper, and said we could all be joyful now. All the **symptoms** was first-rate.

He'd been sleeping like that for ever so long, and looking better and peacefuler all the time. Ten to one, he'd wake up in his right mind.

So we set there watching. By and by, he stirs a bit. He opened his eyes very natural, and takes a look, and says, "Hello! Why, I'm at *home!* How's that? Where's the raft?"

"It's all right," I says.

"And *Jim?*"

"The same," I says, but couldn't say it pretty brash. But he never noticed, but says, "Good! Splendid! *Now* we're right and safe! Did you tell Aunty?"

I was going to say yes, but she chipped in and says, "About what, Sid?"

"Why, about the way the whole thing was done."

"What whole thing?"

"Why, *the* whole thing. There ain't but ont. How we set the runaway nigger free—me and Tom."

"Good land! Set the run—What *is* the child talking about! Dear, dear, out of his head again!"

"*No,* I ain't out of my HEAD. I know all what I'm talking about. We *did* set him free—me and Tom. We laid out to do it, and we *done* it. And we done it elegant, too."

He'd got a start, and she never checked him up. She just set and stared and stared, and let him clip along. I see it warn't no use for *me* to put in.

"Why, Aunty, it cost us a power of work—weeks of it. It took hours and hours, every night, whilst you was all asleep. And we had to steal candles, and the sheet, and the shirt. And your dress, and spoons, and tin plates, and kitchen knives. And the warming pan, and the grindstone, and flour, and just no end of things.

"You can't think what work it was to make the saws, and pens, and inscriptions, and one thing or another. And you can't think *half* the fun it was.

"And we had to make up the pictures of coffins and things, and nonnamous letters from the robbers. And we had to get up and down the lightning rod, and dig the hole into the cabin. And make the rope ladder and send it in cooked up in a pie. And send in spoons and things to work with in your apron pocket—"

"Mercy sakes!"

"—and load up the cabin with rats and snakes and so on, for company for Jim. Then you kept Tom here so long with the butter in his hat. You come near spoiling the whole business. The men come before we was out of the cabin, and we had to rush.

"They heard us and shot at us, and I got my share. We dodged out of the path and let them go by. When the dogs come, they warn't interested in us, but went for the most noise.

"Then we got our canoe, and made for the raft, and was all safe. And Jim was a free man, and we done it all by ourselves. And *wasn't* it bully, Aunty!"

"Well, I never heard the likes of it in all my born days! So it was *you,* you little rapscallions. You've been making all this trouble. And you've turned everybody's wits clean inside out. Not to mention scaring us all most to death.

"I've as good a notion as ever I had in my life to take it out on you this very minute. To think, here I've been, night after night, and—*You* just get well once, you young scamp. I lay I'll tan the Old Harry out of both of you!"

But Tom, he *was* so proud and joyful, he just *couldn't* hold in. And his tongue just *went* at it. She kept a-chippin' in, and spitting fire all along. Both of them was going it at once, like a cat convention.

And she says, "*Well,* you get all the enjoyment you can out of it now. For mind I tell you if I catch you meddling with him again—"

"Meddling with who?" Tom says, dropping his smile and looking surprised.

"With *who?* Why, the runaway nigger, of course. Who'd you reckon?"

Tom looks at me very grave, and says, "Tom, didn't you just tell me he was all right? Hasn't he got away?"

"Him?" says Aunt Sally. "The runaway nigger? 'Deed he hasn't. They've got him back, safe and sound. He's in the cabin again, on bread and water. And he's loaded down with chains, till he's claimed or sold!"

Tom rose square up in bed, with his eye hot. His nostrils was opening and shutting like gills, and he sings out to me, "They ain't no *right* to shut him up! *Shove!* And don't you lose a minute. Turn him loose! He ain't no slave. He's as free as any creature that walks this earth!"

"What *does* the child mean?"

"I mean every word I *say,* Aunt Sally. If somebody don't go, *I'll* go. I've knowed him all his life, and so has Tom, there.

"Old Miss Watson died two months ago. She was ashamed she ever was going to sell him down the river, and *said* so. And she set him free in her will."

"Then what on earth did *you* want to set him free for? Seeing he was already free?"

"Well, that *is* a question, I must say. And *just* like women! Why, I wanted the *adventure* of it. I'd have waded neck-deep in blood to—Goodness alive, Aunt Polly!"

If she warn't standing right there, just inside the door, I wish I may never. And she was looking as sweet and contented as an angel half full of pie.

Aunt Sally jumped for her, and most hugged the head off of her, and cried over her. I found a good enough place for me under the bed. It was getting pretty **sultry** for *us,* seemed to me.

And I peeped out, and in a little while Tom's Aunt Polly shook herself loose. She stood there looking at Tom over her spectacles. She was kind of grinding him into the earth, you know. And then she says, "Yes, you *better* turn your head away. I would if I was you, Tom."

"Oh, deary me!" says Aunt Sally. "Is he changed so? Why, that ain't *Tom,* it's Sid. Tom's—Tom's—why, where is Tom? He was here a minute ago."

"You mean where's Huck *Finn.* That's what you mean! I reckon I ain't raised such a **scamp** as my Tom all these years not to know him when I *see* him. That *would* be a pretty howdy-do. Come out from under that bed, Huck Finn."

So I done it. But not feeling brash.

Aunt Sally, she was one of the mixed-uppest-looking persons I ever saw. Except one, and that was Uncle Silas. He come in and they told it all to him.

It kind of made him drunk, as you may say. He didn't know nothing at all the rest of the day. He preached a prayer-meeting sermon that night that gave him a rattling reputation. The oldest man in the world couldn't have understood it.

So Tom's Aunt Polly, she told all about who I was, and what. I had to up and tell how I was in such a tight place when Mrs. Phelps took me for Tom Sawyer.

She chipped in and says, "Oh, go on and call me Aunt Sally. I'm used to it now. 'Tain't no need to change."

Then I told how, when Aunt Sally took me for Tom Sawyer, I had to stand it. There warn't no other way. I knowed he wouldn't mind. It would be nuts for him, being a mystery. He'd make an adventure out of it, and be perfectly satisfied. And so it turned out. And he let on to be Sid, and made things as soft as he could for me.

And his Aunt Polly, she said Tom was right. Old Miss Watson had set Jim free in her will. And so, sure enough, Tom Sawyer had gone and took all that trouble and bother to set a free nigger free!

I couldn't ever understand it before, until that minute and that talk. But now I knowed how he could help a body set a nigger free with his bringing-up.

Well, Aunt Polly, she said Aunt Sally wrote to her that Tom and *Sid* had come all right and safe. So she says to herself, "Look at that now! I might have expected it. How could I let him go off that way without anybody to watch him?

"So now I got to go and come all the way down the river, eleven hundred miles. I got to find out what that creature's up to *this* time. I couldn't seem to get any answer out of you about it."

"Why, I never heard nothing from you," says Aunt Sally.

"Well, I wonder! Why, I wrote you twice. I asked you what you could mean by Sid being here."

"Well, I never got 'em, Sis."

Aunt Polly, she turns around slow and severe, and says, "You, Tom!"

"Well—*what?*" he says, kind of cross.

"Don't you what *me,* you impudent thing. Hand out them letters."

"What letters?"

"*Them* letters. I be bound, if I have to take ahold of you I'll—"

"They're in the trunk. There, now. And they're just the same as they was when I got them out of the office. I ain't looked into them, I ain't touched them. But I knowed they'd make trouble. And I thought if you warn't in no hurry, I'd—"

"Well, you *do* need skinning. There ain't no mistake about it."

Aunt Polly says, "And I wrote another one to tell you i I was coming. I suppose he—"

"No, it come yesterday. I ain't read it yet, but it's all right. I've got that one."

I wanted to offer to bet two dollars she hadn't. But I reckoned maybe it was just as safe to not to. So I never said nothing.

Chapter 43

Nothing More to Write

The first time I catched Tom private, I asked him what was his idea, time of the evasion? What did he plan to do if the evasion worked all right? What if he managed to set a nigger free that was already free before?

And he said he had it all planned in his head from the start. If we got Jim safe, we would run him down the river on the raft. And we would have adventures plumb to the mouth of the river.

Then we'd tell Jim about his being free. And we'd take him back up home on a steamboat, in style. We'd pay him for his lost time. Then we'd write word ahead to get all the niggers around. They'd waltz him into town with a torchlight procession and a brass band.

Then he would be a hero, and so would we. But I reckoned it was about as well the way it was.

We had Jim out of the chains in no time. Aunt Polly and Uncle Silas and Aunt Sally found out how good he helped the doctor nurse Tom. So they made a heap of fuss over him. They fixed him up prime, and give him all he wanted to eat. They give him a good time, and nothing to do.

We had him up to the sickroom, and had a high talk. Tom give Jim forty dollars for being a prisoner for us so patient, and doing it so good. Jim was pleased most to death.

He busted out, and says, "*There,* now, Huck, what I tell you? What I tell you up there on Jackson Island? I *told* you I got a hairy chest, and what's de sign of it. En' I *told* you I been rich once, en' goin' to be rich *again.*

"En' it's come true, en' here she *is!* There, now! Don't talk to me. Signs is *signs,* mind I tell you. En' I knowed just as well that I was goin' to be rich again as I's a-standin' here dis minute!"

And then Tom, he talked along and talked along. He says, let's all three slide out of here one of these nights and get an outfit. We'd go for howling adventures amongst the Injuns, over in the territory. We'd go for a couple of weeks or two.

And I says, all right, that suits me. But I ain't got no money for to buy the outfit. I reckon I couldn't get none from home. It's likely Pap's been back before now. He'd probably got it all away from Judge Thatcher and drunk it up.

"No, he ain't," Tom says. "It's there yet—six thousand dollars and more. And your pap ain't ever been back since. Hadn't when I come away, anyhow."

Jim says, kind of solemn, "He ain't a-comin' back no more, Huck."

I says, "Why, Jim?"

"Never mind why, Huck. But he ain't comin' back no more."

But I kept at him, so at last he says, "Don't you 'member de house dat was floatin' down de river? En' there was a man in there, covered up? En' I went in en' uncovered him and didn't let you come in? Well, den, you can git your money when you wants it, 'cause dat was him."

Tom's most well now. He's got his bullet around his neck on a watch guard for a watch. He's always seeing what time it is.

So there ain't nothing more to write about. And I am rotten glad of it. If I'd have knowed what trouble it was to make a book, I wouldn't have tackled it. I ain't a-goin' to no more.

But I reckon I got to light out for the territory ahead of the rest. Because Aunt Sally, she's going to adopt me and sivilize me, and I can't stand it. I been there before.

THE END

YOURS TRULY,
HUCK FINN